T0147022

BEGGING
4ATTENTION

BEGGING 4ATTENTION

CRACK OF DAWN

JOHN COLLINS

BEGGING 4 ATTENTION
CRACK OF DAWN

iUniverse books may be ordered through booksellers or by contacting:

iUniverse
1663 Liberty Drive
Bloomington, IN 47403
www.iuniverse.com
1-800-Authors (1-800-288-4677)

Because of the dynamic nature of the Internet, any web addresses or links contained in this book may have changed since publication and may no longer be valid. The views expressed in this work are solely those of the author and do not necessarily reflect the views of the publisher, and the publisher hereby disclaims any responsibility for them.

Any people depicted in stock imagery provided by Getty Images are models,
and such images are being used for illustrative purposes only.
Certain stock imagery © Getty Images.

ISBN: 978-1-5320-7269-7 (sc)
ISBN: 978-1-5320-7270-3 (e)

Print information available on the last page.

iUniverse rev. date: 03/31/2020

I Had a Dream

Single Mother of 3 kids struggling became a way to live,
No Father figure grew up in our crib.
Deep in my mind I felt as if Life was the most precious gift!
Eyes witness pain That could never escape these lips.
Living to change, how did it come to this?
Honor Roll student dreams of being a Doctor or Lawyer no
Father.
Brother whispering life isn't a movie!
After my mom's death I became the ghettos orphan,
I felt useless!
Was I born in a coffin before my death?
While many are playing checkers all I had to play was chess!
Choice after choice had to be the best.
Living in a world where we seldom exist!
My cuffs had been hopes, listen to the words being wrote?
Lynching starts before your (2nd your erased) neck visit any rope!
They instill failure to choke out any form of hope.
I had a Dream to lift my mother from life familiar handicaps
that us as blacks visit, attack after attack!
I felt as if my dream was tarnished by realities monster.
The poison of pain has been eating at my conscious.
My dream turned into a nightmare!
It went from desiring to be a doctor to choppers flying everywhere.
Life isn't fair?
So, it seemed, whom I valued was my only Queen.
The world turmoil tried covering something totally royal it pressed
her into a dope fiend.

———

1

In my eyes it was an ultimate sin, broken wings earth had abused my
Angel!
Many nightmares became my reality, in various Angles.
Filled with anger my dream was in danger.
No stranger to truth, lies became alibis after my mom's died I rewrote
my dream.
I became a ghetto hero to many fiends in a world of concubines I was hailed King.
Many times you can drown if you stop swimming.
I notice I was killing everything around me, intoxicating many with my venom.
Wait how did I grow into someone I held a distaste for?
Closing my eyes, I seen a snake on the floor!
I had a dream..
...it was to help my kingdom rise, so as you become the guide to open your nation eyes.
If one divides, he subtracts, if addition isn't given you're vulnerable to attack.

Engulfed in memories from my childhood, Sincere was well pleased with reminiscing on New York. Nina Simone was her name, his childhood sweetheart. Which was to him his best kept secret. Even though he was no longer with her nor corresponding. He embedded her name over his heart forever securing a spot in his soul. This day was her birthday, 6 years and counting since he spoke to her and 8 since he seen her. Sincere was a hot head that played cool, raised in Syracuse New York on the Southside. Home of the notorious Boot- Camp click on (M.C) Midland and Colvin. Young renegades who had nothing to lose yet everything the gain. At the time we were at war with almost every hood, we would only stay on our block but on weekends Salina at Deb's. If you were anybody or desired seeing anybody this was the podium. In route to Deb's walking up Colvin on a Friday. This night a cripple guy arms drawn up on his right side, legs dragging looking as if he was recovering from a stroke. Wearing a black hoodie, black jeans and black Tim's kinda fresh. Yet, this wasn't unusual in New York. We had to be about 15 to 20 deep. Messing with crippled people all the time this was Rated R. He goes to push the guy, in arm reach of the guy rated r looked as if he seen a ghost. It's Slick! The cripple guy pulled the tec from under his hoodie, sending shots at rated r. Rated R running down the street in a zig zagging motion. I almost shot myself trying to get my cannon out my hoodie, while diving over hedges. Slick had done it again! On many occasions we've bumped head yet slick was Bruce Willis. Exhausted hiding behind the church, Sin called Nina. Nina, come snatch me up I'm on the camp where you always pick me up. Posted in the shadows by the church that's sat on the corner of Midland and Colvin, I stepped into the light when seeing Nina Acura integra. Sin, you all right? You know Sky just called me and Author did as well everyone blowing my phone up. Author was my best man the streets called him King. He was given the name because he spoke words of wisdom that fell from the lips of any book plus he could create thoughts in any girls head just from his presence alone. Nina was a rich chocolate total pureness, innocent all around the board. Thick as molasses, possess a body that held more than milk. Not from the hood she stayed in the suburbs. Meeting her I took my time knowing honestly, she was different. Always opposed crowds and disposed certain hood cats or attention grabbers. On a Sunny Tuesday getting off work early morning I was leaving Loretta nursing home. It was a little after 10:30 because I stayed late trying to help the shift catch up plus, I had this nurse who work mornings I was interested in. While riding through Colvin I seen this thick girl and redbone both who truly were beyond beautiful, easy. I was thinking like I seen these chicks so I turned around. I pulled up and was like excuse me? Do you all need a ride? The Chocolate thick one held a beautiful aura, yet her response was no! We don't even know you! Sincere, began smiling because it was true. The redbone instantly said I'm tired girl, let's get this ride. I pulled over, stepped out the car to where as she can see my complete work attire. I responded YO! Both of you mad beautiful but kidnapping you after getting off would be impossible I'm exhausted! The Red chick attacked me like full court press, hitting me with many questions. I interrupted hello I am Sin, what's your name baby girl? Instantly the other friend was like your momma didn't name you Sin? I laughed and said what did your mother name you, Desire? She smiled for the first time. Then the Red chick said no my mother named me Desiree the body of desire. I smirked yet realizing Desiree was the aggressor in my desiring her friend she desired me or my car to the least. Suddenly, Desiree interrupted my thoughts and said its pleasure in sin so you must be a bad boy? Then I realized she was eyeing my car 1997 Acura Legend forest green white interior wood grain dash with new feet that stood out like Jordan's. I was still a young bull, but many took me to be still a yougin because I held a baby face. I came from a great family even though life tried stripping me naked on many occasions. My biological moms have died but her coming from a family of many kids, she was the oldest girl the next oldest girl took custody of us. No kids a RN as well as Evangelist married, she accepted us openly. I can say she was my motivation to excel and do things in an appropriate manner. Thoughts interrupted by these five words, So what hood you rep? Desiree, I work I'm not on no block. Even though I was familiar with what I was surrounded by and from time to time ventured to my hood. It was nothing I desired promoting, my representation would be of strength which in my eyes was sound etiquettes. I wasn't raised like that I am not that guy, then her friend instantly said my name Nina. Ding, ding, ding jackpot. What's your name and don't give me no nickname? Sincere Hollis I blurted out quicker than a new breath of air. Nina laughed I didn't need your entire government! Sin started laughing realizing he almost gave her his social security number as well ugh this was what he needed, all in all she was drawing to his spirit which was a plus. Nina said do you always pick up strangers Mister Sincere. No ma'am is there any danger in being helpful this sun can be disrespectful! Not at all!? Nina overlooking Sincere realizing his demeanor wasn't of the norm, suddenly Nina was the aggressor move Desiree he is not from the hood you such a groupie. Desiree brushing her off, girl whatever. You know I love a hard head i don't want anyone soft as me. Skating thru traffic R. Kelly you Remind me of Something was blasting thru my speakers. Vibing more so than talking that's how our journey started. Nina riding in the front while Desiree was riding in the back. Nina said were dropping off Desiree first then we pulled up to her house which sat behind Manley Field house in a quiet area. Thanks, stranger, for such a great deed. So, are you ready to pay me? Huh, looking back before exiting the car she snaps, now you want gas money Sincere? Before leaving the car completely Sin grabs her arm. No ma'am pay me with a portion of your attention if that's not asking much? Sincere, I've given you that? Don't be mean babe, I'm not go stalk you? Her response kinda startled me, what's your number Sincere Hollis? Sin use to getting what he wanted wasn't used to not being in control. 315 450 1000.

Sitting on the top of his car hood surrounded by flowers, freshly manicured grass with a tree stomp. Vines growing outta nowhere. Sincere, would always meditate on the thought. Even during death something is birthed in the same cycle. This was peace from madness, beauty even amongst the chaos. Interrupted by a sweet voice Mann, how long you been out here? My mother was the only one who called me Mann she told me at a young age she viewed me as her only Man that's how my name came about. I've just been here a second, love. You must be going fishing gotcha fishing gear on babe?! Blushing shaking her head see said Sin you're such a charmer. All white alluring dress, white hat, gold trimming looking like a preacher's wife she is an Evangelist. Boy I'm headed to church. You have not surprised me in years I'd love to see you? Send a prayer up for your baby boy, prayers of the righteous availeth much. Smiling she was comfortable knowing regardless of his actions he always desired growth. On her way to church she recalled the time she seemed to have lost her baby boy to a world she held little knowledge of. Arriving home early she began noticing the difference in his routine she worked nights his younger sister stayed at her mom's (granny). For some reason he'd always come to my job bringing me lunch and talk with me? Many times leave me with a gift always stating if I could add value to how I view you you'd lay in treasures but for now all I have is love. Sin would always state aloud Lord; I know time isn't forever just keep me throughout life journey....in Jesus name Amen!

This had become a repetitive prayer daily for Sin. His mom she always stressed the power of prayer. Many nights Sin slept thru the fights and bickering. Even Though mom was adamant about God, my Father was in a tug of war. Wrestling with different vices, convicted felon he always felt incompetent of being the Husband he desired being. Which left him bitter. Sin fed up! His room being on the first floor leaped over 3 steps a time before reaching the second floor. As he reaches the door to lift up misery skirt the door is locked, he knocks down the door. Yo, get your hands off my ma! Boy go to your room, mom torn how could I leave her helpless. I was all over him before I could remember hearing all moms cries, rambling and the bruises covered …. hearing echoes in my mental attempting to snatch his soul from his body the only chant I hear was die nigga which derived from me. Paramedics lifted his body from the closet he was rushed to the hospital, heart attack was his diagnosis. Sincere, couldn't think straight. He went straight thru the trenches in the city. Throughout it all dad wanted me to see him. He said love is love I'm done drinking. Mom embraced us said forgive me. I'm done with whining and tripping. Sin, riding blowing his pain in the clouds. Thoughts running rampant, tuned into another channel. Love crawls thru the teeth of hope grasp. Savage, mind state in which is a constant reminder of my past hurt leads to berserk outcomes. Riding passenger seat with Ace who was like a brother to me. He was my grandmothers neighbor, so I'd always see him constantly. Hazel eyes chestnut complexion followed by braids which always flowed backwards. A boxer so his physique reflected his dedication. Which he covered in jewels and excess name brands which he held an abundance of. Being raised up around him and other people who were looked upon as pretty boys I wouldn't describe myself as a pretty boy. My physical makeup consisted of being well groomed, attentive to detail. I held what many lacked because they exploited their strengths, so I obtained mine thru creating me. While me and Ace slid thru the South Side, we ended up on South State Street. Sitting at the light on South State Street and Colvin a car pulls up next to them. Damn! Sin slips from under his breath. He snatches his steel from under his shirt quickly exiting the car he walked towards the driver side smashing the butt of the gun to his window. Not in a rush to kill him because he needs to see my face, is how Sin felt. Dude fell and mashed it running the light. Blah, Blah! I ran to the car and scream catch em Ace. Sin began his Dukes of Hazzard stunt to where as he began clapping rapidly while hanging from the window. After turning or attempting to, Ace crashed into a fence. Sin jumped out giving chase! After chasing him I get off three shots and realize we were in his hood Brighton and Brigade, that's when I saw flames which came from various areas. Running back to the car I was relieved to not have gotten shot, but I won't rest until he's erased for my presence. Finally, at home in solitude this is where me and Nina lived, Dewitt. Higher than clouds my head laid in the lap of Nina. Racking her fingers thru my waves I asked? Yo, why you with me? You could be with anyone, yet you chose me? Nina was a nurse totally focused on life to the point where I've been with her since I was fifth teen now nineteen, she still was a virgin. Sincere, listen do you remember my freshman year in high school? We promised each other a family and a house with a picket fence. Nina, remember that? Wow, that's real. Now let me ask you why you are yet with me you can be sexing anyone? Here it is You still respect how I feel and choose to walk it out with me. Taking thought choosing his words carefully. Sex easy to get even though you promised never to indulge in sex til you married doesn't make me view you as awkward. Lol, why because you got all those groupies? Nina not desiring to just believe all Sin truth, yet his actions reflected his true desires, which was me all in all. Doesn't nobody want me Nina but you!? In thought Nina felt safe with Sincere private school student who held a hood appeal yet was opposite of just that. A student in college mother an evangelist he was an ideal mate raised with morals and prove to be more than different than the masses. Sincere Hollis was the husband of my future the father of my kids and more so than anything my soulmate. Sincere was a young guy who tried to better his future never settling. Thoughts of Nina knowing he tried to escape all she hated was what his essence was familiar with. His biological moms died from aids, it helped him to become brave. Yo, this isn't living he uttered aloud! Understanding his desire is not to be of hurt more so help. I never approved of this life I was given, God always said you didn't choose me I chose you! Refusing to break or bend thru life adversity he embraced his challenges. Interrupted from phone ringing Sin reaches over Nina answers the horn to be startled by familiar voice that was followed by thoughts. Laying sedated in pain chased with soft cries. "Caviar dead Sin! They chased him on the hill, and he wrapped the car around a telephone pole!" Sounds of silence! Cav, didn't fuck with anyone!? Sucking up all at hand I grabbed my tool and whispered "FUCK, FUCK, FUCK!" Phone slammed on the bed and Nina asking talk to me Sin come on and talk to me? What's wrong? Tell me, this not real!!!!! You know I got this! How by killing them? Sin, it's a domino effect tic for tac. I just want this to stop! Phone rings and Nina answers, and says Ok, Sky let me call his mom I'll hit you right back. Big O, G-Loso and Finesse were a few heads I called asap. "We are riding is all Whitey White kept repeating." Numb to all logic, revenge was the reward of such an act nothing less. After a few jumped in the jeep and another crew filled the other car. An army would draw attention, yet we needed to come face to face with these individuals. Thoughts would not birth no form of victory the Camp gotta ride. As we approached Cherry Hill the strip was thick as they normally were known for being. Two heads slumped in the back of the jeep and two in visible sight riding in the front. We obviously appeared to look like smokers. The other car trailed a distance. After sliding down Maple St. sitting on the corner of East Genesee Street. A few heads tried deciphering who was going to catch the play. As White held money out Ching, Ching all things cashed out. A wiseman always said money can confuse logic and drop the guards of many. Not prepared to wait for him White held the pistol to the door of the car invisible to the ppl standing outside and before anyone grasp what was at hand White released 3 shots that left the first guy canceled in his tracks. Body twitching until lifeless. The alarm had been set. Camp nicca was all you could hear after each shot, instead of running from the fight White ran to the fight. Ejecting himself from the car while walking towards the opps, death tip toed in the eyelids of Whitey white. It was if the light from the heat startled roaches because some responded in gunfire, but most ran trying to avoid getting sprayed by raid. The car behind us had pulled out stopped on Lexington Ave. where Red jumped out with no understanding a Camp general who refused to allow any form of attack to go unmet thru out the city in his eyes the city belonged to the Camp. Red vested up screaming MC fuck nigga forever live the camp.

Each car sent shots rapidly then we rode back to the South Side. Confused hurt torn I rode to my mom's house where few if any have the knowledge of. Pulling in driveway pistol in my lap around 4 in the morning. As if it was a pattern whenever he was unsure about anything, he'd head straight to Mom's duke house. No one could tell him different that his mom was his safety net. Flying through the night lights escaping the South Side to Lincoln Ave on the shores of the Westside. Instantly Sin realizes mom Car not home. He calls her job hello Upstate hospital Carolyn Brown. Ma! What's up Sincere? I need to see you it's important! Can you wait till I get off? Do you get off at 6? Yes! Okay meet me at Denny's we can grab a bite! Music blasted Sin getting intoxicated off tunes and lyrics. Feeling forced to live in the manner his Spirit never would agree to. Dazed and Confused by all the events transpiring. Unbeknownst to Sin he was followed leaving Lincoln by a green tinted van. Sin recognize he'd been sitting in the car for some time. He gets out to grab a table before his mom's pull up at any time. One person steps out the back of the van around 5'10 stout what a hoodie and Avirex jacket followed by Tim's everything black. In route to the door Sin is stop by his name being called. Off habit as if it was a casual breath Sin reaction was clutching his rocket. Seeing a familiar face Sin became more at ease. Bounty! Bounty was Sin cousin two brother children. What's good? Sin was open to seeing his fam. Bounty getting closer to Sin hands in Pockets protecting himself from the weather, so it seemed. A lady steps out the maroon Alero covered in hospital smocks. Sin mother had just pulled next to the green van. Bounty arms coming from behind Sin he showed the Heat and stuck it in Sin ribs. You know what it is and make any move I'm go kill you, brody. Heading inside of Denny's she notices Bounty hugging Sin walking in her direction. Sin knowing Bounty and him being in the blind he was left exposed. We're going to walk to this van, and you go get in it if you try anything I'mma gun you down. That's just what it is. In route to the van Sin sees his mother crossing the parking lot. Refusing to invite her to this chaos or her been exposed to any harm Sin takes a chance. Ma let me talk to Bounty one second. Bounty seeing his Aunt he hesitated long enough for Sin to grab his fire and empty five shots 3 in his chest 2 missing its target. While instantly running off anger, betrayal not wanting a hair to be touched on his mom's head nothing mattered but removing every threat. Gunning at the driver side window of the van. Get down ma Sin started screaming. He felt like a walking lick; all he was trying to do was live. That alone drew a great distaste from many. Then instantly flames of fire came from the back of the van. A ripping feeling as if heat soaked thru my arm. I dropped my fire and was hit in the stomach after collapsing I heard nothing but a silence that laid dormant in the pit of my stomach. A guy wearing a ski mask pointing a 357 revolver in my face, prepared for death to rest upon me all I heard was click, click, click as he disappeared so did my sight. Everything faded to black. Sin mom's laid over him crying hurt broken not understanding really what was going on, in her heart she feared someone ever calling her in response to Sin and his street life. Never did she believe she would be an eyewitness to such madness.

Nevaeh was heaven when I was living backwards in my emptiness, she always spilled within me passion. Laying in the hospital unsure of my next act because I wanted this designed perfectly without error. My ideal vision of a woman who complimented all I felt equated to the essence of a woman. Sin met Nevaeh thru passing. Young, reckless and rich the world in Sin eyes could never do him no harm all things flowed in unison of what it was he believed. One-night sliding thru the town grabbing his friend a bite to eat, who was left at her house. Pulling up to Mickey Dee's which was packed because it was Friday high school football night. As Sin step inside because the line wrapped around the store, he chose to walk in. After placing his order Sin sat down in the crowded forum where he heard someone call his name out. Looking up unbeknownst to him it was his cousin Bounty. What's good Cuz? Sin asked as he walked up embracing Bounty who had just been released from Prison. Welcome home my guy cuz get this money this go around robbery is a broke man hustle. If you wanna eat eat fuck with me, I am not rich by any means but I'm living and have no worries ya heard. Sin, I'll take you up on that movement. Suddenly Sin and Bounty was interrupted by his cousin Baby Doll. Cuz, how you been I haven't seen you in a minute you stay out the way for real huh? That's the only way to move, baby girl. Ummm, who your friend? Baby Doll was attractive and aggressive she wanted what she wanted she never waited on a dude to choose. Looking Bounty up and down straight out the can he was fresh. 5'9 rich chocolate full lips that reminded you of Malik Yoba with time on his side he was chiseled like Tyson Beckford. Licking her lips what your bout to do yall go chill with me and my cousin tonight. My father had a big family I was kin to her on the Hollis side. Which open the gates for Bounty who I was kin to on my mom's side. Bounty I am about to get my meal who you with Sin. Nawh, I came with my homies. Well tell them bye. Listen Sin you get him to ride with you and were meet up at the hotel. That's cool with you, Sin. Seeing the glow in Bounty eyes as he sized Baby Doll up. I obviously don't have any choice. Say Cuz? Sin said looking towards Bounty let me grab this food and drop this off and we go head in that direction. Jumping in the Tahoe Bounty was in amazement. Dam you eating fam! This my little shorty shit my car at her crib but I'm aite. I'm not making no noise for real. Pulling up to the house that was well put together. Unfamiliar with this level of living unless he was kicking the hinges in, it all seemed foreign to him. Looking over the inside of the car it looked brand new, omg Sin living I gotta fuck with him I know I'll be straight. Cuz always been about his coins, women and hustling. A loner but many never tried him because he had 7 brothers outside himself who was a tribe by themselves. After making in the house Sin gives Jennifer her food. Say babe I'm bout to make a couple plays and one of my young bulls made it home so I may slide in here late if that's cool with you. Jennifer was a counselor at a woman's prison and she always had a thing for bad boys. That was the makeup of Sin. Kissing him as he placed her keys on the dresser. Oh, you must going to see one of ya bitches and don't want my car to be seen, you get on my nerves Sin. Yo, chill out I just told you my young bull out here babe. Oh, I didn't know he was in the house? No, he is in the truck babe. This his first day out I just wanna float around in my toy can I do that DAM. I get it I get it, it's an ego thing. You got ya key to the house right. You know I do babe. Ok, I'll see you once you get home. Sin jumped in his car while motioning Bounty to get in the car with him. Running back to the truck to make sure it was locked securely Sin jogged back to his car. I don't smoke Sin told Bounty but if you wanna burn something we can grab you something. Nawh, I am good you know I'm trying to stay out. Stopping by the liquor store Sin asked, "What you drink white or brown?" Whatever you get. Grabbing a bag of ice, cranberry juice, grapefruit juice, sparkling water and some grey goose. It was time to set the night off. Truly Sin didn't look at Baby Doll cousin but knows Baby Doll rolls with hittas, his agenda wasn't based off selfish intent. All he wanted was to make sure Bounty enjoy the life on the side of the wall and reward him for his stance no longer a prisoner of war (lifestyle). Pulling up seeing Baby Doll truck at the hotel, Sin turns his music up. As he pulls in Baby Doll steps out the room signaling where it was, they were roomed at. Arriving to the room bringing out the drinks Baby Doll didn't press no brakes. Bounty seemed hypnotized by the movement of events while Sin sipped and vibed with Nevaeh who was quiet but holding a demanding demeanor. Eyes chinky as an Asian, lips full as a fresh plucked tulip. Caramel complexion with a shine that held a glow. Two beds they got straight to it. Placing themselves under the covers with the lights out. I sat on the end of the bed while Nevaeh laid back one leg stretched and the other one propped under it securely in a half butterfly manner. Cuz fuck that I can't get right like this excuse me while I take this nigga in the bathroom. Bounty and Baby doll closing the door. Nevaeh, you don't mind if I prop myself against ya leg. Go ahead, Sin. I aint go bite you. I know because I know how to bite back Sin said after both laughed in unison. Sin placed his head upon her inner thigh. While laying there watching tv Nevaeh placed her hand against Sin cheek bone touching him gently in a seductive manner. Sin turned around looking in Nevaeh eyes said if I do anything that makes you feel uncomfortable stop me? Ok! Lifting the bottom of her shirt with his lips as his fingers began unbuckling her pants. Slowly removing her legs from her pants Sin left her with t-shirt and panties on. Throwing the pants to the side of the bed. Sin covered his head with the Covering of the bed linen. Leaving them both submerged by the blankness of the sheets, hiding secrets that only was deserving of their eyes. The vodka had his mouth numb but somehow, he could feel the flavor of grapefruit each moment his tongue peeled back the peeling of her fruit. Was this the manner one eats fruit? Nevaeh pulling in my every thought in her palms as if she wanted me tattooed upon her heart's mental rolodex. Staining me with the core of her existence. Looking behind her eyelids seeing more than stars, blackness and war with flashes that leaves me grasping her nails in the neck of this tree not wanting to fall down. The gift of crowning him with my milky ways as I completely escaped while screaming as if I was calling all my ancestors from the grave.

Now fast forward a few months in time here it was that the same avenue I met Sin almost was the same route that tried leaving him for dead, Bounty. Nevaeh was Detroit bred Muskegon at heart.

New York was her summer vacationing spot she'd visit her family at. Torn, exhausted and confused Sin contemplated his true reasoning for being in this place at this point. Room phone rings in hospital Hello? How is my greatest Sin doing? Sin started smiling because he knew that was Nevaeh punch line know one called him his greatest Sin but her. You know I am cheesing from cheek to cheek a hug would be so clutch right now. You think so? Yes, indeed that would be life. The dreamer the great dreamer, are you prepared to pull that off? How so? Close your eyes? Do you see me in your mind? Sin eyes being closed, yes, I see you. Open your arms and receive me I believe once you close them with your faith its possible. A nurse arriving while being followed by balloons. I am normally breaking meds to cure your aches and pains let's see what this Love can do?! Sin caught completely off guard as he feels a soft fluffiness which was a bear. Opening his eyes, he witnesses many balloons and flowers the nurse brings a dozen of roses 4 white, 4 yellow and 4 pink. Growing up I am completely into detail; I've come to find out Pink represents unconditional love and understanding as well as compassion. Yellow represents honor, loyalty and joy. White represents Sincerity, protection and humility. 4 represents completion and 12 represents faith and divine rule. Sin, Sin, Sin coming back from his window of thoughts he realizes Nevaeh was still on the phone in tears "Yo, hello?" What's wrong Sin? Someone just showed out and showed the kid mad love. How so, Sin? I got mad balloons and flowers. What does the card say, read it or you scared to expose one of ya thots or ya cut buddies?! Faith the size of a mustard seed is beyond amazing. Yo, how did you just do all this? Realizing Nevaeh was the sender. Nevaeh walking in with the phone to her ear said you know the wind tends to blow me from here to there as well, you not the only one can fly state to state on a drop of a dime. Hugging Sin while he was in his lowest mindset. Yo, you always on time. You always know how to fuck me up emotionally ugh I am so in my feelings now yo. Enjoying the idea of it all she just continued holding on to Sin as if they had traded energy. You know you would've killed the world something happens to me. I am just glad you still breathing. You know death isn't visiting me any time soon. It's not a part of the plan. Right, so now it's time to start moving more so towards the plan. Wiping Sin face from the tears along with trying not to allow her make up to run. I love you to death and losing you would be the death of portions of me, I just can't allow that. Since you're a walking bible I'm going to hit you with some of your soul food. Luke 5:37 "And no man putteth new wine into old bottles; else the new wine will burst the bottles; and be spilled, and the bottles shall perish." Its ok to let this lifestyle go. With all the movement and events going on around Sin everything was mute. This is not living. A wise woman once said every action has a reaction, be slow to speak swift to hear those who have ears will hear. Life currents can force one's hands cause in these trenches its kill or be killed. No matter what no one thought, retaliation was necessary because Sincere promised his mother on her dying bed he would never allow no one to hurt her baby boy. Now Sin became activated! Nineteen currently in the best place in his life, Sin who was rising at a quick pace financially but lacked control of his temper. Easily could've paid anyone racks on racks to erase any error that stood in his way. This was personal, they had to see him face to face. Fresh out with hospital bracelet, mind only seeing one outcome ridding himself of anything bringing harm to Blondie son. 2pac screaming Hell Razor as the song stays on repeat tip toe-ing thru the streets. Finally, home thumbing thru his stash after overlooking 200 different piles of franklin's rubber banded plus 29 racks. He had all he needed being that his plug fronted him what it was he got, he had a bird and quarter bird left. Sin never ran off on the plug he always finessed the plug, after 2 runs his face was clean. Then by the third run a lot of things got ugly which was believable cause I always kept my face clean. So, it was nothing to get a whole fresh thanksgiving. No pressure nor heat but this time Sin wanted to run the bag all the way up. So, he opens the heating vents while breaking everything down like transformer to keep it in his great Aunt Mamie house who rarely had visitors. After Sin and his cousin Florida boy left the hospital, he had broken down 2 zones for CaveMan & Shunna oldest brother DirtBag. Pulling up on CaveMan they jumped in the car. Sin, anything you want we on it I'll tell you where Bounty is right now. Sin, already holding his tec-9 under seat with his Taurus .357.

On his waist like a belt. Turned around instantly. Talking to himself, you mean to tell me I don't have to find him he just falls in my lap just like that! We'll ride with you and have him come out. Jingle bell and Christmas carols played thru out my head. You go die today my guy that's on Blondie!

Shunna just getting off work desiring to go to the club with her team of friends. Kinda rushing was interrupted by opening her door to Sin with money covering her floor & a couple, not a lot of zips bagged up. With bowls full of bud as if he was the chef of greenery. Sin sitting at the table lost in a trance with a Taurus 357 in his lap.

Matthew 6:21

For where your treasure is, there will your heart be also

Sin was a traveler he could go anywhere on God green earth and create from zero. 4 states he stayed handling business in were New York, Georgia, Carolina and Florida. When one spot slowed up, he went to the next stop because the wave doesn't bath upon the same shore daily. Mind of a go getter. Yo, you never happy you got all things anyone could want hands down. You are sexing most of the city. You got racks on racks in front of you clearly. What else is it that you want? You got pounds which is more money, I really don't get it? You blessed; God loves you Sin! If God loves me, he won't allow me to die if he so real. You believe he real, let's see! Suddenly Sin leaps to his feet and empty a few bullets out his revolver he puts it to his head & looks Shunna in the eye "Let's see?" As the trigger is pulled Shunna closes her eyes and her heart drops listening to the clicking sound she not believing what was taking place right in front of her. Then outta nowhere another clicking sound goes off after failing twice as if he was clearly attempting to make God outta a lie she slaps the gun outta Sin hands. Both were startled by a gun sound that cause both to duck. As Shunna was on the floor Sin begins laughing & crying at the same time immediately he lights the Dutch that was once lit in his ash tray. Talking aloud to himself, Sin you crazy! Shunna screaming "Really Sin!" "My house full of drugs, guns and money this the time you choose to see if God with you or against you. You gotta be the stupidest nicca I met since they started selling water. You need help you really crazy." For real clean up this stuff while you think everything so funny and don't care if you live or die. Your crazy crazy dude, lord knows you can get a check. Eyes watering while turning away not knowing whether she should snap or cry. Shooting holes all in my ceiling ugh you get on my nerve with ya craziness!" You need help! As Shunna was fixing the pillows on her sofa she grabs the pistol & realized instead of one bullet Sin had two bullets in his pistol. In awe and taken by what had transpired she ran to her room in tears talking to God.

Later during the night Sin gets a call while he is in the shower. What's good, Trap!? This dude just hit my line and said I'm a dead man he catches me in traffic. Who? Cash, he said I won't live to tell anybody I took from him. Immediately I began to laugh, you scared?! Trap responded come on yo! Dude got a squad. Sin numb to understanding, its consequences when ppl choose to play roles that they know nothing about. I never invited you to this life, you said you wanted his sack I said no never rob a dude unless he doesn't show you love. In the event of him not showing you love; the reaction was you took his hold sack. Now you scared for your life you funny my dude…. hold on tho, we go call him on the three way. (as the phone rung, Trap listens on the three way) What's haddin Sin? What's good with you Cash? Cooling! You still got some lime on deck? Yea, I got a lil something! Can you fix me up an elbow? Yea, how long it'll be for you to come thru? I'm on the way! After hanging up with Cash Sin tells Trap come to my crib I'm getting dressed. Sin at the house twisting up some fine gas hears a knock at his room door. Yea! Shunna yells Trap out chea! Aight Babe give me one minute. Sin, yelling thru the door Trap don't be trying to holla at my girl neither bae don't make me act out. Sin stop playing with me you know I don't play with kids and Sin started laughing I am playing bae. Cuz I don't allow people in my home. I'll kill you if you touch my baby momma anybody else open field but this one-off limits. After undressing the bed Sin sticks his arm thru the mattress in a concealed hole. Grabbing his tec 9 he walks out the room with the tec covering his abdomen while putting his shirt on. Yo, you brought the stick with you? Gotta know that cuz, it's in the car! What you do run over here, let me find out Cash got you on house arrest straight scared out chea. I swear yall be wanna be street but aint built for it I'm done saving yall for real for real. Cuz, stop trying me loc! I don't bang nothing but my fye do! Don't loc me if anything bee's popping. Sin began laughing because he knew what his cuzn repped didn't like those who repped from the other side but those were Sin family no matter what. This the move, we sliding over here you in the back seat, leaving front open to him to perform the stunt ya dig? Trap said cuz you be trying niccas all up. No cuz its real out chea in the field. Once you jump off that porch what Gotti say Aint no turning around. I get it cuz! Pulling up to Cash house I tell em fall out cause I'm trying to go O.T (outta town). Cash comes out jumps in whip with bookbag ask me do I got time to burn one? I said Yea so he pushes me the blunt already rolled. So, you gotta one stop shop, huh? That new thang you just hit the strip with running like water I heard about you. Yea, just trying to keep that different gas in they mask ya dig! Oh, you know niccas getting outta hand its time Cash make examples word. I know you heard! Sin car so dark Cash not realizing its another party in the backseat ducked off. So, what the lit read Cash, talk to me?

This nicca name Trap from the bottom violated I gotta have his head. Sin interrupts, let me get that elbow? I'm listening? I'm sorry caught up in my shit I forgot about the cake, ya dig! Cash pulls out 4 suppressed glad lock bag Sin rips 1 open & sniffs it. Throws the closed 3 in the back seat stating yea imma get it i love that its real fruity. Cash states you can cash in now or later you know how we give it up! Sin said you know the cat Trap who you said robbed you. Yea, you know em or where he be at cause once I catch em its off with his head. Trap mother is my daddy oldest sister. Huh? While lighting back up the blunt Cash passed. It wasn't registering to Cash just yet. Let me say it slow, Trap mother is my daddy oldest sister. Finally catching on he looked in amazement Sin I don't got no problem with you my guy? Aint nobody go touch me and get away with it?! You think, Sin said while smirking instantly like jack in the box Trap popped up with the stick to his neck. See Cash this my City homie it's a fee to do business here. I allowed you to eat off the strength of ya ole lady Key but that's a bridge you burnt its neither here nor there not my issue and now you not with her ya pass has been revoked. What Trap was doing was just picking up land taxes. Before he robbed you, he allowed you to show him love first" Sin on God I don't gotta problem with you homie he can have that we better than this. I know it's no problems I'm letting you understand my truth. Empty ya pockets and put everything in the bookbag. Then get out my car, I'm not go kill you can live but if you ever get hungry just know it's more than one plate at this table. Instantly Cash dropped everything including his cell phone & I didn't even ask for it. After Cash got out the car, Trap was in awe like Cuz. You stay on ready you see how cats pay homage to you. Sin, listening to Trapp instantly snapped you think I wanna live like this bruh. Stop watching them movies and shit, this new rap got yall fucked up. Streets birthed this in me, today you rocking with me tomorrow you could be on the other side of the table. "Never Cuz you forever, real never dies." Sin started laughing lil cuz when the situation flips imma remind you of this same conversation. Enough of all that fam let's get our club on. Instead of heading back to the crib they head straight to the club as if nothing occurred. This was Sin! Cutting thru traffic and arriving to the club. They began sliding towards the door and Trap askes Sin cuz you sliding in with the fye. Sin looks at Trap in a manner only that was fitting for a fool. This apart of my uniform I never take it off under no circumstances. I'll never be naked under no conditions especially not chasing no shorty do better lil cuz always know you are more important than anything. Going in the consoles a bag of pills was revealed Sin popped 3 triple stacks chased with some orange juice. "Showtime!"

Let's get it fam! Lit his loud threw on his Cartier. Numb to the serenades of life Sin escaped in a world of the cold rugged dungeon of his thoughts. This was Sin when Sincere wasn't present Sin was go sin again & again. The curtains he has tried closing repeatedly. Caught up in the moment Becky came on Plies was roaring thru the scene & Becky from the hood was stuck to me as if she was a sponsor. Pussi grabs Sin full fledge to her deserted island. Him & her locked in a trance as we were literally sexing in our private space. It's as if her essence sneaks me to heaven. After dancing she grabs my hand and leads me outside. As I jump in the car she tells me I've lived for this moment. Drowning in my lap filled with thoughts that blew more than bubbles I was taken away on a wet ride. As Sin dug his hands in her scalp releasing his pain this was his outlet. Slumped & drained statue giving more freedom than liberty while yet holding the torch fully erect. Pussi tells me I wanna fuck? Sin pushes seat back puts his legs across the seat as whispers would drown the scene as suctions of rain matching my pain thirst, release after release souls speaking in tongue every ride is another high. Windows fogged, bathing in us. Feeling areas of stains unhealed passion covering every wheel the thrill of satisfaction is unmatching. Who would think minutes would feel everlasting saturated with ecstasy? Fingers crawling upon the pages of her body writing notes in secret. As hidden spots respond, communicating amongst one another. Sin got right and left.

Brains out so everyone was easily in his business flushing thru the city music banging pulling up in Lil-Miami he is interrupted by a call. "Hello!" "Sincere" "Yes, ma'am!" "You busy?" "Not really just twisting up some good!" "How have you been?" After looking over his car choppa over the front seat somewhat covering the floor 45 on his lap 40 cal under the driver seat Sin smirks "Yes for the most part I am good, how are you?" Behind Sin hid Sincere the side many never witness, maybe few encounter the flip side of him in totality completely. To his mom who was a Prophetess Sincere was always present and those whom grew up around his mother more so. Outside of his mother church family Sin existed 2 different people that was totally opposite of one another. That lived in one body. Strange yet true! Only Saskia encountered the depths of both worlds, yet she never would allow Sincere to disappear she pushed Sin to the back of his mental, around Saskia he could be gentle. "So, when will I see you Sincere?" Sass blurted out! "Keep your eyes open I maybe under your nose!" "You not go act right Sincere?" It's like the more a cat try & do right, the evil is present with me. I'm yet striving for better in Keith Wallace voice. All things hold pro's & cons until your forced to face them.

A fighter of the norm the loud kept Sin engulfed in deep thought. Desiring to understand why many didn't fulfill Real in the manner that he perceived it, I analyzed many from their original state. Realizing many was only a reflection of mass ideas & thoughts they entertained with strong desires. Pulled from his window of thoughts Saskia tells Sincere "King asked about you?" How he doing he got shot six times last night he in upstate. "Huh?" "Say no more, let me hit you back!" Instantly Sin hung up Crunk up his whip and slid to the Nolia parked on P-street grabbed the choppa emptied the whole drum screaming to the heavens. "Lord these niggas go die, touch anything of mine death will visit ya! Yall really think this a game." Screaming to whomever could hear him. Less than eight hours Sincere was walking thru Upstate hospital doors. After not speaking nor seeing King in over seven years Saskia always kept him informed of King wellbeing and Sin felt it was his job to watch over King whom wasn't even from the streets. A lifestyle he seemed to have embraced after college. Which seemed weird to Sin, yet all people make their own choices and in saying that Sin never judged who King was but guaranteed he'd protect him in all the events of his life. A big brother he felt he was commissioned to be. King mother seen Sin somewhat in shock probably not understanding how or where Sin came from after seeing him, she hugged him seeing she was shaken Sin just consoled her to the best of his ability while taking all things in. They almost killed my baby he has been fighting for his life never seeing people whom he deemed as family broken and torn. Sin couldn't accept such an act. Sin, silent as tears inside fell upon the cheeks of his heart. Once Sin witnessed King, he was hesitant at the sight of his strongest Souljah filled with tubes battered and abused. A fighter the first one to teach him how to fight against life by taking me to the gym preparing me to war against the many casualties that I never saw unknowingly. In my eyes my hero before I looked to anyone as a role model. Eyes seemed closed face swole standing next to his bed Sin was hurt deeply. Eyes watering not desiring to break in front of anyone he swiftly looked away as tears rolled down his cheeks as he whispered to God. How? Why am I constantly placed in such a position? You know I love him, and I will do what needs to be done for those I love. Suddenly King grabbed Sin hand. Startled, eyes yet puffy King said like Bruce Willis I'm hard to kill Champ. Sin gripping King hands refusing to release it responded Kings cannot Die Brody you built for this. Sin, pulled away stepping quickly to the window weakness wasn't in his pedigree and refused to be looked upon as anything close to weak yet he was dying inside fighting not to allow anyone to see that he indeed felt pain or even cried in hurt in his eyes this wasn't the essence of a Souljah. Tears flooding his shirt. They dead King I promise! Immediately Sin left & went the long way so no one could witness tears from a grown man. Pac his nephew in Georgia was sitting in his car blasting his idol 2pac as phone began ringing. "What's good?" "Say nephew?" "What's up, Unc?" "You remember the construction job we did in Florida?" "Say less" "Bring the tools the same way we did for that job, this job contract for this week." "Four helpers are all needed." "Over stood!" "While in the cuse 2002 the city reached record breaking homicide with 20 murders in one month 5 people died mysteriously. Walking on campus at S.U Sin jogging thru thoughts as soft hands cover his eyes from behind while grabbing the body of his .45 against his stomach beginning to pull it out when suddenly she said guess who? Sin pushed the fire back in his pants trying to figure who knows him in such a manner to feel comfortable to touch him without his knowing. Sin grabbed the arms trailed up the collar bone of the mysterious body. Feeling the face, long hair & fullness of her body eyes yet covered she kissed him. Saskia lost in all completeness caught totally off guard engulfed in a passionate kiss after opening his eyes he is greeted by Saskia. Quickly Sin pulled Sass towards him so she doesn't witness his confusion. Sin was taken away by the magnitude of such passion. They hadn't kissed since middle school. You're a different breed I can honestly say I am appreciative of the support you've shown King and what's crazy is the guys who did what they did died look at karma. The idea of them turned Sin spirit yet he rolled with the events that rolled off her tongue just being an ear. You know they say time heals all wounds. Now here it is their full-grown adults mixed feelings followed by a lot of excitement. I maybe feeling you Sin a tiny bit not much, but I believe you can see the difference. Oh, you think so, huh? Are you speaking from your heart or your mind? Sin stop that! What? Always asking me riddles that leave me stuck in mid-sentence just ride the wave stop trying to drown me in the wave. Lol, yo why you think someone is always trying to bring harm to you or is it I just want you to encounter truth in its purest form. Sin said Its always something unique about you. your nothing like no one I ever experienced. Hmmm, should I be normal? Then I'd feel like you're always left to feel the idea that I leave you with butterflies. As well as keep you on your feet should be enough to allow you to indulge in something outside of life's pain ya dig! Sin feeling somewhat out the loop yet in harmony with his own tune which was the melody he was truly familiar with. Sticking his index finger in her back pocket as she becomes his human G.P.S he follows full stride. Tugging somewhat gently Sass looks back "What, Sin?" "He uses his other index finger to insinuate he wants to whisper something to her. "Have by any chance have I told you your super sexy not just sexy I mean sexy, sexy!" Blushing she kisses Sin on his cheek and says thank you Sin you're such a gentleman. Really!? I guess if you say so. Sin and his sarcasm were so fitting to who he was. Jogging thru his thoughts in all honesty Sin was in awe of the beauty others saw in him cause in truth Sin knew he wasn't who he could or should be but ok if they dig it, he dug it. It was crazy how in my eyes I never seemed to look at myself like others did and felt he wasn't healthy for those he deemed as greatness. He never pressed Sassy, not once not ever could he nor would he tarnish such beauty in such complete form. Recalling moments of complete despair to whereas Sin felt lost at times unknowingly there were moments life pressed hope to its hopeless state & in the moments Sin would cry out to God for help from God's Angel's. Staring about in complete nothingness Sass spilled life into Sin whispering" Looking unto Jesus the Author & finisher of our faith; who for the joy that was set before him endured the cross, despising the shame, and is set down on the right hand of the throne of God. Hebrews 12:2 God is our constant reminder to us hold ya head King!" Life demons constantly attacked Sin outta all the good many seen it was dark

---

nights many don't see, and it can snatch one in a window of depression that seems as if it's an aroma that derives from nowhere. Feeling pulled living in two different mind sets many times Sin felt hypocritical to whereas how could he feel so passionately one way yet live recklessly in another. Sin was truly at war with himself to where as he had become so familiar with many habits that many adored which he saw as strength. Addicted to become the best him he ever could witness nothing nor anyone else was in site. After Sass and Sin gets to her car Sin thanks her for blessing him with her beautiful energy which he needed. Walking to his car Sin pulls out his tool and leans his head back exhausted from a lifestyle that was draining to him completely. Lord I am tired of this I shouldn't have to kill to live this not life. Shoving the tool under his seat soon as his turns up his music his phone begins ringing. "What's good?" female voice. "Sin, when am I going to see you & you go stop playing?" Sin unsure of the voice on the other end just sat listening "So obviously I'm talking to myself?" "You called to talk to me so I'm doing what a person does when he is being talked to, listening!" "All those girls you got you may not even know who this is...this Malika." "Lil Mama…" Sin blurted out "Yes, Sin!" "We on the same page." "So, when you trying to chill with me or what not?" "Whatever is best for you, matter fact hit me up in an hour or two and we can link up Sin." "Say less, are you go play fair?" "You will see tonight my phone going dead here's my number at the house I'm there 315-450-7884. Sin, cutting thru traffic blowing on a Dutch that laid in the ashtray he was sitting righteous. Hanging up Sin goes to hubs liquor store in the hood grabs him a personal bottle of Remy Martin thoughts of King flooded his mental cause this was where he was struck at, it seemed as if Sin wanted to burn the hood down even tho the issues had been erased. Sin & King had been best friends when he was 11 years old never argued, fought or fell out it was naturally love. Caught in thought Sin always swore he would aide his friend in any & every way right or wrong. Pay back exhausted Sin mind he truly felt that was justice only reward. Blowing clouds in the park off Glenwood & South ave cats hollering as if it's an altercation at hand. Taller dude slapped another dude who then punched the taller guy & as if it was natural the 40 cal. appears fire leaves the barrel, yet the body tumble isn't the opposer his brother dove in front of the shot as he holds the pieces left from his brother. After observing the scene Sin reflects on thoughts of the most common demand for survival "Eat or be eaten!" Unsure if it was the bottle or gas Sin no longer wanted to be a part of the problem which was killing his people. Galatians 5:13-15

13 For you were called to freedom, brothers. Only do not use your freedom as an opportunity for the flesh, but through love serve one another.14 For the whole law is fulfilled in one word: You shall love your neighbor as yourself.15But if you bite & devour one another, beware lest you be consumed by one another!

How is it that were placed in chaotic circumstances were looked upon as aggressors because we refuse to die! Juggling ideas in his head Sin wanted out, familiar with a certain way of living for years became habit. The only way to break habit is thru a greater practice. After removing himself from his past life style isolating himself to focus on what's the greatest thing for him to grow as a man. Finally, standing prepared for life priorities which involved fam and friends more than ever his kids was deserving of his totality. Raped spiritually abused mentally while left empty emotionally. Refusal to give up and die after life has beaten you numerous times takes a will to live not just breath. To be of essence to the makeup of life story line which we are the only authors of. It takes courage to change it don't happen overnight change can be painful if one isn't open to it. One must be fully prepared to face life and its circumstances don't be afraid to lose it's the only way one creates room for winning. Wind milling thru various thoughts Uncle Pete said Sin how can you judge someone because their sin different from yours while toaking his blunt. The question was on repeat in my head then words spilled out without thought. I am not the man to judge you in any manner what difference am I from you question isn't that I'm judging you cause not once have I rendered a statement or question to you that represented judgement. What it is the walk of my reality offends the typical being make up because one is forced to measure themselves, I'm not the one using the measuring stick. I measure who it is I desire to constantly grow into. Uncle Pete digesting the response given he then replied, "Deep & something that leaves ones reflecting on many things." Nothing is more exhausting than the refusal of the truth it causes one to hide in its own shell. In thought meditating on the conversation at hand Sin was finally seeing Reality isn't reality. Should I say everyone reality isn't drawn up the same many people look outta different lens. So many are willing to aide the greatest lie known to mankind. Leading the unled sheep to the slaughter unknowingly without obtaining any guidance. What's so crazy is "They'll eat with you, sleep with you & yet try to keep you submerged in the foolery." One must understand there is a price for each level of foolery. Those around you will distaste you for the courage they could never grab.

Head leant in the back seat of the van Major slumped off the white rhino straight out of it. Rose a thotty off the Westside beautiful as ever caught Sin eye and instantly Major said she some straight cut, let me show you! Rose look here for a minute what you got going on? Puerto Rican and thick as ever Sin was completely feining for what this kush hits like. Looking in the van not knowing Sin she asked Major who ya cute ass friend? Major said ask him. He got lips. Then in response she said what's up poppy. Sin, taken away by her accent and her lingo started cheesing and said what's goodie, ma!? How are you? "I'm cooling you not from here huh. Let me guess what gave me away my accent? Ummm, yes, it's cute tho poppy I love that country shit. What yall got going on? Sin lifted the bottle of Rémy martin then passed the Dutch and asked you smoke or drink? "Do a bear shit in the woods and wipe his ass with a rabbit? Sin laughed hmmm you love my guy Pac I see. Answer my question

don't run from it. I responded you must fucking with the kid? That sounds like the move, scoot over!"
Blowing in the back seat as Major drove thru the town Rose and Sin was cracking up kicking it with
one another. Instantly she said ya lips as soft as they look? I don't know. Fuck it, I'll see for myself!
Rose began kissing Sin while rubbing his abs she quickly moved with a goal as if she knew what it
was that she desired in truth. Sin, a slave to what was at hand he desired nothing more than receive
whatever it was she was willing to offer. Unbuckling his pants while the car was yet in motion
stroking his manhood as he stood at erect attention. "Dam poppy you big as a horse are you human?"
Sin intoxicated didn't even respond and in the event of things she attempted to perform magic like
none. Sin whispered make it disappear since you are a magician. Not able to take in all 10 inches
she said I need you personally this car will not let me be great, Sin began laughing and said I can
dig it! Leaving thought after thought in Sin lap leaving his statue full of ideas. Creating more than
dreams leaving visions that Sin yearn to walk in. Floating in his own realm his statue free as liberty
she placed his weapon away. It yet bulging fighting for freedom she said I want you to fuck me Poppy.
Are you a runner because I am not into chasing anyone?! I got too much weight to run I am a big
girl it's a difference. Rose began biting on the bulge that tried busting out his jeans saying I need you
to feed me poppy. After Major had rode us all thru the city, he had parked whereas we just sat back
laughing and tripping. Intoxicated from the gas Major falls out. Me and Rose vibing in the backseat.
Drawing up what was to occur the rest of the night and my Phone began ringing I didn't answer it
then Major was awaken. His phone began ringing after my phone stop ringing and fell off the console.
It began vibrating and playing a ringtone, Saskia asking Major what you got going? I'm not doing
nothing real, what's popping with ya babe? Nothing I was checking to see if you and Sin wanted to
go up on the U and get a bite or something you know how we give it up. Where Sin at anyway I just
hit his phone up. Oh, his phones right here he outside blowing with King politicking or what not.
As Major looks in the review he realizes Rose wiping her mouth shakes his head smirking. I am going
to grab him, and we go slide thru. Putting his hands up Sin gives him a thumb up and he proceeds
to say he said he with it. Major cranks up the van and ask Rose where you going ma? I guess you can
drop me off at my crib. As he slides thru the tenth (hood), Rose begins asking Sin you go stay with
me or what? I can wait on you if you're going to come back thru or you just go get rid of me. I'm
with whatever you up for! Sin began moving towards the front seat and said ok I'll hit ya horn later
that's cool? I guess, kinda feeling brushed off. Passing thru the camp heading towards the Ph. Major
stops at the hub to grab a bottle. Sin, I'm bout to get a bottle what you go do my guy? I got half Brody
it's no pressure. After leaving the Hub Major push down South Townsend and turns on Harrison
Street heading towards the West. After riding down West Onondaga Street heading down West street
Major drops Rose off in the projects. After Sin was slightly slumped in the front seat not aware of his
destination Rose hits him like Sin are you going to come back or what don't have me up looking for
you if you not coming back. Ok, I gotcha ma imma come back let me go bust a few moves and we

will go from there, that's cool with you? Yea just call me just in case I fall asleep. Yo, if you go fall asleep, I'm not coming so what is it going to be let me know? Ok Sin I'll be up! Say less! After Major pulls off Sin daps his guy up and say you never fail me big brody I love ya for that. Already! You know I will always hold you down no matter what. Also, we about to go blow some more gas so let me run to the crib and get us some more pressure! Sin calls Sass "What's goodie babe?" "Nothing Sin what you & Major got going on?" Nothing real we just tip toeing thru traffic trying to skate with you up here on the U. Bored nothing else to do. Just doing what I do, blowing on this propane and sipping a little. I'm in the mood to grab a bite you still with it. "Yea, we can. I'm up for it aint nothing else to get into. Where Major? He in the crib! Oh, yall right by the crib then ok let me finish getting myself together. "Ok ma we'll meet you up there we in route just hit my horn up? Ok, Sin! Sin attempting to adjust his demeanor didn't wanna be totally outta pocket. While sliding thru the hood Sin reminiscing on Sassy. Pictures and thoughts of Sassy were beyond words. A creation God truly took his time on in my eyes, her entirety spoke volumes more so divine than anyone I have ever witness in all my twenty-eight years of living. I was a fan of God artwork internally as well as externally I don't believe many knew the depths of her beauty. In the crevices of the valley only darkness has been death shadows no one desired to face during any moments yet in my case she was indeed a light to my path. Help me escape some of my darkest moments my grandma always would say light under a bushel can't be hidden. I was given more profound understanding by Sass it was many of nights darkness invaded the confines of my mind only desiring to walk deeper towards darkness but as if she was a key towards my freedom. Words of the truth we always encountered as children were seeds, she would water even when I believed death was fitting for me. Matthew 5:15 -16"Neither do men light a candle, and put it under a bushel, but on a candlestick; and it giveth light unto all that are in the house. Let your light so shine before men, that they may see your good works, and glorify your Father which is in heaven. "Sometimes I go too far I am not an Angel but I have had Angels save me from me cause the world can cause you to be as cold as it just to stay warm, so it was never any need for me to stay bundled up. I was indeed my heat. Sass held a uniqueness which was rare the swagger of the streets flooded with grandma's storyline indeed an old soul. The totality of her essence was alluring, demanding yet humbling. Being in her presence was soothing to a Beast only low lives could understand the depths of such a reward. Someone who was needed in the field. As a kid i constantly desired her attention which she blessed me with openly, smiles and endless laughter. The idea of my laying my head in her lap as she ran her fingers thru my scalp was refreshing to my spirit even though it occurred as kids it was on repeat in my mental like my favorite script. I'd fall asleep, wake up late go home after the time which was well spent. Let's leap to the future. Sassy, who became a clothing designer for celebrities who were marquee names or b class. Always told me I wanna make your first custom fitted suit for the presentation for your photography & canvas painting. I'd blush because it was something I long to do outside of these streets. No matter what she always spoke life and detached my street life from how she seen me up until I seen what she seen. I'd only give attention to it in my privacy. Music vibing listening to Mali Music candle lit displaying dim lights as fire dances thru out my eyelids. Bristles feeling like drumsticks as I'm in tune to the music the canvas becomes instruments giving melodies that seduces the eyes as the brush flies without stopping or missing a beat. Shadows roaming upon my thoughts praying upon the beauty of Art totality. I was an Artist and I adored it. Room flooded with paintings reflecting on a letter I received from Sass during a depressing time in my life pertaining to women. Before anything Sass was a friend first & foremost in my eyes a person whom protected my heart no matter what never leaving me blind to the trickery women possessed.

1) *To my friends that are...single.*
   Love is like a butterfly. The more you chase it the more it eludes you. If you just let it fly, it will come to you when you least expect it. Love can make you happy yet often it hurts. Love's only special when you give it to someone who is worth it. So, take your time. Always be your friend….and choose the best.

2) *To my friends that are...Not so single!*
   Love isn't about becoming somebody else's "perfect person," It's finding someone once in a blue moon...who helps you become the best person you can be.

3) *To my friends that are...playboy/girl type.*
   Never say "I Love You" ...if you don't care. Never talk about feelings if they are not there. Never touch a life if you mean to break a heart. Never look in the eye when all you do is lie. The cruelest thing a guy can do to a girl is to let her fall in love when he doesn't intend to catch her fall and it works both ways...

4) *To my friends that are...Married!*
   Love isn't about "it's your fault" more so "I'm sorry." Not "where are you," clearly "I'm right here." not "how could you?" sincerely "I understand." Not "I wish you were," definitely "I'm thankful you are."

5) *To my friends that are…. engaged!*
   The true measure of compatibility is not the years spent together but how good you are for each other.

6) *To my friends that are...Heartbroken!*
Heartbreaks last as long as you wanted & cut as deep as you allow them to go. The Challenge is not how to survive heartbreaks but to learn from them-Tricks of the Trade!

7) *To my friends that are…....Naive!*
How to be in love: Fall but don't stumble, be consistent but not too persistent, share and never be unfair, understand& try not to demand, & get hurt yet never keep the pain.

8) *To my friends that are…. Possessive!*
It breaks your heart to see the one you love happy with someone else. Yet its more Painful to know that the one you love is unhappy with you.

9) *To my friends that are…. afraid to confess!*
Love hurts when you break up with someone. It hurts even more when someone Breaks up with you. Yet, love hurts the most when the person you love has no idea how you feel.

10) *To my friends that are…. Still holding on!*
A sad thing about life is when you meet someone & fall in love, only to find out in the End. That it was never meant to be & that you have wasted years on someone Who wasn't worth it? If he isn't worth it now, he is not worth it a year or ten years from now. Let go! Men lie, women lie but energy don't!

11) *To all my friends….*
My wish for you is a man/woman whose love is honest, strong, mature, never Changing, uplifting, protective, encouraging, rewarding & unselfish.

No moment with Sass is normal even in thoughts she tends to walk me upon beauties cloud that alone is life to any dead bones. Major and Sin kicked back on the U as Sin sits in the car listening to 2pac Do for love. As he watches Major in a crowd of women laugh and uncontrollably act out. It was no one nor nowhere we would go Major didn't fit in. As light flash behind Sin he looks in the review as he sees Sass in the review mirror. High off her essence as if she was a drug Sin loved indulging in, he exits the van jumps in the passenger seat kissing her on the cheek as he hugs her. How are you babe? You know I get butterflies still, we too grown for this, but your aura is everything. Touched by her as if they were still kids butterflies indeed were constantly laying in the bosom of his ribs. "You be doing the most, but we'll go with that, Sin!" Karma by Lloyd Banks ft Avant serenading the atmosphere. How you feeling Sin? I am good love trying to enjoy this mini vacation. "You the only one I know who has no job but travel more than Diddy." Both laughing in unison you know my job doesn't intel me to be in one town you dig! I get it you ready to invest some of these business ventures I've blown in ya ear? Knowing this was the only way to try and get Sin outta his situation with his lifestyle. I refused to give up on him life has been crazy yet great at the same time. You must go customize our outfit for our wedding? Laughing out loud, no one caused my spirit to be at ease in such a manner. Sin, Sin, Sin after leaving my hypnotized state she ask "Got a few days for me to kidnap you." Where are we going, if you don't mind my asking. You know I blow like the leaves it's no telling where I maybe. Sass going thru her & Sin conversation the other night. You know this life is exhausting. Sass said that's why and stopped mid-sentence. Choosing just to listen. Sin high off more than pain he was intoxicated by life. A group of kids slid up on me before I came here, I really don't like what I represent so I take myself out of the eyes of many. A group of kids slid up on me & told me Sin we wanna be like you. Confused but understanding the reality of his truth. Sin carefully examining himself a light 2 racks sat on his eyes wearing Cartier glasses with wood frame covering his eyes. Polo attire Rugby shirt followed by the shorts with Sperry covering my feet in Society I was chameleon in the hood I stuck out. Understanding money & class seldom follow one another in the hood. A full time Street pharmacist with Shakespeare wordplay How could I blame them for looking up to me. Looked upon as a role model to many nope cause I'm not perfect. I'm human in my eyes I always depict myself as a real-model a model of reality hopefully many grow from my mistakes in hopes of being a better person. "Lend me your hand, you will always have my heart. We go always build each other up we not go tear each other down." Bringing Sin back to the reality at hand by pulling him outta his thoughts. As her words interrupted me outta my place in my mental rolodex. Holding my hand reassuring me that she was here in the present sense. While hands clasped she took both of our hands while her index finger turned my face to look at her "I apologize Sassy, I seemed to stumble in my thoughts constantly." "Sin you always apologizing & thanking me. Do you recall when I once was in a dark place & you shed your light upon the shadows of my life." "Yes ma'am." "You just left the light on, it never was dark you just had to walk back to the light. "Wow, Lord its certain people you surround me with that are truly refreshing to my spirit. I thank you, father!"

Love Is the Language

I've felt so much pain from the hate I've injected in my veins.
Was I insane or familiar with the picture that's been surrounded by my frame?
Again & Again I've drunk from this same cup.
That was given free of charge.
Attention was the fee that help me look past the scars of my heart.
Thoughts began walking from the dark.
Language of love began to talk.

The Ark that kept me during flooding moments.
Love is greater than hate I've embraced the promise.
Faith lies in my stomach giving birth to something far more honest.
Even lust attempts to mumble the same Ebonics.
Love defends itself; love forgives, love is here!
It's the only language I express so clear cause in the end Love always win.

Sin Mother was an Evangelist no matter how far he ventured in the deep end of the flooding waters God stayed close. Reason being he was taught how to converse with God thru prayer a tool he became familiar with but didn't fully understand up until he grew into a man. Many times jogging thru thoughts Sin felt as if no one understood him. Crazy truth I soon would learn to embrace faithfully. He looked at no one as adversary everyone was helpers of where it is, he was destined to be, some seemed harsher than others being that wasn't the direction that was chosen by the most high. Things were becoming more vivid after embracing life adversity.

No that's not it at all Solace, what it is that people are to look as society puseudes them to and we're being pushed from Real to unreal wearing the make up to remind us we look like the role. Yo Sincere you be going too far! Explaining that you say that when our men are walking around looking like women and I women are walking around looking like men but they're not going too far. It's a difference between freedom of choice and force, this has been forced on us from fear. Fear of what Sin? One has become comfortable with familiarity in saying that one has become dependent upon a structure so you believe something can change that. No, I kinda see what you're saying it does make sense?! So do one live or die then? It's crazy that you would say such a thing, were forced to choose one of the lesser evils. So, you believe its fear? What else could it be? Maybe they were raised to believe as you were raised to believe what you feel suites you, correct or incorrect? I agree yet in my seek of what's real I came across God! It was the closest thing to Real. Hmmm, ironic that you said that? What? You were looking for real and you found God! It was the most consistent thing I witness that was more loyal than man.

Do you believe people look at you as hypocritical? Honestly that at one time was my issue i no longer worry about what others deem as what's best for me I am the only one outside of God who holds such power dealing with myself, that would be too much power to give any man outside of self?

You can be the remedy and people will still reach for the poison…!

Complacently tried knocking my doors down unbeknownst to me pride always tried being the anchor of my journey. A father of a tribe with the responsibility of complete governing none. Only partially from time to time never consistent. Money, I felt was the premier identity of fatherhood. Up until the point I believed women job was easy. My son is fourth teen his mother has been dead over two years. Life pushes me beyond my normalcy. Fear of failure, fear of not being a man. Various people would whisper some form of guidance. "Go to D.F.C.S they will help you!" Were the words played in my head? Not over being looked down upon, Sin seldom encountered circumstances to whereas he'd allow life to consume him in his heart its always been by any means necessary. Over the loud speaker numbers "5545TW!" Sin leaped up hearing his number called goes in to speak with the lady who open the door. "Hello, Sincere!"

"Hello, how are you this evening ma'am!" "How is it can we help you today?" Looking in the face of a black woman who seen defeat conjuring in his eyes. Asked how can I be of help, I'm here to be assistance? Yes, If all the paperwork goes thru two weeks you'll have back pay for this month & the up and coming month. Living in a world where tough is only a running mechanism to where as one is afraid to look at their own flaws & sharpen what is dull. Proverbs 27:19 "As in water face reflects face, So the heart of man reflects man."

We question our truth, yet we only push it as far as the eye allows which deprive one's spirit man to excel with no limitations. The ability to walk on water God son performed such a task yet let's look at the law of logic Sun has the ability to fight from afar yet walk on water crevices nothing hindering such intimacy. The idea of creativity in itself is one in the same. Fighting to understand what was at hand Sin somewhat rattled by the events that was transpiring. These words residing in his spirit & constantly echoed, after leaving his ex he was shattered someone whom I dared to see in any other manner held no regard to how I would perceive her, all she wanted was me submerged up til a point death seemed as if it was ones only means. In my thoughts I felt its either love or death nothing more. Many have always questioned Sincere ability to endure strenuous encounters, after every fall, he'd get up all over again. If you never knew love you could never fathom Sincere to the least to know him is to desire love equivalence.

Walking inside a pub that held open mic the words that derived from the other end of the mic was intoxicating. "Love has sat at my rib cage yearning to breathe, pain has tripped up love strut daring one to believe!?!?!

Yet, after every fall Love yet leaps! I feel your feet when you're walking to me…

...like a sheet you keep me covered whether you're in my thoughts when I'm in bed or even when you serenade thru out my head, I'm led to YOU. So if it takes me in complete totality ....Incline to spit a piece Sin begins thumbing thru his phone trying to decide. When the gate became open Sin attacked the mic. Normally, I could spill on any topic but being mental illness is at an all-time high. I will drop gems that could aide some in a sense.

Salvation Helmet

I was always told kill the head the body dead, never neglect wisdom shared.
After every fight, each scar!
I looked upon the man in the mirror, the picture became clearer.
Smitten as a kitten fears driven walking thru a prism that seemed like Prison
Seeing reflection of a lion.
Peering in haunted houses whispers of many wanting out.
Desiring to help my fellow man every moment I turned my back I was attacked by the shovel in his hand.
Many yearning to leave.
It's impossible to retreat with treasures that won't squeeze thru the doors!
Can one ignore the writings on the wall?
It's hard to fall if you keep your helmet on.
All is fair in LOVE & War; enemies keep their weapons drawn.
So, who are one's Allies?
Love grows stronger by & by; it causes deaf to listen?
It wipes smut from the blind eyes!
What's wise?
No, what's foolish?
Understanding Peter before the rooster crowed 3x or trusting Judas?
Disaster in itself is beautiful!
So, let the music play!
I'll continue wearing the Helmet of Salvation as usual.

Snapping and many standing at ovation, I was humbled that many were. This was more so Sincere I no longer desired embracing Sin.

Waking up witnessing a few missed texts no one matter in this world of Sin but me and my girlfriend. In my mind Nevaeh was mine no matter what portion of the earth she resided in. A woman who poured in me just because, I never asked intrigued by her world of beauty she was nothing less than amazing. Drumming to her number a Muskegon, Michigan native I met thru writing. Let's look outside ones physical a moment a brook with refreshing water in the midst of sunburns she became the umbrella to shade me from life storm. I never was familiar of nature precipitations. This was the thermostat of my life, blessing me with coats of esteem when quitting seemed like an addiction a picture nor words could describe such abundance. Before I ever understood how to face my monsters and demons, she was my ghostbuster. The gems when my vaults were empty the director to my peace when the world storms tried offending the melodies that held me ever so gently. My Poetry when pen lost lips, there's no question this was much more than a gift. Sin receiving a text from Nevaeh.

Nevaeh

Just up and horny thats all....July 2nd to the 6 th im in Ga, you feel like coming feeling my urge?

Sin

You play 2 much yo!

Nevaeh

Im tryna to make it happen. Cum get me? Im in Gainsville. Sin Wya?

Nevaeh

At least I'm trying!

I really need to know how far u are from gainsville.

6/2/14, 4:21 PM

Sin

I am 2 hours from you, give me three hours ill slide your way. It's nothing i know where you at, im down here in middle georgia handling bizness somewhat.
4hrs

6/6/14, 2:58 PM

Shunna

This how we doing? I haven't seen you nor heard from you in 4 doors. You gotta be tricking, i cant stand ya ugly ass.

Sin

Money over bitches cause they breed envy is what i was taught. Got out ya feelings im check chasing. This how you get what you want with no problems.

Shunna

Im so tired of you throwing money in my face. This all we are? I love you Sin do you not get that but i guess you comfortable with this arrangement.

Sin

You must need some pads? I stay at this bag you knew that walking in, get out ya feelings were better than this

Shunna thing was learn or hurt either way the responsibility lies before you. The penalties of desiring growth and one not being in their best state of mind is a form of suicide. If one true desire is to create the most perfect fire. Treasure who was Cee Cee sister had just moved to Georgia outta Fort Myers, Fla. The home of Plies, Sin punch line would always be Bussi Baby. Treasure stood 6 ft tall chest stuck out as if the S on her chest was 3D. Caramel complexion chased with a spoon of honey. A woman of simplicity who never desired to stick out but, stood out. Round cheek bones that seemed as if they were handed down from one of granny stove tops. Crown that was full as Foxy Brown in her best acting moments, she was a natural. Quiet offish demeanor never seeking attention, but the reality of life stills remains true. Often times for the most part those who never desired attention somehow grasp the most attention. As Sin walked up on Treasure who would stay wrapped in her thoughts whenever Shunna came thru. Baby Momma & Baby daddy nope I'll past in her voice! Cee-Cee and Shunna was sisters who had the same mother the streets. Treasure and Cee-Cee was sisters who held the same father. In truth Shunna & Treasure wasn't sisters but their bond was decent enough for you to consider them as being family. Treasure could feel the ice in her veins from the hurt and past betrayals. How is it for one to receive or be of help to one in such a state outside of listening so Treasure just sat and listened as Shunna rambled and poured out her feelings as if she was a facet. Years of faithfulness seemed to be up in the air how was it that the only person I truly loved or loved me for the most part was to leave me and just marry someone else like really who does that? Never saying a word Treasure knowing the story ever so clear, what could she say she just continued listening. Sin caught between two lifestyles that no one could seem or refused to understand. It's a flip side to every coin, one forgets that the head looks away from the tail so it's clear both sides view is completely different. This was a moment Sin deemed as progress or stagnation. So which baton does one take?! Shunna who have been the life of his world pushed him beyond the adversity of the jungle was a lioness easy in his eyes. No longer having a desire to hurt others when in all sincerity I just wanted to evolve. Maybe people never seen what I seen. Shunna & I held an open relationship to where as we could be involved with whom we saw fit the only guidelines we sat were respect the others presence (I know how crazy is it or how can respect be present when we both were clearly disrespecting one another but in truth this was our level of understanding.) If one was to see the others immediate family or their team whoever they chilled with they were to separate from among the madness openly. Nothing more nor less! At this point Sin had never been in a true relationship because he loved his freedom. Never wanting to pretend nor openly hurt people in his mind he felt as if I tell you who I am openly. You are given a choice if you don't wanna deal with it cool. It's a million people who would still rock with me. If you did, its nothing I wouldn't do for you in return. It was clear to say I was offering stability and protection. All required of you was to not harass me or press me with the extra and for the most part who wouldn't want such an opportunity? Shunna would always tell Treasure everybody cheats the hurt comes from one not knowing what's taking place but when you know, and certain guidelines are permitted I believe you can't be hurt and if so look at me. It's nothing I don't have my own car, my own crib, I go anywhere I wanna go I am living. Who wouldn't want that! Treasure still listening couldn't believe what she was hearing but was thinking in depth about the reality of Shunna truth. Wow, who is faithful? Then out the blue of you dragging me the entire relationship you ask me to marry you. Damn, right I said no cause you're not ready! Treasure never knew that she just assumed Sin had decided to leave Shunna cold turkey. In search of an exit Sin no longer desired to be trapped in the confines of killing everything around him. As the 40 cal. Covered his lap Sin whispered to himself "Yo, I don't have to live like this & made a decision that day. Words played on repeat in Shunna head all she remembers is "Either you move forward with me or get left behind! What's it going to be? Shunna was listening to Sin on the phone as he was in New York.. Sin, then what? What's after now? A brighter future yo this not living, dude I fuck you and anybody I want even your friends stay at me. You call this living? Listening to Sin harsh reality which was undeniably true. All she could say was, you not ready and I am not ready. Hurt beyond life this is who Sin wanted to be with forever the most consistent female that ever existed in his life. Loyalty was an understatement!

You sure this how you feel? Bathing in thoughts of hurt she knew she would never love like this again for anyone and Sin was just leaving her. Sin caused her to feel, outta pain Shunna pops off and gets white girl wasted. Wakes up with another guy in her bed, unbothered she felt what Sin don't know won't hurt. How true is reality slogan what's done in the dark will come to the light? A few weeks no menstrual Shunna was worried she was pregnant & it wasn't Sin child. How could she tell Sin?! Shunna had been involved with Sin so long til it wasn't no secrets between her & him. Cee-Cee and Sin was super tight their bond was crazy and Shunna knew that so as she arrived to Hope house Sin was on the phone laughing & joking with Sin. Shunna tells Hope to put Sin on speaker. So, you loving New York Sin you crazy is what Hope states. Yo, how about I am fucking with this officer and let me tell you how crazy this is no flex. The police tries killing me in the car with her because I tell her I don't wanna be involved. You too controlling and she say she pregnant! What Sin? Yea, she said she pregnant. I'm all on the phone calling my momma like ma she trying to kill me. Yo, I jumped in the backseat she flowing thru stop sign after stop sign never hitting the brakes. Hope cracking up, while Shunna is bathing in tears. Shunna gets up and goes to the bathroom crushed. This nigga is no good is all Shunna mumbles to herself I hate this dude, ugh! While Shunna is in the bathroom Hope tells Sin you know Mann been staying with Shunna? Huh, was all Sin could say. What, yo stop playing with me. Sayless! Sin, hangs up instantly while riding thru the town taking in all the events at hand the reality Sin was in a whole nother relationship. Never considering her possibly being pregnant Shunna wanted to walk away from all this madness. Sin calls Tinka phone and it began becoming clearer after 9 she would not answer his phone calls. Sin calls his sister Bleu which was his real sister same mother and dad. What's up Sin? I need you to do me a favor I need you to go get all my things from Tinka house. My clothes, shoes don't worry about nothing outside of that I'll get everything else but get that I need that asap. You sure I won't have a problem getting your stuff? Sin said why would you? Call her on the 3 way she just may not answer my call but if you call, she just may answer. Hold on Sin? After the phone rings Sin hears Tinka voice "Hello?" "Hello, Tinka?" "yes!" This Bleu Sin told me to come get all his stuff… Tinka interrupting mid-sentence no why? Sin tripping! He said he calls, and you don't never answer your phone he's been calling over a week, he said you've gotten to comfortable." "Comfortable, I am not doing nothing tell Sin to call me." "For what Sin interrupts you haven't answered my call for a minute!" "Surprised and caught off guard her response was Sin don't do this please." Do what? Just give me my things and you can live lil buddy no pressure. No Sin I need to talk to you? "You got 2 days to erase everything you got going on I'm on the way asap. Play with me and think it's a game." After hanging up Sin head is running in circles unsure of what to do. Currently in a great place my mom just got me a job to where as I would be working for the state driving transit vans. I can finally leave this life and do better than this ugh. Fuck that! Phone ringing Hello this is the Airport "I need a ticket for tomorrow!" Head throbbing unsure of what to do and King slides thru and picks him up. What's good Brody we bout to go to the Casino get ya mind off the worries we go live. Texting while in route to the casino. Sin tells Shunna you got 10 hours to get all ya niccas out the way on God the outcome won't be pretty that's on Blondie tombstone.

If you think it's a game you go hate me, you've been warned! Shunna wakes up with Mann lying next to her knowing that if Sin gets a weft of this he acting out. After taking a shower her sister calls "Shunna the streets talking bout Mann been all on you in the Club you know Rocky asked me who Mann is?" "Ugh, this nicca got a million eyes on me I cant never move." "Girl, you know Sin is Sin and people know he get to acting Loco its curtains you need to chill." "While talking to her sister she began reading her text after reading her text from Sin she screams girl I'll call you back frfr I gotta go." Get up get your stuff you gotta go hurry up yo." Why you acting out Ma?" "I don't got time for Sin get ya shit and get out for real for real." "This nicca do what he wants to you and you act like he God!" "Believe me Mann you don't want them problems sit ya hummingbird ass down now." Don't let a few nights of pleasure get you hurt." "Hurt shorty…" Mid-Sentence she stops him, you heard me get ya shit and go right now." Realizing the text was 4 hours ago that meant he'd be here in 6 one thing she knew for certain that Sin don't tell many people his business but when he moves, he moves it was nothing for him to be in another state in hours that's just who Sin was."

Tinka was having breakfast with her mother and she was telling her mom's about what was going on and didn't know what to do. "Sin, said he was leaving the streets alone ma!" "This dude left me in the middle of my being pregnant to go flip some work, fuck all that!" I am supposed to be this ideal shorty ok so what he dropped a few racks in my account that don't make it cool to fuck over me." "Plus, the streets say him & Shunna still involved." I am not go be around here being nobody fool while they do them." "I can sit here and tell you a million ways to fuck over Sin what would that do?" "Growth is a process you must be willing to work together." "You know you been dead wrong for what you been doing but you grown you gotta bump ya own head a few times to know how it feels not to hurt it again." "Nobody is perfect but respect someone that's trying, many times we can be a man fuel to push beyond anything in life or you can drain one's battery to whereas the engine doesn't move anywhere you choose?" "Yes, I can hold ya hand but some decisions you must make as a woman." Tinka rambling thru her thoughts refusing to let life get the best of her, winning was her only goal by any means. Sin, plate was never full in his eyes. Attempting to lighten the load Sin was sure with no restrictions on call he had over 50-100 women he could call on faithfully who would aide him as needed in any manner he wanted. A dope boy was a star to any hood they walked thru, money & power went hand & hand. Sin, always said I get more money & cut up more women than most rappers they living our lives without the reality. Those gunfights, those unsafe circumstances they are speaking on isn't their lives its mine. A rapper that came from the same city as I did, asked me to rap with him I refused to live a lie and give up game for fame. This not Vegas but what goes on in the trenches stays in the trenches. Even though many people could never grasp our lingo we speak in codes only we know. I can never expose my brethren to be deemed as a boss. The reality was this lifestyle is more exhausting than ever and Sin was at his wits end. Walking in normally its only two

---

ways out death or jail where one is deemed a legend but how can I fight many years of my life to get rich just to brag about it and never see freedom I just don't get that part. I really don't, realizing he signed up for more than he was willing to encounter, and endured Sin no longer wanted to be a part of the problem he wanted to be a part of the solution of our reasoning of familiarity to our existence. I embraced a lifestyle for ages because I yearn to encounter real but this wasn't real it was a fasuage. All the many people he was among that always chanted real nicca, real this wasn't adding up. Was Reality real? Questions after questions stayed flooding my thought process in seek of what was truly real. Waiting for his flight Sin sat outside blowing clouds feeling disappointed in what he seen as real, finally within himself he felt as if he was representing a falsehood he wanted no portion of. Looking up towards the clouds Sin spoke sincerely "Lord I don't know you but help me understand life truth I know this some bullshit." Ready to board his flight the weather rerouted the string of events he had to go to the windy city and then to Atl Sin was ready to go home. Arriving in Chi-town Sin had a layover where he was delayed about 2 or 3 hours because the weather and while waiting Sin bumped in to R. Kelly whom he thought was the God of r&b. Never one to be celebrity struck cause he felt his hood and generals in the jungle was people he looked at as role models. What's crazy was R. Kelly had spoken to Sin after going thru the metal detector Kelly said I guess it is real. Unsure of what he was speaking on Sin said what? Ya chain looking down at his chest Sin wore a Cuban link flooded with diamonds that would remind you of 2pac but the only difference was diamonds were filling half the chain when 2pac chain was flooded with all diamonds .2pac was someone Sin really admired in the music world not because of his fame but his truth he gave out to many. Sin laughed "You not the only one eating." looking up to Kelly who was a bit over 6 ft tall and Sin was 5'9. Never the one to be intimidated by anyone presence Sin continue pushing thinking yo he has the guile to attack my demeanor. Sin nonchalant acts was typically who he was and instead of desiring to grab any form of attention he disappeared thru the doors of his flight.

"Prepare for landing we have now arrived at Hartsfield-Jackson Atlanta International Airport this is Delta Airline thank you for your flight"

Butterflies laid in the pit of his stomach and Sin was really moving under the radar this was how he moved outta everyone's eyesight. As Sin was walking towards the lobby, he stopped to text Ree-Ree whom was to meet him in the lobby. "Hello, Sin where are you what Terminal are you at?" "I am at the second terminal." "You were flight DL1808 correct?" "Yes ma'am" "Well i am at the baggage claim." "I am wearing a yellow kinda goldish top." "Ok." Sin seeing Ree-Ree who was a Parole officer. Ree-Ree who was from Brooklyn, New York moved to Alabama and recently began working Atlanta her and Sin had been friends over 8 yrs. and their relationship was unbreakable. In his eyes she would always have a place in my life. Anytime I needed a place of escape I'd disappear in the confines of her presence from time to time. The story of Sin life was he had a female friend in almost every state bathing against the east coast as well as mid-west. The many reasoning in his disappearing he could never be found where was one to look? Always positioning himself for the feds when or if they ever came, he resided in many locations.

As Sin walked up behind Ree-Ree he poked her in her side turning around startled wearing a scarf he pulled her in by the ends of it. Eyes closed believing Sin would kiss her he drew her in close enough, so the warmth of his nostrils laid upon the crevices of her lips. His nose upon her nose he begins rubbing them together. Lips gently touching one another he pecked her then kissed her forehead I love everything about ya thank you for everything you do. So, you ready to go back to Macon tonight I need you to hold me tonight? "You told me your guy was at the crib, so I didn't wanna intrude or bring any madness to your doorstep." "Sin, I pay my bills no one tells me what to do! Matter face what we will do is I will go get us a room. So, I can be close to you. Is it ok if I just hold you close to me if anything? "Yes, Sin that's what I need I don't need sex in every situation. If my listening to your heart beat isn't the greatest form of sex the physical doesn't match. Placing her fingers thru Sin he quickly says did you feel that. Arms brushing against one another in such a delicate manner leaves goosebumps tip toeing against the entirety of her body she kisses Sin knowing that no one else left her with such a feeling. Asleep in the room after both shared a jacuzzi and massage each other with hot oil. Sin, is awaken as he begins to crack his eyes open Sin realizes he is fully erect and Ree-Ree is spitting more than truth as every word touch deeper and deeper Sin doesn't wanna walk outta such a dream the TV screen is the only thing that gives away her silhouette I witness her going back and forward towards the mic giving spoken words unmatched to any def poetry event. In tune with the current conditions Sin begins encouraging her by the ouuuu and ugggggghhhhh. Then in mid performance it seemed as if she was in Nelly video tip drill standing behind the center of attention it was far to say this was a wave that one could never pass on. A good girl that's bad don't get it confused. It's fair to say she thicker than clay dough, easy. After I fainted on the bed from her standup performance my legs were gone and wasn't coming back. Let me clean you up Sin? How can spoke words turn into someone who indeed had a bounty placed on her head, a quicker picker upper lawd you real. Dutch burning Sin always keeping bud close to him as if he was the personal plant dropping the seeds. Play ya Cardz right humming thru the background as Ashanti & Pac serenades the atmosphere Ree-Ree tells Sin you know imma do my job easily. You know I know this you moved to Georgia because I told you I need you closer and I am forever grateful to everything you have done for me in every way. You deserve a place on my body I just gotta figure out where to put you. In Sin eyes he was a walking billboard that only posted people whom he loved at heart. Where will you put me where I put you. Rolling up her shirt while driving on forearm was a tattoo of my lips surrounded by the words Walking on the lips of Sin. Yes, I may put it there because I have nothing on my left forearm. You go get in trouble for your actions next time I see you go have a black eye. Sin started laughing after making such a statement. As Ree-Ree continued looking on lips poked out she, shaking her head she began racking Sincere waves cuffing the back of his head pulling him towards her kissing him passionately as Sin peeping out the side of his eye as she held his bottom lip in her mouth stated Yo we go crash with you doing all this babe. Eyes back on the road she laughed I am a veteran you know I can multi task in a great way. That you are correct about thinking on all that Ree-Ree was speaking on. Why didn't you tell me you got married Sin? No one knew that I ran away to South Carolina. Married my baby's mother maybe I did it for the wrong reasons, but I no longer wanted her to kill my kids. Do people assume because I'm in the streets I can't be a father or cannot love? Maybe I don't express my emotions enough? Growing up in a world where weakness is vulnerable one is left with a choice of staying strong. That's not true Sin. Ree Ree please don't talk just listen, its certain things I care not to speak on. Piano and guitar strums as Lyfe "Must Be Nice" fills silence voids. Once in Macon they went to the mall and Sin had to spoil his homie she was his life outside his world. While holding bags on top of bags Sin phone rung and he answered it "What's up Sis? "Where you at in the mall? Oh, I am in the food court once she came in Sin introduced his sister to Ree-Ree actually Yvette was his sister Husband sister who loved him as if they were kin because they been in one another life their entire life. Making it to the car he places bags in the car and said hold on she about the bring the rest of my clothes baby girl! After she pulled up in the Infinity SUV, she drops off Sin bags while kissing him holding him tight. Yo I may need to touch you sooner than you know? Sin, you know I am open to you at any given moment I love who you are to me for real …. know that! Kissing him one last time before releasing him. Leaving the mall in route to Warner Robins Sin calls Tinka "Hello!?" "Hmmm, you must've did what I said do?" "Sin I heard all you told me; ok I get it! Omg I feel special for some reason I guess because I been gone for a minute and you answer the phone for the first time." Meet me at Texaco with the Taco bell I'm in Warner Robins you for real how, never mind I am on the way!" Hugging his sister now being she had his undivided attention. So, you feel she was outta order or cheating on you Sin. If so, it's no pressure I am not go trip life is what it is I am not mad by it in any manner. Are you go stay with her or leave? I believe I may stay with her none of us perfect what's done is done, what's did is did that's how the cookies crumble so may the cards fall where they may. I can dig it in your voice lol. Kissing her on her cheek it was fair to say she was closer to him than his biological sister than were tight. Arriving 2 Texaco running in the store to grab cigars Sin comes out ready to burn to keep himself in a righteous state. A gold Altima pulls up and suddenly he hops out grabbing his bag but as he approaches the car Tinka unlock the trunk uninviting and numb. Sin felt it clearly which answered more questions than any words. On the ride to Hawkinsville Sin was silent as she was once, they arrived. Sin told her don't tell anyone I am home I am staying under the radar and don't want anyone to know my business. Matter a fact pull up to my Uncle house as they pulled up on Jelk Street he asked her to pull in the drive way then once she pulled in Sin asked her to go get his fye from his Uncle. Huh? Sin why you... never mind! After leaving to go get my fye Tinka phone vibrates and once it vibrates Sin doesn't read the text message, he reads the name and sits the phone down. As Tinka gets in the car handing Sin the 40 cal wrapped in a sweater he asks her who is Dirty she states oh he just a friend. Cool! Leaving Jelk street they head to Arrow head Apartments where she stays in the back. Soon as he gets out Mailman who goes with Tinka sister Hollers Yo Sin get at ya boy asap. Ok, homie let me put my things away and I will be on my way. After throwing his things on the living room floor Tinka says you running straight over there Sin said I'm just going to blow this gas I'll be right back after this blunt. Once Sin arrived at Mailman door, he hollers its open come in Bro! Playing the PlayStation which was his thing Sin was a video guy money & women were the only thing held his attention. Roll up and get off the game frfr, after he chopped it up about Cash calling him about Trap Sin said you know I had to handle him so kinda way right. I already know how you give it up homie that's just who you are. Oh, yea I thought I saw you the other day since I begged you not to cheat on shorty, I will be the first to tell you shorty aint shit! Sin, already felt that was the case but he was listening not saying a word. Then Mailman was like I thought it was you the other night I am hollering Sin, Sin and dude slides up in her front door then immediately I goes in the house and check my girl. Yo what type of a game ya sister playing and she said this just how she gives it up you just now knowing this Mail. As Sin was taking it all in after gassing one another down Sin told Mailman he was sliding to the crib. Once Sin stepped thru the doors, he smelled chicken parmesan which was his favorite dish she definitely was on time. Fresh out the shower Tinka was definitely eye candy 6'1 thicka than a blizzard that couldn't fall out the cup. 30 inches giving her butt a massage bosom bursting outta her shirt as if they were fighting each bra she wore. Legs that stretched out longer than a catwalk, Sin couldn't take his eyes off her beauty. Full from his plate almost full of his lust Shooti filled the background imma turn the music up and TV down. As she arose from Sin lap, he smacked her butt and said get the what and leave the what? His favorite line from Shooti had just hit the screen. Lil Wayne and T-Pain studio was on time. As she began straddling Sin everything disappeared concerning them both, her headlights gleamed spilling light into Sin lips he continued allowing all of her to spill in & out of his lips. As she unbuckled Sin belt, she grabbed his weaponry as if she was scared that it would misfire, so she treated it delicately. Pushing what seemed to already be exposed to the side allowing Sin to fill up all areas of her insides and outta nowhere a thought of the guy she had been with invaded his thoughts Sin tire went flat instantly. Hitting Sin on the chest she cried you don't love me no more. Move yo you right I'm not feeling you it's time for me to go. No Sin please don't do this please I love you I know I fucked up no Sin why so you can go back to Shunna on her knees in front of the house door. Sin not wanna cause any issue was just pleading for her to move!? I'll do better I promise. Nah, I am not feeling this we good! Hurt and torn Sin pushes her to the side and leaves everything. What is really crazy was Tinka stays in the back apartments and Shunna stays in the front as Sin slides to the door Shunna askes who is it "Sin!" Walking in Sin tells Shunna I am leaving shorty you were right this crazy. Rolling up as if it was his oxygen this was Sin outlet. Confused and felt as if he was taking advantage of Shunna really in a vulnerable state Sin tried leaving as he felt unequipped Shunna grabbed Sin & said don't leave you wanna stay here right! While approaching him she blocked the door "You know you got me Sin." "Love who loves you when will you get that." Looking for clarity everywhere she kissed Sin and said you're stronger than you know you are I need you?" Things of this nature confused Sin he needed support, but everyone viewed him as the warrior of the world. You think, huh? Brushing against his groin instantly Sin was aroused. You still my kryptonite I haven't seen you in forever. Shunna fell to her knees as if prayer was what she was running to as she unbuckled Sin pants, he tried stopping her she grabs his hands as she placed every inch of him in her mouth. As if Copperfield was her father everything disappeared. Head leaning against the front door Sin began releasing all his pain as she became the sponge of his misery. Laying in the bed sleep as knocks at the door echoes thru the house. Again, more banging Shunna doesn't move someone riding their car horn as I reach the door bags and clothes laid all in front of the door. Confused Sin looks towards the car standing in the doorway wearing only his boxers "Tell ya bitch my man can stay there too since she is fucking him. Sin being familiar with such situations and circumstances goes to Shunna and tells her take ya friend or whatever ya call him his clothes yo shaking his head. Embarrassing him for what? Knowing she going to be back fucking with this dude! I hate all that ugh. Shunna kinda confused cause any other guy would've been ready to fight and all type of chaos would have been at hand. Laughing out loud running thru her window of thoughts she said that's the difference between Sincere and Sin. Sincere is gentler and loving as ever but Sin has no feelings. The strange thing is you never know which one you will get up until that moment. While riding to drop off Tec things Shunna phone rings. "Hello?" "Shunna your brother down here him, Yung & Cut Throat beefing!" "Huh!" Turning her car around she mashes the gas to get to where it was that her bro Dirt Bagg was standing behind Yung while Cut throat held his fye out. Without thinking she jumps out without questioning anything and screams you not go do nothing to my bro. Cut throat turns around and looking Shunna in her face and says, "You got more heart than ya brother he Pussy!" As Cut Throat raise up the tool Yung without thinking was not going to allow his nephew moms to die like that pulls out his fye and said nawl Throat. Cut throat turns and doesn't hesitate he lets 3 go as Yung is hit. Throat begin jogging off as the smoke is trialing the barrel that yet lies in his hand. Dirt Bagg holding Yung not understanding how so much has been lost from his refusal to correct something that should've been addressed. Digging thru his thoughts his general had been killed protecting him and his sister. Shunna hollering in tears "get him up, Dirt put him in the car we gotta get him to the hospital. Sin vibrating as he received numerous texts not in the mood to be bothered didn't even desire to see who was on the other end. Phone began ringing various ring tones and suddenly Shunna ringtone grasp his attention then he knew something was right getting up he goes to grab his phone. "What's wrong!?" "Sin, Yung is dead ugh?" Not really grasping the depth of what was at hand she just said Throat did it! The reality of Sin truth was that's not my team, so their issues didn't concern him until she said Throat drawed down on me and Yung tried stopping him, so he shot him. Sin response was sayless! Hanging up Sin first call was to the streets which he would comb until he was dead. Putting on his clothes acting as if he could save the world with his S on his chest. What Sin number one thing always have been was to protect those whom he loved sincerely the first place he pulled up to was Cut Throat moms house. Tooty who was Cut Throat sister runs out to meet Sin asking who he looking for, don't bring this to my mother house? It had to be a little after 9 and it was just getting dark outside. Sin looked at Tooty and said where ya mom? I don't care bout was going on Sin don't bring that to my house. Sin looked her in the face and told her its cold out and when its cold out people need to bundle up looking over her, he said don't you think. Knowing Sin was with the fuckery she instantly ran in the house told her mom's Sin was outside. At one-point Sin stayed here when he was on the run, they were good friends. Barbra walked out on the porch with her scarf and her robe looking me square in my face really Sin?! You know I was on the way that's why he not here, you know me! Its lines that you don't cross in the jungle. Heavy lies the head that wears the crown! Juggling should I pull out my fire, but I walked closer to tell her that death was at her door step. Unsure how to respond with water in her eyes she said Sin that's my Son please don't bring this madness to my house. Sin turn away because even tho he held a loyalty to her he never would turn on Shunna. Walking away he left her with only one thought, every action has a reaction know that! Clutching his fire in his hoodie he then turned around and said he not even safe here I don't care who his momma is. Ralo stood outside the fence where Sin told him to stay because this was personal, and he didn't need anyone else energy involved in this situation but him. Ralo said you still saving them, Sin said I live by a code of ethics. Unsure of the outcome of the way things were headed Sin escaped to be alone and in his being alone this where God spoke to him to bring a sense of what was at hand. Even though Sin was dedicated to the streets Sincere held a more in-depth bond with God, so he was constantly at war with himself between recklessness and order. The only way Sincere could control Sin was placing him alone in a cave with God. He had no choice because Sin truly craved for blood. Sin was heartless and in his eyes, he was protector of Sincere, Sincere felt as if Sin never held common sense he only rode off of the hate from his opposers. In his eyes he only desired matching the equivalence in his palms alone their difference and his difference was he desired ending anything in his path they tried scaring him which never did anything but ignite Sin bullheadedness. While in seclusion Sin could never live so Sincere gave life to the reality of who he was which was love. After he stayed there reaching out to God, he ran in fear of Sin ignorance. This was a constant fear that Sincere jungled until God chasten him in such a manner to whereas Sin held no oxygen. Sin was never known by his mother because she kept God before his face, but Sin never had to encounter God because he was living in hell on earth so all he *knew was pain. He was taught the word and knew how to pray Sincere, but he never forced God on Sin only thru music which represented good to tame the beast that always tried rising. Remembering what he was taught thru conversing with God as a child Sincere knew how to pray. It was one secret he held close in the field if God never could hear him, so he heard him closer was too fast. A gem he has held close to heart as a kid. During the isolation Sincere began speaking the word in his spirit saying it aloud Ephesians 6:12 states For we wrestle not against flesh and blood, but against principalities, against powers, against the rulers of darkness of this world, against spiritual wickedness in high places. Devil you must flee you will not win here. falling to sleep while in his word he was sedated by God verses and brought in stillness. After living the room late night he was walking and talking to God aloud in the stillness of the night thanking God for his many blessings and praying for a revival in the midst of where he lived. Sincere desired to heal others because he knew about the many monsters he faced so in saying that those who knew Sin never understood Sincere those who knew Sincere never believe Sin existed. Once he arrived back to the room, he seen Y'uata who face had been burnt and he reached out to her in concern. Y'uata was someone who was beautiful, but her face got burnt in a fire and she was recovering. At this point Sincere had been in the room over 40 days phone off no one knew where he was so when Y'uata seen him she addressed as Sin. Sincere believes that's its power in words so he detached himself from Sin name stating don't call me that. In saying that many people knew when Sincere tells you not to call him Sin he is in a better state no longer thugging so she would say oh you are living righteous at the moment. Laughing Sincere said why I gotta be all that because I don't wanna exemplify this evil. I was told by a wise man evil is living backwards the only thing that is backwards isn't of God. Live /evil, evil/live you do the math. You and your philosophy, you the only one out here in the streets that's a philosopher. You call it philosophy I call it good and the great book says the only thing good is God. You should be a minister! How is it that I am not ministering now, think about it? You'll caught up in the messenger not listening to the message. When in truth the message is more important than the messenger. Yadda, yadda, yadda in your voice laughing out loud do you even know what you are saying oh gosh what now Sincere. I don't use words wastefully everything I spill holds substance because if I can't be edifying, I am not doing what it is I was called to do. Tell me this Sincere for real how is it that you can be so loving in one instance and be cold as a doorknob in the next. Forgive me for my lack of control Sin feels as if Sincere is soft and allows many people to push him over. Why you feel that way? In the jungle its cold out here you and everybody else gotta stay bundled up aint no love Sincere love and many lay on that. Sin doesn't like me to be taken advantage, but I believe Love conquers all things Sin just don't get that. Laughing to herself yea Sin is numb to the reality and everything. He is a protector he is not a bully that's never lived in my spirit bullies are his prey he live to encounter bullies and numbers he feels its him surviving the wave of it all but I can admit he has to know God exist because he has been placed in face to face encounters where he has openly questioned and he always show up. Sincere that's why you be looking like a preacher when you're Sincere and when you Sin you look like the streets. Don't judge me! My greatest moment of being tamed was me and Shunna was beefing. About what Sin or should I say Sincere cause you know you was very whorish, in honesty I never believed I was whorish I believe I gave people freedom of choice I can't force you to be the whore. I told everyone from the gate my lifestyle was complimenting a woman and commitment because I move strange and in saying that I dealt with many outlets so I could isolate myself to one person so not willing to bring anyone in to any state of falsehood I told them if you deal with me here is the options if not that's cool too so everyone knew what they were walking into. It didn't benefit to lie that's to much energy and work would I can tell the truth and if you choose, I never misled. That's a catch 22 Sin. Y'uata seen Sincere looking strange ok, ok I get it Sincere. What happened tho? Shunna was involved with a click of my lil homies I knew it openly so being she was my heart outta all the women I ever involved myself with I grabbed her and lost it talking loud knowingly so the dudes would know I knew then I pulled out my fire I said you ready to die Shunna in tears trying to calm Sin down asked him to walk her to the room so no one would be all in their business. Shunna was no bible wiz but she saw how Sin controlled himself in certain situations. Grabbing the bible she went to 2 Corinthians 10:3-6 [3]For though we walk in the flesh, we do not war after the flesh: [4](For the weapons of our warfare are not carnal, but mighty through God to the pulling down of strong holds;) [5]Casting down imaginations, and every high thing that exalteth itself against the knowledge of God, and bringing into captivity every thought to the obedience of Christ; [6]And having in a readiness to revenge all disobedience, when your obedience is fulfilled. and Sin started crying as she read verse after verse falling asleep, I woke up she was gone. That's what taught me how to control Sin it wasn't me in all completeness she helps me understand what it was I was dealing with. You crazy nicca. I would've hollered, screamed and act out. Sincere grinning said nawh Sin aint right he wouldn't have cared about nobody not even the police he crazy yo for real. So, answer this how is it you deal? I trust God he is my fence he really is. I don't walk around talking positive for yall I do this for me because I minister to myself first you gotta understand a lot of us hasn't learned how to control their demons I've made peace with mine. When they arrive, God do too because I don't desire to do wrong, I truly want better. Wow, you really ride a deep wave Sincere why don't you tell anyone about it why don't you get help. Sincere started laughing help, God is my help. Man can't tame demons it's no logical formula to stop demons. Once you know what you're up against you handle it accordingly, but you must want it. It's no cake walk. So why don't you like Sin I'm confused Sin has everything the women, money, people fear him I'm talking about clicks and you still have ya sanity. People don't fear Sin! Huh, you don't get it people can't go outside of God authority and Sin knows that he can't die so he wears it like a badge. If people could kill Sin don't you believe he would've been dead, he one man against numbers. So how is it that he knows that God revealed it to me while I was in the field. My homie picked me up and said I've tried living like you, but you know you're outnumbered right. Me not being mature spiritually I grabbed my pistol and pulled it out and placed it in my lap. I said yea they might out number me but how many go die first everybody in a rush to kill me but not one is in a rush to die. You do the math it's me and God matter fact let me give you free game what God showed me out here I know its numbers against me but God revealed his truth in 2 King 6:16 And he answered, Fear not: for they that be with us are more than they that be with them. My trust lies with him. Unsure of how to take it he said I don't know who God is but somebody walking with you cause you walk boldly in this field alone. Head held high after many try keeping you suppressed. I am not alone he walk with me. Y'uata then says Sin you be tripping I be thinking you out here on all kinda drugs. The drugs are used to control to people Sin doesn't like Sincere so Sincere pops pills to get him to be more aggressive Sin is on weed to keep him calm it's called balance. No Sin is crazy and Sincere is saying you point blank. After sitting outside on the car Y'uata ask Sincere to come in the room but, he is still married. Sincere goes in the room and Y'uata turns up all air conditioner and Sincere seats on the edge of the bed watching the movie and she was under the cover. Sincere starts getting goosebumps and she invites him to get under the cover. When it comes to women Sincere is naive. Knowing better he tries putting the cover over his arms at the end of the bed. Still freezing Y'uata say boy I aint go bite you so Sincere places his legs over her back with his back to the wall to avoid placing himself completely under the cover. Eventually Sincere gets under the cover and she scoots her buttocks towards Sincere knowing the attempt of things and Sincere yet being a man, he was aroused but scooted closer to the wall in return Y'uata reaches behind her and says you ok Sincere. Mute to all at hand Sincere couldn't respond she began unbuckling Sincere pants. Dude you don't look retarded. This is not human, are you half man half horse? Placing her mouth upon his greatest topic the subject was a sloppy outcome. Like Mary J. Blige I'm going down played thru out Sincere thoughts. There was a banging on the door next to them which was Sincere room and low and behold his wife pulls up. After seeing her car Sincere runs around yo I can't explain this and not only this Sincere felt as if he cheated God instantly, he ran to the bathroom crying. Y'uata gets up and grabs the shampoo and place it in her hair and goes to the door. Sincere sitting on the toilet looks up and she's his wife and Y'uata confused not knowing what to say Y'uata begins saying Sincere got some shampoo in his eyes while shampooing my hair looking at his wife it was clear to say she believed it or believed in me at that time. Scared because his wife was a fighter Sincere gets in the car and realize it's no ill energy. Sighing within himself Sincere goes out to eat with his wife and kids. The only time Sincere was able to be completely involved in his kids life was whenever Sin was completely dead she never brought Sincere among his kids nor did Sincere desire to be among them in his eyes he never wanted them to know about that portion of him.. Angel the kids and Sincere after eating went to take pictures. Angel looking at Sincere loved the idea of him not represent that Street mentality this is what she adorns. Waves falling, well groomed, not high and desiring to be involved in his kid's life was golden in her eyes. Looking as if he was a man Sperry's with the bubble gum bottom, creme polo jeans with an all-white polo rugby with a creme horse as a creme polo hat cover one half of his waves. The reality was Sin was married while still in the streets. In taking a role as a husband, working full-time as well as full-time student.*

Was this Hell Kitchen being served the devil's pie that convince me to make a u turn on a one-way road. At war with my soul betraying my own ghost, how can something so hot be so cold. Out of balance trying to manage the scale I no longer wanted to bargain. In moving forward listening to all it was to gather. Angel constantly snatched me outta my hell letting me know that nothing mattered outside of becoming better. No one ever help me believe in me the truth is all I desired was the street, it was home the land of all my brethren. So, it seemed! Angel was different she was the preacher's daughter and dealing with me I'd have her out past her normal hours. It wasn't beauty that held him intact, more so her essence spilled something outside the norms of anything he had encountered up to this point. Life was her conversation peace was her breastplate that I was allowed to lie upon during my moments of madness. A safe haven definitely. Up until this moment no one could quiet the demons that constantly rattled my cage as if they were attempting to leave but played in my bosom as if pain was my antidote. Violating all her rules to keep me at peace she was the only piece I was missing. This particular night was school night. Angel was a senior in school seventeen and Sin was twenty-eight, what was disturbing to Sin was she had an old soul. Valentine's day Sunday and honestly so I don't cause a problem at my house don't send nothing I'm good with any gifts. Sin said you sure. You been everything I've needed I would be less than a man not to bless you in the event of that. I'm good Sin honestly and without hesitation she kisses him and says I got school in the morning so I may not be able to see you because you be having me out outside my school hours that is not what's up. This my lifestyle it's all I know. Sin stop saying such ignorance you have an amazing mind you not slow you're very intelligent you don't gotta do all this cause it's what you're familiar with. Truly not understanding such a statement Sin looks as if she stated something questionable. Pulling Sin closer Sincere she said slowly each one of her palms touching Sin cheeks drawing him in kissing him. I am going to show you we going to school together. Ok babe as her lips were covered over his. Leaving Sin to go back in the house where they were gambling, unbeknownst to Sin he had left a whole zip of his personal on the gambling table. Before his leaving he noticed passing June that he was walking and was non-responsive it alerted Sin, but it didn't alert Sin. Asking others who sat at the table about his gas others was looking as if no one knew nothing. Reaching and patting his pockets Sin realized that he didn't have his rocket on him and found his kiss jumping in his car almost tearing down the mailbox. Doing the dash just trying to get home to his fye hoping anyone would challenge or question him death would definitely visit anyone's doorsteps. I don't take from no one unless they violate me it's open season and no one would take from me. Pulling up to the crib running into the yard overacceeding the driveway. Sin jumps out not able to get in the door quick enough Shunna comes to the door what's wrong Sin. No words Sin high off more than any form of drug, this was the side he never liked because no one could calm him down. Pushing pass Shunna getting the .40 cal Sin shoved it in his coat. Shunna lips moving but the words that played in his head were louder than love low tones Pain placed everything on mute accept revenge which sang betrayal in the earlobes of Sin as he was getting full of the things on the other side of the track of love. One city that once divided by the track each one opposed one another like many ghettos we all witness. As Sin pulled up at the gambling house what seemed like 10 seconds, he kicked the door open looked at both gambling tables and said he got my shit he can die, or everybody go get it that's on Blondie grave. Family was there, friends were there in Sin eyes everyone was opps in his sight. If one isn't with me, they're against me is how he always felt. The person of the house stepped towards Sin and never exposing the fye just gripping the trigger and aiming from his pockets Sin press forward to his gut and says something gotta give. Instantly people began putting money together to appease Sin demons. Yo, Sin was his cuzn words. Sin not knowing who was who at that point turned around fuck dat I want the head of who got my shit if one is man enough to take from me be man enough to stand up for his life ole coward ass nigga. Mole was one of Sin closest cuzn, but he knows how reckless Sin gets when he blacks out there is no understand trying to draw him back to reality and not stuck in the bosom of Hell's fishnet. I keep that gas cuz what you need as he pulls out a zip lock of over a quarter pound. Sin looking at everyone seeing who would question or indicate they were the man. Mole grabbing da Dutch he had at the table said you know I keep that gas as he fired it up people placing a few hundred in his hand after pulling the blunt Sin said you know I aint on no bully shit but I can be a bully stop fucking with me. On God if you wanna live leave me the fuck alone I'll take you to ya maker. Walking out the door getting in his car weed and money intact Sin felt horrible this isn't what he desired to promote but, in this jungle, you'll get ate alive if you show any weakness. Then in when he realized he was at war with himself, for Sincere to live Sin must die. The next morning Sin wakes up it was Valentine's day and he had so many women til it was crazy this was one of the most creative days of his life, but he was the ghetto Santa clause if you meant anything to Sin, he cherished ya existence in completeness. You didn't have to only be his girl, or should I say one of his girls. If you were a woman in his eyes you all were to be placed on the greatest pedestal that's just what he felt regardless of ones flaws imperfection was not a flaw in his eyes it was a treasure that many deemed as flaws but he felt it was a birthmark that represented strength, courage and drive. No matter the waves and currents that was sent to drown us in any manner if one didn't have flaws one wasn't fighting to live cause in fighting bruises occur and if you leave unbruised you were not fighting you were sparring. If one desires to live it's a fight once you step in the ring of life giving up isn't an option to a champion one only becomes a champion from winning. Losing doesn't denote failure if one continues fighting, get back in the ring win, win, win its the feet of endurance. Actually, Sin had been preparing for Valentine's day for over a week because he knew it was many people, he

just desired bringing heaven to the steps of their door. A smile is so enriching and contag
one places a smile on the face of others it spills into your spirit and two people have been re

A wiseman said in Proverbs 3:7-8 Be not wise in thine own eyes: fear the Lord, and dep
evil. It shall be health to thy navel, and marrow to thy bones.

With all that being said Sin was a giver and he got joy in giving others joy and bringing ea
situation. Life prepared me in many ways as a child my mom use to give me and m
allowance, she would spoil us abundantly, but Sin lived to reward her in the manner she
us and it was spilled down how her giving nature was radiant to many lives. No one kne
would measure his life to his mom's greatness and not meeting the equivalence in his eyes
her embarrassment and lived by the means of his understanding using the tools he was
never had to live in the manner he chose to live but he never desired failing so for the m
was appreciated in this level of life so he embraced it in all fullness not to promote it but g
a greater foundation and try to become better than how or what many was used to. Sin
church boy who just didn't accept the guidelines in his rebellion he was vigilant for th
assigned to. First, he was a child of God Second, he was a Man Third he was protector
loved on and women were the essence from where he came. So, it was natural for him to
women easily his family held more women than men plus no men ever was a leading piece
Women became his teacher, he learned in every encounter no matter who they were they
his eyes. After every fall he seen before his eyes he constantly ran before than to replace the c
their temple to remind them not to forget who they were when life tried sabotaging then
were worthless or less than who they actually were. Pulling up to Angel father church car
balloons, flowers and a bear the size of Sin with a bag that held other gifts Angel loved fro
to Victoria secret to starburst of many flavors. Not knowing how she would get the gi
around the church trying to figure it out and on his coming around the second time. Tr
was a girl who was around Angel age going to her car looked up. Can you do me a favor
try! Can you put all this stuff in your car and give it to Angel for me please? Already
dozen of roses that he used to give to random women he seen in passing one for each pers
Trina a rose thank you. Smiling she hugged Sin and said this is so beautiful tears trying
her eyes he said now you know you all are more beautiful to us we love you women as a wh
her on the cheek, jumping in his car he goes to get a sandwich from Subway but he de
Angel reaction she was a new asset in his life and he wanted her to feel how she made him
grabbing a bite and backing up across the street Sin began rolling up and waiting til chu
I saw Trina walking outside and holding one hand while her other hand covered her
turning her around before revealing to her all the gifts her reaction was beyond any nor

drove passed blowing the horn and she was everywhere emotionally and mentally that in itself was refreshing. Actually, Sin nor Angel knew she was carrying their first child and the world wasn't ready for this. Sin heart and core was Joy she was his cousin cousin they weren't kin but called one another cuzn. All his gifts were at her house which was his honeycomb hide out. The safety vault he never had to question she kept everything his work, his tools and his money loyalty was never a question they had been thru the storms of life standing behind one another edification is all they desired in truth. Pulling up to da Nolia Sin didn't wanna expose everything so he would get different gifts so he could drop them off accordingly. Oh, and Tinka been calling me all day asking have you made it to town yet because she still thinks you're in New York. Giving Sin a high five but I must say that you showed out for her and don't even got a month under ya belt you will spoil you a woman. As I should, do you believe I shouldn't? Turning her lips up, if you weren't my cuzn I would have to have ya whole bag to myself cause you spread ya self everywhere you are a hoe. How so and I am Single? Sin, you stay with a girl! I pay all the bills there and more of my personal items are there than here I am here more than there don't do this cuz. Ummm, whatever! I said what I said you just love ya freedom! I mean how can I be obligated to just one under the circumstances I'm everywhere around the board. I can't get from here to there it's just like family dollar you must have a store on many blocks cause if not someone goes to the store that appears before reaching your store. So, all these women family dollars? Sin laughing aloud for the most part and they stay renovated, rite. Rite! No one lacks you stay feeding anyway you deem as a part of the family tree. Are you lacking? As he draws her in by her collar, face to face feeling the warmth from his nostril. I ask do you lack. No Sin humbling herself cause she never felt vulnerable are butterflies never swarmed in the pits of her stomach. As you never will. I love you mean more than words then Sin kissed her upon her forehead. Jogging slowly upstairs to get some more bags. Joy felt herself perspiring and was confused to how and why she felt the way she felt with Sin whom was her ugly big head cuzn. Waving her shirt and wiping her forehead Sin came running back down stairs. What you think? This for Tinka! Holding a handbag 2 dozen of roses and a hand full of balloons and a Victoria secret bag. What you think? That's fye that bag big and deep what kind is it? Metamorphoza Tote bag look inside? Looking inside she sees perfume by Ralph Lauren, Dolce & Gabonna with a card with twenties running out the inside of it. You think she would like that? Joy mouth fully a gaped she was in awe of his free will to create heaven for those he loved. In tears she said Sin you are amazing for real. I don't suppose to be. I grind for those I love this aint for me if it was for me, I'd be satisfied this who I do it for, ya over stand me! Sin was someone many held a distaste for in their lack of understanding because many perceptions deems upon one's character if one lives in the jungle there are no rules Sin lived upon principles that was contrary to the beliefs we were taught to uphold. Who was told how one was designed to live or move? God design is beyond man concept of thoughts so he rules apply in every area of life with it being the way many has looked at it as being or whatever it could be. God has

the last say, Sin held a heart that was created to love under vigorous circumstances and he did it sincerely cause he would always tell Joy my happiness is in witnessing you being happy nothing outside of that matter. We are in a place where many are selfish and when one becomes selfless, they are looked upon as weird, opps and hater. I thank God for Sin spirit of holding a loving essence. Love is helpful to us as a whole don't miss out in encountering love because someone else distaste for love. Allow the appetite that suits you to eat was healthy to you because everyone intake doesn't receive the same things. Sin pulled up and to Tinka door while calling her phone honestly, he hadn't called in two days cause his movement didn't permit him to. That being said Tinka felt as if he was really playing her, he sexed her left the state and hadn't texted nor called she just wasn't open to such foolery. Sin feeling irritated left a message on her phone to let her know if she was in her feelings he would fall back and throw everything he bought her in the trash before he left it was nothing. Giving her ten minutes to respond Sin was going to throw everything in the dumpster one thing he never wanted was to get caught up in roller coaster feelings his phone rung in two minutes. You got me something, what a hand size teddy bear you not fucking with me for real if you were you stop dissing me. I stay busy I'm out here chasing this bag I don't have time to stay still I told you this coming in. My Sister said she sees you can you please drop my stuff off to her? You cool with that? I got money for you too I was hoping you'd be open to getting ya own gifts. Sin, you really fucking with me. Nope, after I drop this off, I am not calling you any more cause you stay in ya feelings I'm not into all that. Hanging up backing up to her sister house Sin takes the gifts to her sister house and in doing so her sister said Tinka want you on the phone. Not the one to be disrespectful among others he took the phone what's good yo? Sin, I'm sorry I am in error I'm here at my mother house and I want you to stop here please? No, I'm not in the mood right now I am irritated you win! Music blasting not desiring to be taken outta his space Sin was feeling good as it seemed everywhere, he went everyone was smiling that alone allowed him to smile thru all things.

Shunna was the fighter, the warrior the person who fought beyond all challenges. Broken seemed to become a beautiful birthmark that Sin adorned, strong seemed simply invincible with no resistance, so it seemed. Carrying the world burdens, she constantly stayed afloat as if wings were always there. Sin first thought of her was she was a beautiful nightmare if it made any sense cause even though darkness was very much present, she dealt with it beautifully. They were beefing and had been for weeks she was sick and tired of the freedom and people always bringing extra madness to his house so after weeks of not answering his call he was not going to intrude. It wasn't abnormal for them to fall out he just didn't understand when he couldn't spend this day with him, so he was going to escape all madness and what better way than rush to his favorite location which was any form of water. He had made reservations with his homie whom they weren't serious, but he needed an escape without the extra turmoil. Jekyll Island it would be! Water was a refreshing for me, something I found to raise my vibrations at my lowest point. Stopping to get Treasure the first thing I asked was she prepared and ready to go? Clothes packed and coming to the car Sin said before we head that way we go stop in Savannah where we go chill momentarily. Cruising thru the interstate Savannah was Sin second home he loved Savannah it held his favorite beach which was Tybee Island. Flipping thru his phone he found Camoflauge bumping Raised in Da Ghetto from his album Strictly 4 Da Streets. All my Port babies already know how Dirte' give it up. This was our Pac, voice of the street. Died in the streets tryna escape a lifestyle that tries drowning us all. Rest easy Flauge! As he screamed from my speakers talking for many who held no voice as "A Letter" on repeat. A world if explained one couldn't understand unless they witness in the purest form, so in saying that witness the closest encounter in the stories of rappers & writers to journey to a place many couldn't live 16 seconds in. Treasure rubbing Sin neck bringing him back to the reality in front of him which was a little under two hours on the road. Finally arriving in Savannah after passing thru Georgetown Sin jumped out on 36th and Waters Avenue going Live I'm here the land of head hunters my home away from home. As Gotti crowded the back ground Aint No turning Around as the strip joined in unison this was the accolades of the life not promoting saluting how one stand in the fire of struggle and embrace every avenue of it. No running from the truth, no sad stories or no van coming to save us here. We accept the truth not receive the lies that's been thrown out. To many our truth we live with, others sabotage their true identity taking on a lifestyle they can't walk into. The truth is, they don't mean those standards we accept who we are, do you? Not in the city an hour and my guy beat my phone up, where you at Sin you already know aint no turning down we lit all night. Laughing pipe down Brody I'm moving on another wave its Valentine day I'm riding with my shooter on the side of me ya heard. So, we are caking now, never hoes over bros. I'm go overlook ya energy right now just because you beat up ya women when you get skied up Nicky Trick was a true fool no one was as stupid and my family. The eyes only see what the mind is ready to comprehend. Trick was from the Lost tribe all he knew is violence, but he loved his potnas. Only laws he lived were the codes of the streets, nothing less and getting up with him wasn't a great idea with shawty because he only moved in the underworld of these streets another door few could comprehend. Trick refusing to allow me to leave before seeing him in no time he pulled up blasting Gotti Testimony no shirt tattoos and Mack Eleven laying under the belt of his pants it was a part of his uniform in the middle of waters standing on his hood all white everything you couldn't tell him he wasn't Gotti. Laughing while Treasure was going Live Trick was loving it and as traffic was halting Trick was daring someone to blow the horn, he was throwed just like that a goblin with no understanding as if the world was his. Sin, dancing waving for Trick to come down and mob with him to bring a calmness to Trick mindset rolling off 4 triple stacks the world wasn't ready for a monster of this stature. All gas no brakes and plenty money ready for whatever. Jumping down hugging Sin I love ya Brody Sin knew when they get on the drugs emotions are more deep hugging him conveying the love then, Yo Trick trying to get him out the street and Sin knew he been ready to let loose with a car full of hard heads head flooded with dreads all you seen was guns, gold, bottles and plenty Gas. Many loved the site of this unknowing to many all these cats was ready to kill with no feelings. Reckless hard heads were something you avoid. Losing they life was a blessing to all they believed in. Taking ya life was a part of violation of outsiders stepping in an avenue of life they felt only family belonged in. The love was real, cause being a part of this if you were looked upon as Authentic was what represented medals. Home of Savages, bottom of the bottom. Souljah's this is low life a land no one understood typically. Kissing Trick on the cheek outta respect Sin spoke to him in his ear letting him know they would spend all night together he was for the movement by all means. Later, Trick just give me til later, don't leave my city broski until were together. Brrraaattt, Brrraaattt, Brrraaattt! Trick felt in-depth to Sin in prison Sin saved Trick life when Atlanta cats tried killing him. Sin didn't even know Trick he was loyal to Trick homie so outta respect for his homie isolated in a room niggas tried killing him being stomped out and wet up Sin talked the dudes outta of it. Afterwards Sin told Trick if you let them live you will be exposed as a girl in prison that was the lowest position any man could witness. Prison is a world many don't speak on. The world of the lawless its killed or be killed. One must move very strategic if one choose not to move in numbers. Inclined to believing in God in all completeness refusing to embrace or fall under the subjection of anything that opposed God mindset. I stood among many who only concern was to survive among many men. The greater your capacity to Love, the greater your capacity to feel pain. In an environment where love was looked upon as the biggest wound among heartless tribes. Unsure of what to gravitate towards his oldest brother was O.G of Gangsta Disciple and well respected he naturally fell under the umbrella of protection because in their eyes he was F.O.F (Friend Of Folk). Separating himself from any title not dividing his freedom he moved as he desired. Titles get you killed in certain environments; some people didn't care they loved what they believed in. Locked up in solitary for 30 days before being placed on the flat top. Sin received a letter from Cole Hart who was his older brother who had been riding over 7 years at the time.

Dear Sin,

May life greet you with blessings and strength to continuously walk beyond the circumstances that challenges us in every area that we may not be knowledgeable in. Knowing that if will trust God in all our ways we will return home safely. Psalm 121:1-2 I will lift up mine eyes unto the hills, from whence cometh my help. My help cometh from the Lord, which made heaven and earth. Bro, this is not a place to show any form of weakness, weakness is an invitation of death. If you don't wanna die stand even when you cannot stand. No one, no society nor no religious group will protect you in the manner that God does so erase running to the safety of anything outside of God. He stood by ya side in the field he will stand by ya side in Hell bosom know nothing can harm you, but it starts with you TRUST GOD NOT MAN! Filter everything you are in the land of the wise, snakes are very wise and cunning they are subject to manipulate you and deceive you easily. 2 Corinthians 11:4 And no marvel; for Satan himself is transformed into an Angel of light.

Stay aware at all times God is vital because he shows us how to move under all circumstances. He is our Basic Instructions Before Leaving Earth. Trust me you can't go wrong he is there even if it doesn't look like it. Stay away from church people they are cons believe me here they only lie under you to magnify your weakness and use you to their benefit and most of em gay on GOD. It's the plot of the enemy you can't trust no one but you must trust that you will walk thru the tides that beat against your shores because God is all and all. Matthew 7:15 Beware of false prophets, which come to you in sheep clothing, but inwardly they are ravening wolves.

Your instinct and intuition are your greatest tools I am only speaking as a man, but I believe its God comforter that aides us that's my belief and I will stand on that. We were baptized as a child and we are believers God knows our heart don't confuse man limitations with God application once you master that God love is infinite, you'll lose sight of man limitations it's a ceiling to control and limit your faith. I Love ya bro and its only so much I can give you. You don't have to kill everyone because you're incapable of such a feat but respect one's desire to stand on his ten toes are the greatest reward. You will receive more assistance from many in seeing your truth. People respect Truth at an all-time high. No one will allow the wave to overtake one who stands for what they believe in, but cowards are up for grab. If you listen to me, you will make it home safely. One more thing kill anything or idea of someone trying to kill the man that lives in you I can't talk like I want because our letters are read but stand bro.

Tears rolling from Sin eyes only nine teen in a world of beast and monsters you just couldn't run from. You have to face em now your here it was his brother was letting him know he had to kill to live, which he wasn't totally prepared for. Looking back towards the letter to finish reading.

I speak to you in love and sincerity I am not there to protect you and I feel vulnerable so I can only give you the truth with no punches. This is not a time to be fearful this is a time for you to become a Man among many never compromise who you are for NOTHING. I will leave you with this and I will write you and have many drop offs sent to you my hands can reach further than you know. I have people watching over ya head that's a command from the Chief you know how I ride. You don't have to ride no wave on that end of things I trust you will make wise decisions I admired this about you more than anything you were a thinker something I lacked because I apply pressure. In your voice its more than one way to skin a cat. Take heed to this last scripture and stay focused, do not receive nothing from anyone I DONT CARE how free they promote it freedom not even free let that marinate. Ecclesiastes 3:1-4 To everything there is a season, and a time every purpose under the heaven: A time to be born, and a time to die; a time to plant, and a time to pluck up that which is planted; A time to kill, and a time to heal; a time to break down, and a time to build up; A time to weep, and a time to laugh; a time to mourn, and a time to dance;

I wrote this letter not trying to be your preacher but God word tells us my sheep hears my voice you know what's going on and its bigger than ones natural eyes can reveal walk in strength and be encouraged brethren. God is there with you he all we got once we master this we can't lose. I love you big head and Momma prepared us for a time such as this walk faithfully.

Sincerely Cole Hart

On his release from the hole Sin first encounter was a trouble dorm which coming in would intimidate anyone. Its stories I wouldn't care to expose to many people, but the reality is this is a home of monster who has no restrictions if Hell held a location this was it. Sin standing in the salad port. Open Salad port door for H-2. Doors open to a dorm that was locked down witnessing people standing at windows measuring what was being invited in their kingdom. Sin along with 4 other guys stood as they were being directed to their rooms. Field of Titans on my first night awaken from screams of Momma reality was mom couldn't save no one in this cage. Following morning this young guy who was deemed as a pretty boy who came in with me was raped and was in PC (Protective Custody). I wouldn't wish these terms on my worst enemy. Walking into a world I lacked knowledge of I stood in my own domain treating circumstances with jungle ethics, everyone wasn't ally and everyone wasn't foe. Seconds crawled into minutes, minutes walked into hours, hours trotted into days as days jogged into months. Pace of times ran into years looking back over 3 under his belt working in the kitchen he met Trick. A young wild Jack Boy who it turned out was infamous with a fuck the world mindset. Loyal to those whom was loyal to him. In truth hustle goes on all over the board and this is where Sin and Trick complimented one another. In dealing with Trick he gave off a notion of loyalty that was rare, in his consistency Sin watch over him as if he was a little brother. Trick was a shooter in the field, behind these walls the closest thing to a pistol was a sword or scratcher (shank). Posted in the dorm Predators plotted on prey. I roamed with the Predators because I was considered dope boy plus jack boy which was pluses for the circle of animals. Reality was everyone move in their own ways for me many always said I have the gift of gab which was priceless in the trenches. My ability to converse with women as my greatest gem and young women or women with vibrant personalities drew into me easily. Chess taught me that you don't move for the kill just because it seems as if it exists because reality is all actions has a reaction so every action must be protected with another action. Game of life, I was always taught run to the fight not from the fight and a pawn is the most powerful piece because it has the ability to become whatever it wants to be! With that being said you are creator of your circumstances, application is key in all ways of life. Pressure does two things I believe it bust pipes and it turns coals to diamonds. Which mindset do you have? The youngins were bragging about exposing someone weakness who they deemed as Strong in the dorm. They picked Trick, me and Trick hustle in the kitchen but we choose not to move in unison in the dorm so we can never be attached to one another plus I had been riding with these young savages for some years. Derrick who was known as Dee Rec because he wrecks things with ease a young savage with no understanding. Watch how we eat this nigga, Sin knowing that if he were to stand on his own feet that the pressure wouldn't be applied yet if he promoted weakness you were lunch; ugh. All of us went in the room and Dee Rec went to the door Yo Trick look here broski. Trick sliding down stairs cause this was a smoking room 2 about 4 of us was in the room I sat in the back on the desk while Rat sat on the bed and Pretty Al sat on the toilet using it as a seat. Room tinted out Dee Rec closes door which locks us in. Standing at the door looking Trick in the face he said tell the truth my guy you a bitch huh? Trick confused not knowing how to answer the question. Worst mistake was question who he was a taste of blood. Dee Rec slapped him and said what I say you'll bitch? Fear and isolation were putting Trick further in the hole no longer were brakes being pumped all the guys in there were ready to expose his man hood and pressed. One throwing blows the other pulling at his clothes all Trick was doing was trying to protect himself no resistance is assistance behind these walls. Trick got beat under the bed holding on to the bed hoping all things would fade away blood puddles covering the floor Rat pulled out his sword Sin jumped up and said Yo its almost count time yo all this blood covering the floor chill we can't get cased up like this all us be put in P.I (Private Investigation) Money over Everything. I got this yo for real for real. Pressing the buzzer to open the door it popped and Sin while pushing Dee Rec and Rat who were the true aggressors Pretty Al just ride how his team ride. Closing the door so no one slip in and the officers see what transpired Sin tells Trick get up yo. Trick lost Sin shaking his head this another world little homie snakes are the only species that eat they own kind. Listen you gotta stand little homie even if you can't fight. Trick was really bruised up, its code. Listen go to the shower and fall so they don't attach your bruises with any investigation on the dorm you don't wanna be looked on as a snitch death will be your next breath. Crying harder, Sin grabbed Trick listen it aint no guns in here but its swords and scratchers plus your will to stand on your ten toes. YOU ARE A MAN, FIRST! Get ya self together do what I say, and you'll live no flex. After a week later Trick eyes finally healed, and he slid in the dice game where Dee Rec was without his tribe or his sword it's no rules in this dog eat dog world. Trick felt he was forever in debt to Sin Respect was the body of the laws of the underworld many don't talk on and Trick held a deeper understanding for love after Sin held him down and guided him thru his 7 years. Sin, despised bullies and numbers in his eyes Hyenas were the only thing in the jungle that rode in tribes they always tried killing the Lion nawh we Lion Hearts over this way we not dying. So, you go let me catch up with you later Trick while I bust this move? You know that I am not going leave you out Dirte'! Ok, chirping on beans Tick said oh yea Plies down here tonight we are turning all the way up! Sin agreed but knew he wouldn't be back tonight this was his escape from the madness. As they left Waters Treasure said they really love you everyone you go Sin you really, I good dude? You didn't feel as if I was? You know that's how I give it up babe! Sin, hitting up a few more people who he knew thru the town. I am pulling up now, give me 5 minutes. Sin riding thru downtown stopped at this custom design shoe store. Oh, this where you get all those fly shoes from, huh?! Treasure looking thru the glass windows they had everything from the Avengers, Flintstones and Jordan's super stupid. Walking in instantly Sin was greeted by a guy whom was familiar with Sin asking him did he want those Pink Panther Adidas who ask to be customized with the all-white Polo Jean and Jacket with Pain panther body leaning against the body of the Jeans and Jacket connecting in unison. Sin you always creating something you got a stupid imagination! Grab whatever it is you want Treasure it's on me, Sin paid 1,800 hundred for his outfit without hesitation and with me looking crazy he said I pay for what I want point blank that's just what it is! After Treasure got some 95' maxes walking out the door Sin said will you just let me spoil you while you kick back? Treasure blushing kinda caught up in her feelings she said yes Sin! Kool let's go in this store! Next door was a jewelry store where an Arab came showing Sin mad love oh this ya Treasure huh? Yea, what you think? Nnaji, looked Treasure up and down and said she compliments ya look you're no slouch you know that tho! Come here Beautiful? Watch it Nnaji you got more money than I do but I know how to fight. No, Sincere we break bread together not bump heads money over everything know that! As she reached the counter Nnaji pulls out a beautiful tennis bracelet flushed with more carrots than a garden. You like that! Almost about to cry Sin said tighten up the day not over yet just chill this just a taste of what's to come we kooling babe. Giving her another bracelet for her other arm she flooded with butterflies, exes and o's. I've learned in walking thru life many people will never witness any portion of love so if it takes me to be sacrificial of who and what I represent, here I am! Treasure, taken by not being familiar with those attentive to her wellbeing helped her look at things deeper than the norm. No hidden agenda nothing to gain outta his being who he was to me showed why is name was Sincere. Sincerity was the essence of his being. That's what he was willing to leave a trail of thru out the journey of his makeup to whereas fame or fortune was things he sought. Actually, he made money to give it away which was so weird to me but hey that was Sincere Hollis. Driving thru traffic Sin began to drum thru his phone and he put on a person talking I never heard before Eric Thomas the Hip Hop Preacher who was speaking on You Owe You. One thing I always noticed about Sincere was he always was checking himself why was he not who he should be in the manner he felt represent his truth not man. Only thing that reflected such an act was Love, so he only craved knowing it in its purest form. Laying in the seat head slightly propped upon the head rest drifting back and forth, Sin grabbed my leg and held on to me to ensure my presence was next to him. Treasure? Yes, Sin! If I told you I dug, you in all truth would you believe me? Nope! Saying it just to see what he would say in return I was lying. Well what would I need to do to exemplify such an act? I don't mind! If it takes me giving you every coin to identify my totality, I'll empty myself in every way. This money, cars, and women don't represent substance in my eyes. Tangible things are physical make up, Love is intangible emotional, spiritual and mental is the substance of life greatest beauty. No flex I am committed to being constant in what it is that I desire to be a reflection of, in truth my greatest example is Jesus I know the typical person will believe awe you think you can be perfect! My first example was 2pac who beyond the flaws of what he represented Love was always prevalent in all his acts. Perfect was never the goal, real was the agenda being who I was not who others wanted me to be. His passion for God seemed to be his greatest balance which reflected love. The greatest thing I learned from watching 2pac was if many disliked him in his act of gentleness what was it that they feared?! Pac had a big mouth he spoke from his heart. So, answer this Sin? Why is it so easy to walk away from pain and a lot easier to run from love? Truth can be a monster to someone that's digest lies the make-up of their lives, it doesn't represent the expectation we felt it should when truth is just that with no expectations. We limit our perception by the expectations we place in people, things and circumstances. Take the ceiling off expectations and expect nothing so if one doesn't equate to the identity you felt one should meet and doesn't affect you as more. In boxing if you see a blow coming without placing your guards up psychologically ya muscles in ya face prepares yourself for the accident but when one doesn't see the blows coming no defense is available. You're left vulnerable! Saying that to say this, my expectation of anyone that's next to me is total edification whether it be for me or for them. Remember this and I stay biblical cause my grand moms kept God before us as a child. Jeremiah 17:5 Thus saith the LORD; Cursed (be) the man that trusteth in man, and maketh flesh his arm, whose heart departeth from the LORD.

If in fact, we always say were blessed how can we be blessed if we place ourselves in a cursed mindset. Pay attention to the warnings God gives us in all truth. Huh? So, you mean to tell me you don't got trust in a relationship? Yes, I have trust in a relationship I trust God placed you in my life for his purpose in all deeds no matter how it looks. Edification is the greatest bridge to understanding. Life is our greatest teacher many of us just doesn't take the time to listen to the many statements that are of prevalence because its sometimes overshadowed. 1 Kings 19:12 And after the earthquake a fire; but the Lord was not in the fire: and after the fire a still small voice." I truly believe that anything that is of abundance in this thing called life I seem to question and microscope it because peculiar things doesn't have a tribe of abundance. You get on my nerve Sincere cause Sin don't be on the philosophy or the passions of life. Sin is more so the savage! Lol, no that's not it. Sin is the protector of the things he loves. His hands began leaving her thighs and he placed his hands upon her shoulder while squeezing on the back of her neck. Oh, you believe I am not a protector of You. Treasure listening but unsure how to answer because she didn't feel as if Sin loved her but running thru his actions, she could only say all Sin has tried to do was build or heal me!? Get your feelings off ya shoulder Treasure I see you're lost in ya thoughts and ya eyes watery Souljah stay focused were enjoying our getaway. Riding across a bridge of water Sun skating across the backs of water lost in the world's arena. God creation was beautiful in all aspects. Arriving to Jekyll Island which was surrounded by flamingos caressing gravities restrictions as turtles patiently viewed life completeness indulging in its wave. Flowers growing upon broken wandered limbs as hummingbirds and butterflies drunken from Butterfly bushes nectar. Witnessing them fly away drunken from intoxicating themselves in the forum of their desires. Tides racing side by side to seashore only competition was to touch every dry area that mother nature would push her to bath upon. Nature harmony was a symphony in itself. Winds flirting with anything in its path, brushing my cheeks pulling me into a rhythm freer than any instrument. His prints were evident everywhere. Treasure in awe of Jekyll make up she loved beaches, but it was different here. As they walked to the Customer Service Center Sin received tickets and two arm bracelets. Sin, wearing a white hoodie with thin material, white jeans and white, red and blue camel toe sandals all by Polo. Never revealing his expressions Sin lens lied behind some black tinted glasses with white trim engulfed in Treasure smiles this was Sin freedom. Treasure body grabbing every portion of a pink body swimsuit with a white bathing suit covering that was provocative in many ways. Witnessing the currents waving at us as if it was greeting our arrival Treasure quickly handed me her towel and ran to the water while it wrapped her up as if it was craving to bath her in its rhythm. Record me Sin, please?! Sin pulled out her phone as the currents bathed upon his feet enjoying the wind flirting with his ears what can I say I was in love with the nature of life don't judge me?! Thru witnessing life activities with all things Sin became a photographer of the many reactions to the tides tickling away the madness that no longer existed this was Heaven on earth. After taking multiples pictures Treasure looking over Sin you all wet your jeans and all. Chill while here our only worry will be what's next ok? Pulling her in kissing her forehead freedom was a necessity that lies in ones will. You ready, Treasure? Unsure of what was to come next, she like yes Sin I am. Walking thru trials that were close to the water witnessing an arena of nature many moods uncertainty was very present. A throw Sin held over his shoulders he placed by a bench that sat off the trial that clearly gave one a beautiful view of the Sunset. Lost in the activities of boats passing, cruises along with Spotted Seatrout jumping into the air randomly as if they were jumping outside of their ceiling of understanding. Indulging in this was soothing and relaxing it was the other side of Sin many never encountered. Beyond the lifestyle he never embraced or promoted. Treasure many times life may give us waves were not familiar with riding does that stop us from riding cause if you don't learn to ride waves the only other option is being drowned by them. Always learn to ride life waves, the same waves press us all. Even in attempting to ride waves the beauty lies in learning to master it cause in falling we forget it's a safety lock on one's ankles that keeps us afloat. Opportunity is life nature if we truly listen. Are you listening? I fucks with you Sin cause you oh my goodness healthy for me in more ways than you know. I am who I am! Getting up looking at his watch he said I got another surprise for you. As they walked out the trial it was over sixteen horses easy, never had she rode a horse let alone on the beach coast this dude was totally in his voice weird. Riding the horse is something I never tried doing they gave us shoes and all. He had put together an arena of festivities I never encountered. Galloping while video me Sin kept saying this what riders do, ride. My ride or die my Bonnie and Clyde its rewards in loyalty to me and that alone is my reward. I love ya consistency and all you have done as well as all you are continuously doing in my life. After the horseback riding and leaving the Driftwood beach Sin and Treasure finally reached The Westin where their room was located. Afterwards of taking showers and changing clothes they went to a grocery store and a liquor right outside of the island to grab some Moscato along with simple things that were light foods that Sin was so into a health trip but blow more gas than Atlanta highways. What you wanna eat Treasure? Fruit it doesn't matter what it is just get a lotta of fruit. Paleo Sandwich bread, I am going to grab some Oscar Myers Sliced turkey get some tomatoes and spinach matter fact hold on I am going to google this strawberry spinach salad.

2 bunches	*spinach (rinsed and torn into bite-size pieces)*
4 cups	*strawberries (sliced)*
½ cup	*vegetable oil*
¼ cup	*white wine vinegar*
¼ cup	*white sugar*
¼ teaspoon	*paprika*
2 tablespoons	*sesame seeds*
1 tablespoon	*poppy seeds*

So, is this all you want love? Grab me some whip creme and we good! Oh, my goodness so you really feel as if you're exhibitionist spirit is poking out. I don't know let's find out. Sin, holding Treasure pinky trailing behind her as if she was the link to the biggest and greatest delivery. Basket full of fruit, bread and slices of turkey a bottle of Moscato. Oh, Sin loves Peanut butter and celery plus his favorite he had to have his box of nutty bars. Do we call this a ghetto vacation don't judge me I love what I love! Treasure walking with the basket to Great Dune Park where they prepared their eating area and Sin was vibing to the night lights of the stars. Peanut butter and strawberries was new to Treasure and Sin placed some on the strawberry and went to feed her opening her mouth prepared to enjoy the fruit and Sin placed it upon her nose ugh and Sin kissed her on her forehead as well as kissing her nose while licking the peanut butter from her nose. You do the most Sincere Hollis why is it that you can't be romantic and not humorous in all you do. Let's take this walk, so I can blow this pressure from around these white folks. Ok I got you Sin you and this gas you need to give it a break. Please don't do that I don't tell you how to live your life so don't go on with the extra things that to where as in you'd try leading me to be who you want me to be. Control is something I have never been a partaker of I have done what I have done because freedom is something, I've always been in seek of. Treasure lost in the window of various opportunities this has been an epic night that one would never forget and was unmeasured. After indulging in their getaway and riding back to Savannah she asked Sin why it is you're so honest you can lie to everyone and many will buy into it with the many qualities and attributes you are blessed with. Truth is you can't trust you, speaking of myself I know I am not perfect, so I rely on the guidance of God. Think about this, do you notice how when someone tells you different lies and you grow to believe in them. Once that lie has been attached to your spirit you open the door to more demons, I fight enough demons now to not keep inviting them in. Saying that to say this ya emotions are everywhere people seem altered in every mind set. If one keeps doors closed, they don't have to worry about being attacked by many demons. It's a real live war going on out here the greatest demon I face constantly is Sin dying daily but then again Sincere too soft for this field work. They both began laughing in unison and meditating on all Sin had said he was wise beyond his years. Do you not feel as if Sincere wisdom has helped you all live so long cause I constantly wonder how you still living? I was chosen for this life God knew what he was doing. I may not put all my armor on every day, but I try and keep that belt of truth and I am not talking about this Forty I wear faithfully.

Sin waking up going thru his Facebook was taken away by this inviting picture. Women beauty was life but one's mind was the greatest forum he ever visited because after one's physical make up what is it can someone give to you. Reality is anyone can be sexier, more alluring and breath taking but everyone couldn't tattoo your mental with the reflection of it being stained upon ya heart. That's another window of water that runs deeper than the abyss. Aura was her name her uniqueness was captivating. Intoxicated from the window of her beauty he jumped straight in her inbox.

11/11/10, 3:13 PM

GhosstfacePoet
Wow...ur pics shows true foundation, will u go help me build my house?

11/11/10, 3:31 PM

Aura

I'll be as helpful as I can!!!! :)

11/11/10, 3:53 PM

GhosstfacePoet

U must eat good or is it working out?! Then again sum ppl born wit a silver spoon blessed

Aura

I am certified born thickumz....

11/11/10, 4:11 PM

GhosstfacePoet

Thank ur parents 4 blessing my eyes :).... How long have u been writing if u dnt mind my asking?

Aura

I don't mind. I've always scribbled things down.. But in the last year I've been writing more cohesive things not just streams of consciousness. If that makes sense to you...the notes on my page are the first time I've let anyone read anything I wrote ever!!!!

My mom said you're welcum!!!! Lol

11/11/10, 4:30 PM

GhosstfacePoet

Wow...eye understand cause writing is therapy just gettin our feelings on paper...so do u do Spoken words ur delivery is beautiful.

Aura

Thank you...I have recently been asked to?

Don't know if I have the nerve to do it though!!! Did you read them all or just "Selfish?" I absolutely love how u express yourself as well… There's nothing hotter than a man that's good at wordplay!!!!!! For me anyway…I keep most of the real guttah stuff to myself though!!! Lol

11/11/10, 4:47PM

GhosstfacePoet

Spoil me wit sum eye just give ppl what they want it cud be 2 deep in most cases….im a thinker and love my art so eye try and do things unlike others call it true passion….ur going to share em wit me, eye use 2 rap but their isn't content n songs anymore

Aura

Feel free to share whatever is goin on in that beautiful mind of yours…I would love to read more…

I have a request and it may be askin to much, but can you show me what u look like…I like to know who I'm talking to…and when I'm reading ur words I don't want to think of the scream mask…lol

GhosstfacePoet

Song eye did…Dirte the topic u cats need to stop it….rolling solo smokin exotic hating on me ur girls is a target she keep me in her mouth like brand new gossip…a young chosen prophet keeps a big object open ur lid up like a fuckkkking running faucet…tell me why the system got all da real niggas hostage Dirte got da heat u know I'm go pop it…Love da streets & at da club blow da profit laughn at u niggas like hater top dis…yall my motivation nuthin but God can stop dis 13 and a half dats da odds bitch fuck da system eye won't quit crooked ass America eatta dick

Aura

This is going to be an interesting friendship!!!!!

11/11/10, 5:20 PM

GhosstfacePoet

Keep it interesting eye don't show da face cause I'm ugly cause eye want u 2 want me totally not just da physical

Aura

Whatever ur probably not...and I'm not that shallow!! But I respect it I didn't show my face for the longest on here, because of the same reason I would rather someone get to know me for me not what they think I am from a pic on Facebook...

GhosstfacePoet

So, you Spanish descent? That status is an unfamiliar language enlighten me if you would?!

Aura

it's not Spanish its French...it says: You take me for a wonderful trip through your mind with words and I enjoy every minute!!!!! You'll see a lot of French from me better set google translate as one of ur favs.... when I'm mad I rant in French or when I'm turned on...

11/16/10, 4:06 PM

GhosstfacePoet

Lol eye love it and ur love magnetic mental

Aura

Drink me in....the juice of my fruit, let it explode honeyed on the vulva that is your mouth with full lips and hurricane tongue leaving my true nectar...dripping down your chin and onto your chest, but never taking your lips away from the divine sweetness of my fruit. Feel it wash over your palette and creep down your throat into every cell of your being.... My aphrodisiac takes over like Absinthe your now drunk with desire. Take it Ghost drink me all in drowning yourself til you are completely full of me. Wanna Taste????

GhosstfacePoet

Yes, put it on my status

Jumping up from his laptop after indulging into the world of Facebook Sin rolls up and goes to sleep while watching Treasure sleep quietly. Tossing and turning in his sleep Sin rose up scared from the dream he was just given. Looking at Treasure who laid next to him he couldn't see what it was that was being brought to him because she was everything to him during his lowest point which was when he was on the run. No one knew that Sin was on the run but a few in hand. Treasure who had fell asleep listening to Yolanda Adams the battle is the lords. Treasure began to realize than Sin was irregular than a lot of people she came upon because he always said God told me and I don't wanna do this who go believe me? Treasure was older than Sin and she was very spiritual many looked at her in a condemning manner because she had 8 kids and was known to be promiscuous. Sin was the only person who always looked at her in an empowering way to where as he saw more than others saw. Treasure and Sin met thru Cee-Cee, Cee-Cee and Treasure were sisters Treasure moved to Georgia after her other kids had been taken from her custody and only had her oldest son who was 19 and her daughter who was 15. Fighting to position herself to be a great mother she would always say I'm not getting my kids back they took them. Sin never a person to allow someone to hurt around him tried figuring out how to aide her. So, in his eyes she was his Angel in the field but was constantly pushed by the crickets in the field. One thing about crickets is if you pay attention is their very loud when you're in the field up until you get close to them is when their quiet. Attempting to assist her because he honestly felt as if he was in Hell's kitchen many were coming up against him and it made no sense. As Sin pondered different things thru out his thought process Enemy of the State came on and Sin not a fan of tv sat and watched Will Smith in this movie. Treasure sitting across from Sin who was an ear constantly rolled up and grinding the kush Sin began blowing clouds. Now Treasure house was where everyone from the hood came because Treasure even in her having little, she fed many who had nothing. Treasure what you got to eat today Duecy would ask? Hold on let me go whip something up. A gem Treasure always left in Sin spirit was it takes a village to raise kids and ironically many rode Treasure wave and aiding one another as a family so Lil Miami was a tribe that was in unison with working together in overlooking all the kids as well as protecting in every form. Trying to shake off the nightmare Sin felt. He is anxiety seemed to kick in even worst and Sin never believed in random occurrence he always felt all things meant something. Only if one was willing to take time to take an ear to that thing. Sin had a problem with his control and never would like to listen, so he had a habit of always looking up talking to his mom who had died. Ma, I don't know what it is you're trying to tell me, but I hear you. Sin guide was his mother and Sincere guide was his father two different parents yet in saying that things were constantly revealed to Sincere who was the key to our true safety. The greatest fight that Sincere encountered with Sin was his obedience it was many things life had taught him, and he held close to but wasn't healthy for us to live beyond the circumstances of what we were faced with if we were to live strong. Sin loved his mother and he always ran to her in his alone time because she had given him so much as a child, he knew she would never leave him. Sincere always told himself listen for one to live one must die. Sin didn't believe death existed because this was death existence what could be lower than what life was giving us get out ya feelings. The more Sincere instilled God in the rolodex of things the lower Sin power lied. A wise man said every day is like a dogfight in one cage whatever dog you feed the most will win. Sin lacked patience Sincere determination was beyond any norm because he remembers who he grew up believing in he seen it with his own eyes not by word but by deeds somethings he never expounded on to others because he felt you couldn't explain God supernatural ability. That's the difference between psychology and spirituality one lives in the physical form in tangible ways, spirituality lies in the internal its doesn't deal with tangible things. Sin trying to understand things that were being revealed would ask himself how is it that when I look up and ask my mother for certain things I get them but you don't want me to believe and just in that instance Treasure gospel music said something that grabbed Sin I will look to the hills from where my help comes from. As he pondered the statement that grasp his attention, he stated remembering what Sincere told him. Matthew 8:21-22 And another of his disciples said unto him, Lord, suffer me first to go and bury my father. But Jesus said unto him, follow me; and let the dead bury their dead.

In all thru Sin wrestled with such a thought I could never forget my mother are you crazy? The more Sin was grasping he understood he wasn't letting his mom go he wasn't putting his mom before God. In his heart no one was more divine than this woman who birthed him she led me to God truth. So, Sin believed he try to listen the best he knew how. Once he rose up from his sleep Sincere it seemed always said stay focused, so he desired to listen to the voice within for once. Treasure got up and asked Sin do he want breakfast Sin playing everything thru his head remember the voice within saying stay silent do not say a word. Unsure of how to respond Sin shook his head yes and being his anxiety was really bothering him he ran to just soak in the tub listening to music which was soothing to his spirit. Now as Sin was in the tub Treasure cooked a big breakfast for Sin and upon her coming up stairs she asked Sin did he want cheese in his grits and Sin spoke for the first time and said No outta nowhere she slammed the plate to the floor and said you don't appreciate nothing and Sin realized he said something and this is what was to come about but he tried avoiding it. Trying to control the situation she threw things at Sin, but Sin tried grabbing her and she was running downstairs. This was it; the picture was becoming more clearer in her defense she cried and fought against Sin. Sin mother oldest brother stayed next door and she ran to his house and Sin ran behind her naked outside the door confused hurt by his losing control of the situation went in the house to put on clothes. My Uncle had two big sons who were 2 or maybe 3 times bigger than myself. Sin, never feared no one but never desired hurting who he loved so he never thought about challenging his family who if he felt threaten could easily erase it wasn't in his mindset Family was in his eyes the only connection to his mom and he wanted her to exist in every manner of thought. Treasure was laying in my aunts arm completely looking as if she was truly fearful. Sin began pushing his cousin move let me talk to her. Terry, who was the oldest brother, grab Sin arm chill out cuz and Berry closing in said cuz that's a woman. Sin thoughts all cluttered unsure how to register anything was turned around by his biological sister who had the same father and same mother "Stop it Sin, I am tired of this get it together." Never in his in entirety of living did Sin feel such a feeling from his sister she pulled him outside and said I love you Sin but you gotta stop this. Hugging and embracing him he realized he was hurting those around him, and he jogged off never wanting no one to witness him in a weak state. Walking in the graveyard Sin said ma why are you doing this to me? What has I done to be so cold hearted? Breaking down his Dutch and rolling up his phone constantly ringing he placed it on vibrate. While talking to his mom pondering even hurting himself because he didn't desire to hurt those, he loved Sin felt useless. Harmony who was kicked out her mom's house had nowhere to go on many nights and Sin would get her a room never trying to intrude her space or wanting anything in return was the strangest person she met. Walking thru the path she had walked many times when Sin feared killing, she saw Sin seating in front of his mother tombstone. Sin looking back pulling out his fire "It's me Sin, It's me Sin chill the fuck out yo. "Dude you know you don't slide up without making ya self-know you lucky I aint shoot you. Sin sitting back down Harmony leaned down and said I don't know what it is that you're going thru but I love you for real you loved me when everybody abandoned me. I don't know everything about you, but you left a gem with me and I'm going to leave it with you cause you need it more than I do. Harmony went inside her book bag that she was carrying and placed a bible in his lap. Blowing on clouds in tears Sin looked up now you wanna talk to me? Crying and not knowing what he was in seek of Sin remembered what his mother told him as a child follow God not man. God speaks to you if you're willing to listen Opening the bible just him by himself Matthew 28:6-7 He is not here, for he has risen, just as He said. Come, see the place where He was lying. And go quickly and tell His disciples that He has risen from the dead; and behold, He is going before you into Galilee, there you will see Him; behold, I have told you. Sin, arose and was determined to live better than before he wasn't going to embrace his circumstances. He was going to face his demons if it even meant Sin dying.

The Many Colors of my Eyes

Color upon color spill in my thoughts as I reign its seen in your Art
The promise will never depart
I am all in all allow your pen to walk as I talk to you
Give them the picture of every area of my heart
It will become richer & richer even when it seems as if it's no space
I'm sitting here with you so show them my face
How my love is ever more colorful
Even in error you're loveable every puzzle piece must be placed together to fulfill a covenant more better
There's no need for the perfect letter nor tune
I only desire the most intimate bond with you
So, release me in holiness & truth who can create & destroy?

A taste makes one yearn for more as they stand at the door of my pen
The totality of my beauty allows them in
The deaf will not ignore neither will the blind not see cause the creativity that resides inside I gave you to see
So, allow your eyes to be windows they look thru
I chose you
Then only then I'll be the ink as you continue being the pen of many colors.

Sincere Hollis became an advocate to bring about strength as well as support of less fortunate.

Inclined to be of edification in all he encountered he promised himself he'd give his all in the same manner he sacrificed his all in his representation of the life I believed in during his past. Refusing to be devoured by the standards and expectations of a black man from the lowest pole of life Sincere created a Resolution for himself as a Man.

Daily Sincere would say to his spirit to remind himself of who indeed he was and not be erased by an identity crisis he excepted his place as a Man of substance and purpose bounded by love.

Being absent from his writing Sin was able to breathe again so he applied his pen to trot easily. Flipping thru Facebook Sin realize he hasn't been active in days being all the turmoil that was occurring this was his peace. Poetry!

11/17/10, 2:44 PM

GhosstfacePoet
What should eye say I'm lost…
What does ya name mean if i may ask?

Aura
my name……lol come on if we're gonna do this you gotta pay attention……
In Hebrew it means Halo, to praise and to shine. In India Arie voice I am light!

GhosstfacePoet
Go look at ur page I'm ahead of u…😁

Aura

look at my status.....

GhosstfacePoet

Coconut thighs with mango between it....kiwi lips saying eat it banana split without the Sunday... eye wanna taste u everyday of da week starting again Monday...honey trails running down ur back followed by my tongue and nails...If dis was Michigan id been in jail...fruit is a habit but eye was taught 2 toss salad...before each meal let my tongue peel ur juices like bananas...let me marry dis monkey bless wit a tongue wit stamina...cum milky like coconut...my tongue licking ur clit & butt... Now da question is can eye eat from ur Fruit Bar...

Aura

Aura is...wiping her forehead and sighing!!!!! DAMN U!!!!

11/17/10, 4:14 PM

Aura

Where shall we go next lover?

Bouncing back and forth between establishing his vision and networking on Facebook. Sin continues applying the gems that falls from within from the creativity it is surrounded by.

I Sincere Hollis pledge to live fruitful, attentive as well as supportive for those who I sincerely am here to be of help with. How can one fall asleep on hope arise, arise strong man arise? As experience continues being the light walking us closer to faith, sincerely! I've never believed in coincidence either we listening to life or were gravitating closer to death. Being death cause we were given all the warnings & cautions we continued to trigger the alarm. Stand, stand, stand even if your legs feel feeble Stand for a love greater than selfish beliefs. Love is selfless we are protectors as men so protect the value of our greatest substance which is the essence of nurturing. Life gives us what were in seek of, for one to grow water produces life. Water is soft and ever gentler the complete body of a woman. God is controller of all things, yet we consider the journey as being difficult. Light afflictions, in comparison to any before our time. The review is small so one sees what's behind the windshield is broad so one focus on what's ahead. Focus, focus, focus should be abundant and consistent grab ahold of your truth and blossom into the Man that you are. Look how far you came! Smile, its a reminder that joy is well worth holding on to.

Sincere, was in the barber shop talking to a few men and at the chess board him and a guy who was playing chess while holding a discussion. What was the first petty act that occurred in history? When? Sin asked Digging in thought Sincere was confused. I don't know, what you believe it is? The design of manipulation, it was orchestrated for Eve to point the finger at Adam. It's been spiritually instilled that man & woman have blamed one another! Huh?! You're a trip for real! Sin responded So Young Cricket, who was the blame? It's clear, Eve ate the forbidden fruit because the devil deceived her! The wiseman asked Did not the devil do his job? I guess, I don't know. Okay, we go stay biblical, so no assumptions are made. What does 1 Peter 5:8 state and read it aloud. "Be sober, be vigilant; because your adversary the devil walks about like a roaring lion, seeking whom he may devour." Sincere immediately began laughing because it was nothing that this old head didn't know. You correct! Okay now let's go to the beginning Genesis 1:26 what does it state "Then God said Let us make man in our image according to our likeness; let them have dominion over the fish of the sea, over the birds of the air, and over the cattle, over all the earth and over every creeping thing that creeps on earth." So, is it fair to say that one was born into authority to where as he was ordained King? DaJule stated Dominion is authority so I agree in all truth. Yes! Before we go any further, we are clearly laying things out, so we understand he was Petty Crocker, Sincere. Laughing still how Jule broke things down in a great uniqueness so a baby could rasp it. Which was an Art that Sincere admired most. Are you still with me Sincere? Yes, Sir! Go to Genesis 2:15 read it aloud "Then the Lord placed the man in the garden of Eden to cultivate it and guard it. He told him. "Stop, who is he talking to? Quickly Sincere responded Adam! Okay continue. "Of every tree of the garden you may freely eat; 17 but of the tree of the knowledge of good & evil you shall not eat, for in the day that you eat of it you shall surely die." God is a God of detail & order keep this in mind as I thumb thru these verses Yes, sir! Now go to Genesis 2:21 read Sincere anxious to see what each verse would reveal he was with grasping truth in whatever he did the knowledge too. So he began reading it aloud "And the Lord God caused a deep sleep to fall on Adam & he slept; and he took one of his ribs and closed up the flesh in its place 22 Then the rib which the Lord god had taken from man He made into a woman, and he brought her to man. 23 And Adam said:

"This is now bone of my bones and flesh of my flesh; She shall be called woman, because she was taken out of man." So now here is my next portion of understanding for you to know a husband or wife one must know is God design?! Its only two things God can not do. 1 is God can not sin. 2 God will not be second in no realm. Saying that to say this Adam chose Eve over God cause he was commanded dominium.

When this is broken down one must look at one thing woman was created for man many confuse creation with control. Look at God divine plan one is given freedom to choice. Choices stem from influences, I leave you with this and I am done. What influence will you leave the one you love with? Check mate DaJule states as the guy he was playing trying to see where his error was, as DaJule gets up greeting all as he leaves.

Returning home thoughts rambling from the soul food he was given by DaJule. He needed a poetic release this was something he naturally did which was blow clouds while allowing nature sedation to talk on higher plains that was misunderstanding to many. These are the many reasons I am glad God is nothing like man if it was up to man I'd never be able to rock with God on my terms and we grow closer than anyone could ever convey.

Eve, I apologize!

I love the existence of your creation, I asked for you in the garden waiting for help. My lack of focus of you left me a mess. I allowed something to slither close to what God created best for me. I confess my error!

A wound that yet bleeds, I grit my teeth; at the thought of my selfishness.
Then another me was born.
I am Selfless!
As time progress I look at my truth, surrounded by pain my thoughts return to you.
You've been the glue when all things fell loose.
You're proof that your existence is the only vision i see.
So, many think my respect for the essence from which I came from would allow me to brandish any form of pain in return.
I yearn for you in every way, I desire to earn your totality by God grace.
What could replace my greatest gift, even when the world tries pushing me down.
You've been the one to uplift me with ease.
Is it fair to say without my rib I cannot breathe?

Sigh of release after Sin was able to write the piece that he was capable of writing. While rambling from window to window Sin began roaming to Facebook. Where he met Aura in his mind, she was Life and light her name represented her make up in totality.

11/17/10, 8:47 PM

GhosstfacePoet

Where eva ur mental allows im there deep n ur thoughts

Aura

Thanx lover!!!!

Sin greatest enemy wasn't the d'evil cause naturally so he has a job as we do as individuals. He was at war with himself so after going thru various things. Sin desired to understand things on a deeper level, pulling up in front of the church. Overlooking himself didn't feel as if he fit the church attire but Sin recalled what his mom would always say. God said come as you are. After taking a deep sigh, walking thru the front doors of the church Sin located the restroom and went in to do a self-assessment of himself. Butterflies filling his stomach and anxiety started to paralyze Sin as he grabbed a napkin wet it, so he'd calm down. Taking a deep breath and gravitating to facing his fear of attention, he begins to walk in the church and sits in the back pew, so the attention doesn't become distracting to not only him but the church as a whole.

A young minister was standing behind the pulpit the church was full but not wanting to be distracted nor altering others reception, so Sin focused on only the preacher. If you all would turn to Nehemiah 1:8-9

The lady next to Sin said young man do you need a bible Sin responded yes and thanked her for placing him in a better place of understanding to where as he could read things for himself.

Returning his attention to the minister. Everyone has this chapter and find Nehemiah it's in the old testament for those who may not know. While I quench my thirst give those who is not as familiar with the bible to catch up with us, so we are all on one accord. Amen The church in unison Amen Sin reaching the location of the scripture given. Ok if you all would I truly desire you to follow me as I give you what it is thus says the Lord. Not my word but the words inspired by God in one way or another. Verse 8 states Remember, the word which you commanded your servant Moses, saying, if you are unfaithful, I will scatter you among the peoples:

⁹ But if you return to me, and keep my commandments, and do them; though those of you who have been scattered were in the most remote parts of the heavens, I will gather them from there, and will bring them to the place where I have chosen to cause my name to dwell."

If you have your bible pay attention to Remember. Remember what you say, what God commanded Moses to do. The bible to me I view as a chess board in chess the design of strength to win I was taught every piece protects another piece. Scripture to me doesn't contradict itself. Its one's perception for the most part, which open the door of deception of one lacks the holy spirit in truth. Yet that's another sermon in itself. God speaks in levels, Levels of what? Levels of maturity. 1 Corinthians 13:11 When I was a child, I thought as a child: but when I became a man, I put away childish things."

Typically, the word depends on the one who is delivering it. Example all gas isn't helpful, if you accidently add diesel fuel to a gas engine? In general, your car will turn out sluggish performance before it stops running altogether. Premium and Top Tier gas differs for many reasons. In lamest terms what gas will you place within you? Ask yourself that question before you release what you deem as the appropriate answer. So when one hear various scriptures ask yourself this question how can a high school student grow from continuously learning elementary things that's instilled. Hebrews 5:12 For when the time ye ought to be teachers, ye have need that one teach you again which be the first principles of the oracles of God; and are become such as have need of milk, and not of strong meat."

Even more so many of us have or may encounter condemnation. Now clearly we all have witness or had parents who in error we may feel their overboard or even others whom choose to understand & meet common grounds so the child grasp the difference between healthy & unhealthy actions. John 3:17 "For God sent not his Son into the world to condemn the world; but that the world through him might be saved."

Saved from what unhealthy choices, which is depicted in the bible as Sin. Many times, people are judged by others unbeknown to another person belief.

John 12:47 "And if any man hear my words, and believe not; I judge him not: for I came not to judge the world but to save the world."

Everyone wasn't given or more so witnessed a relationship with God so insensitive acts can easily persuade one not to grasp a desire. Today if I could place a title upon the body of this sermon it would definitely be Lost then Found. Being this could be an endless topic it will be a two-portion meal. I'll give you enough to leave you full and bring you the rest in next week service Amen.

Lost meaning states unable to find one's way, not knowing ones where about. Found meaning states having been discovered by chance or unexpectedly, in particular.

If one is not Lost how can he be found?! Many times, we as people are in search of something, first we must know what we are in seek of? My first question is what is it you feel is absent? No one on earth knows this better than oneself. Growing up in a single parent home by my mother. I can honestly say she didn't instill perfection, she always stressed God love for us. Every morning we would say this prayer to keep us covered from what it was we were to encounter thru out our day Psalm 91(read aloud) "He who dwells in the secret place of the most high. Shall abide under the shadows of the Almighty.2 I will say of the Lord, "He is my refuge and my fortress; my God, in him will I trust.3 Surely He shall deliver you from the snare of the fowler.4 He shall cover you with his feathers, And under his wings you shall take refuge; his truth shall be your shield and buckler. 5 You shall not be afraid of the terror by night, nor of the arrow that flies by day. 6 Nor of the pestilence that walks in darkness, nor of the destruction that lays waste at noon day.7 A thousand may fall at your side, And ten thousand at your right hand; But it shall not come near you. 8 Only with your eyes shall you look, And see the reward of the wicked. 9 Because you have made the Lord, who is my refuge. Even the most high, your dwelling place, 10 No evil shall befall you. Nor shall any plague come near your dwelling.11 For he shall give his Angels charge over you. To keep you in all your ways. 12 In their hands they shall bear you up. Lest you dash your foot against a stone.13 You shall tread upon the lion and the cobra, the young lion and serpent you shall trample under foot.14 "Because he has set his love upon me, therefore I will deliver him; I will set high, because he has known my name. 15 He shall call upon me, and I will answer him; I will be with him in trouble; I will deliver him and honor him.16 With long life I will satisfy him, And show him my salvation."

KINGS cannot die!!!!!

Typically, the format of God order differs from that of the world. Isaiah 55:8 "For my thoughts are not your thoughts neither are your ways my ways declare the Lord."

I want us to allow God to sit and speak to us directly, if one is receptive for the most part their open to receiving what it is their in seek of. Deuteronomy 32:4 "The Rock, his work is perfect for all his ways are justice. A God of faithfulness and without iniquity, just and upright is he."

When one thinks upon a Rock, solid comes to mind. Notice the continuation after Rock, his work is perfect. Work, what work? Work synonyms is service, effort & travail. Let's pause momentarily travail is defined as painful synonyms are trial, tribulation, trouble and hardship. Here is the beauty many of us overlook. Stress, tribulations, troubles & hardship are dealt with perfectly. God can not lie Numbers 23:19 "God is not a man, that he should lie; neither the son of man, that he should repent: hath he said, and shall he not do it? Or has he spoken, and shall not make it good?

Titus 1:2 "In hope of eternal life, which God, that can not lie, promised before the world began;

Hebrews 6:18 "That by two immutable things, in which it was impossible for God to lie, we might have a strong consolation, who have fled for refuge to lay hold upon the hope set before us.

Saying all that to say God reassures he cannot lie yet many probably saying I've prayed & its times God didn't provide. Well he tells us here in James 4:3 "Ye ask, and receive not, because ye ask amiss, that ye may consume it upon your lusts."

Amiss is defined as wrong, out of place, not quite right. Okay if I am a sharp shooter on the court, accuracy comes from molding or forming an appropriate format of delivery. Then one's execution becomes mind boggling. Practice makes perfect, we've all heard this saying. So, what is it one must practice? Turn with me if you would to Matthew 6:33 "But seek first his Kingdom and his righteousness, and all these things will be added to you." Before we move forward to the things that God bestows upon us as a whole. We must adopt a God mind state. Adopt because it replaces ones original mind state which is sharpen first by working ones spiritual mindset. I was always told you don't use something you lose it. 1 Timothy 4:8 "For bodily exercise profiteth little; but godliness is profitable unto all things, having promise of the life that now is, and that which is to come."

Also, I don't wanna limit the ability that God blesses us with yet that's entire sermon in itself. Saying all that to say this if one has indeed adopted a God mind state why belittle God truth with unbelief? Many question God totality at heart cause let's be honest. Its seldom if never we've seen things of such greatness occur before our eyes. That's what were taught to believe, I can say as a steward of God my relationship wasn't always close. I became more intimate in our encounters of life when we fought together. Let's be real with ourselves, in most relationships once we've encountered certain dark moments and yet prevail together in love our bond was stronger after every moment. We can say that's the equation to how we build up our faith. Isn't that how you believe more in your relationship? Stop me if I am wrong. Ok! Now in verse 8 in 1 Timothy chapter 4 reads but godliness is profitable unto all things. First, I'd like to break down something so communication is clear thus far. Notice how God in the bible has a capital G which is greater. Its many portions in the bible God speaks on gods with a small g. Reason being their not greater than him. Its many practices thru out the world & many hold the title of god. So were on course here godliness in verse 8 is God telling us to possess him in spirit. Another indication of God abundance is he states godliness (mind state) is profitable unto all things, it doesn't say some it says all. So how is it that we limit God? Deuteronomy 25:13-16. You shall not have in your bag differing weights, a large and a small. God word isn't a reflection of large and small in his kingdom were equivocal to him not greater. Philippians 2:6 who, being in the form of God thought it not be robbery to be equal with God. The true measure of influence is example. One of God greatest forms of excelling many looks at as the most difficult. Matthew 5:48 Therefore you are to be perfect, as your heavenly Father is perfect." First, I wanna tell you about me helping my son become a greater shooter. What I noticed most about my son is he didn't desire to learn how to shoot yet he was in a rush to be an outside shooter. Which was strange to me was! How can you master deep waves if you haven't faced the waves that beats the seashores? So, the process I would instill is becoming familiar with art of shooting properly. Isaiah 41:10 "Do not fear, for I am with you, do not anxiously look about you, surely I will help you. Surely I will uphold you with my righteous right hand." So, I'd tell myself don't rush the process, I'll aide you in a manner you need if you'll willing to strive or more so continuously grow. Before running to the three-point line I believe one must spill into one self. How so? Teach self to believe what it is that you desire for example Master common shots first. One's mind is like a computer it's up to you what program you store in it. Jude 1:24 Now to him who is able to keep you from stumbling, and to make you stand in the presence of his glory blameless with great joy." Thru out my teaching him I taught him to use his weakest hand and began learning your form as well as your rotation. My reasoning for this basketball analogy is this. I'm the father of my son so it's my job to guide him into growth so its smooth meaning less resistance. In reality that's what God does with those whom he loves. He is our father; he knows for the most part was going thru the process of learning all over again. Constantly inspiring us in every manner. Philippians 4:13 I can do all things through Him who strengthens me."

He is it that strengthens you? If it's only you my next question is when your strength grows weak who will uphold you and help you continue to stand. Man cannot just be of help to self it requires another aide even in your belief system if God isn't whom you believe in one must believe in something more vital than one self. I would never direct one not to believe in God yet if one questions truth totality God gives man freedom to Test the spirit by the spirit. Seek Love in all that you do anything outside of love is a mire distraction May you all go in peace and thank you for allowing me to bless you with God word. I am a firm believer if you are in seek of truth you will return to God word in my seeking, I studied many things nothing represented truth in the manner God word do. Do not be influence by various guides in your journey of living allow God to lead you faithfully. Sin, leaving the church after hearing the sermon was somewhat baffled by the reality of the preacher expressions and he desired to seek the depths of it especially after recalling what his mother told him at 11 he knew by heart Proverbs 2:4 If thou seekest her as silver, and searchest for her as for hid treasures.

With that being said it would just be out in the open it was something only oneself could find in sincerity. Know where your heart lies and all you seek will be given. Looking up to the clouds saying aloud this is why I love ya mom you prepared me for such a time like this. Sitting in the car needing to roll up Sin reconsidered because he no longer wanted to be openly disrespectful as Macy Gray began blasting thru his speakers as Stay woke kissed the earlobes of his mental. Tip toe-ing thru the town watching many that seemed to look like zombies walking dead was never be caught up in his mindset. Bando stood in the middle of the street trying to stop Sin. Sin pulled up as Bando began dancing to Macy swaying his hips from side to side "How you King?" I'm good what's good with you? Nothing major, what was you bought to do? Nothing Bando do you wanna ride with me as I cut a few blocks. As Bando jumped in Sin looked at Bando who as a child lost his mom and was the child. He never seemed to recover! Covering unseen scars that somehow each high seemed to cause demons to dance from pains cymbals. The melodies became so familiar up until pain became the symphony of classic upon classic.

Never desiring to face many moments head on, his retreat became the flames he hoped would burn bridges he uses to see hope cross. No escape from the windows of life truth, this was his way of dealing with the piece's life continued offering him. Sin, only desired to allow Bando to encounter some form of peace if it was only an hour. Always he went beyond his means to put him in a great place. Nope I haven't ate, what we go it? Bando really appreciated Sin cause no one understood the issues of life he felt he could never escape from. Sin never judged me nor made me feel as if I was equipped in any manner, honestly Sin did something no one had ever done. He allowed me to talk to a girl he once talked to because he said I deserved a healing spirit that would refresh me in a manner he felt as if I was deserving of. Actually, I looked at Sin as Brethren more so than anything. The Love was genuine with nothing he desired in return but me being in the best place in my life. As they pulled up to Congo a restaurant to eat some Curry Chicken, which is what Sin ordered I wanted Goat. After waiting 20 minutes both holding a full plate intact. No disrespect Sin I'm bout to sit in the backseat and do me. Yo you and that big ass torch better not burn no holes in none of my stuff for real homie. While being back in a lot of the people in the trenches fucked with Sin because he was the heart of the hood. He did something that none really did, he cared about the interest of others. Backed up to his Auntee house by Lil Miami as Trick Daddy Amerika was beating out his windows. So, Sin why is it you stay solo and you continue to isolate yourself. Sin, thinking before he was to speak trying to choose his words appropriately said Man will never appreciate nothing but only what compliments their appetite. What I eat others may not eat so in saying that I try not to feed people healthy food if unhealthy suits their appetite with that being said God word is right and exact there is no error. Acts 13:46-52 **46***Then Paul and Barnabas answered them boldly: "We had to speak the word of God to you first. Since you reject it and do not consider yourselves worthy of eternal life, we now turn to the Gentiles.* **47***For this is what the LORD has commanded us: "I have made you a light for the Gentiles, that you may bring salvation to the ends of the earth."* **48***When the Gentiles heard this, they were glad and honored the word of the LORD; and all who were appointed for eternal* *life believed. ⁴⁹The word of the LORD spread through the whole region. ⁵⁰But the Jewish leaders incited the God-fearing women of high standing and the leading men of the city. They stirred up persecution against Paul and Barnabas and expelled them from their region. ⁵¹So they shook the dust off their feet as a warning to them and went to Iconium. ⁵²And the disciples were filled with joy and with the Holy Spirit.*

I constantly place the words from God before you because I am an heir of the King Salvation. He seeks many to be saved, sanctified and delivered from one's old ways. Do you believe in your mind set of thinking that what you're doing isn't hypocritical? Sin began laughing aloud and said for a long time I felt as if I was a stumbling block more so than anything until God revealed this using my sister as a messenger, she said bro come as you are. With that being said I had to understand it wasn't one makeup that we embrace cause in this field its more people who has a more personal relationship than God. We are living proof! Yes, brethren I truly agree all in all. Gangsta slid up someone who Sin deemed as one of the strongest people he ever met. Going thru his recollection of thoughts in a dark state of mind when I was married I crumbled spiritually because I felt as if honestly God had betrayed me. I had the idea that in having a relationship was God the reward was blessings upon blessings. Not knowing that if we lack the guidelines the word forewarns us of many things I lacked. Inviting a Preachers daughter to the life of the streets which was something she never encountered compromised love for attention. In my exit of living the streets she was intrigued with something she never encountered in her life. After the divorce I had lost everything my wife, my family, my job and house. No longer familiar with the streets I was left wondering, Gangsta at the time was leaving the lifestyle of the streets to become married whereas he was very well established, and God was blessing everywhere in his life. Gangsta wife Porsha was a woman of God. Complete balance in the event of his blossoming I was falling down the ladder of life. The life and ones fight to escape it is a different ride because the streets don't give one the gift of prioritizing. Your discipline in the corporate world differs because we touch so much money in the streets, we spend it recklessly. In my zombie state of mind broken spiritually, emotionally and discouraged to do anything outside of being traumatized. Gangsta, picked me up during a moment to whereas me being a normally groomed individual. Riding with him and conscious unclear we grab a bite to eat and he gets me a haircut and shave. Giving up on church never giving up on God I chose to live in my place of maturity spiritually. Romans 12:3 ³For by the grace given me I say to every one of you: Do not think of yourself more highly than you ought, but rather think of yourself with sober judgment, in accordance with the faith God has distributed to each of you.

At the point of my marriage I was in the greatest place I've ever been as a man. Once I was stripped of this I was lost! Remembering what the word said God continued reminding me of his glory thru his word. 1 King 17:6 And the ravens brought him bread and flesh in the morning, and bread and flesh in the evening; and he drank of the brook. Never have I imagined my life without God guidance. After reading about you in the bible I saw no greater strength, love, mercy. My desire to understand you drew me to your likeness. I am grateful for all you've done for me. When enemies plotted against me. Many times, it seems were

buried once were in the dark the belief lies in you or what you think. You're buried or you blooming? Yes, at many moments things can be in a disarray. "Bando, You don't understand they want my head. It's no love!" Sin blurted out. "So that's how you feel brody?" Why wouldn't it be how I feel it's clear!" "I love you Brody I'd never stir you wrong, I believe in God faithfully this a real lifestyle never forget that!" Thus far you've shown me no difference. You know my motto A coin has two sides a heads & a tails once you hold the coin do you notice heads looks in the opposite way as tails. Once you hold the coin do you notice heads looks in the opposite way as tails so obviously their perception is different because their views are different. A lot of people don't see what you see, they only see what compliments their perception. I'm giving you that free, next time it's going to cost you. Cost me what? Experience, that's the difference between wisdom and knowledge.

Life challenges us and it's ironic the same person who uplifted me I am here to uplift and hold him up thru the waves of lie. I am my brother's keeper in no way I could turn my back on someone who held me up when my legs couldn't keep me afloat. Sin, you see how these Cats trying me cause I snort and do my thing. Unsure if his ideology was the greatest outcome Sin fed Gangsta addiction to keep him tame. Gangsta name wasn't Gangsta for no reason before he lost his job and couldn't provide in his eyes and ran to drugs which left him hid from his reality. Unknowingly to us he left his family but his wife whom I loved sincerely never gave up on him, but he was ashamed of failure not understanding one doesn't have to quit on life just take a break. Gizzle pulls up blows the horn at Gangsta. Who was close in fact Gangsta sister and Gizzle was siblings? Sincere and Bandoo still politicking. Have you done what I told you to do, you don't gotta still be out here scrapping the land to live it's something better than this? Bandoo grabbing his unshaved beard this was the norms in the jungle, land of the savages. Many of us represented low life like a trophy til it's become a movement that actually is backwards, but many believe because struggle doesn't look like struggling, they have walked into a lifestyle were trying to escape. The ones trying to exit it while others running towards the fire. Bandoo rambling in his bookbag interrupting Sin thought process as he pulls out his personal tablet.

Reading it aloud Bandoo reads his tablet;

Ideas for services

- *Purifying water at the site of wells that may be tainted with abrasive.*
- *(Online Opportunities) Providing guide services to travelers*
- *Developing marketing campaigns for local businesses*
- *Running food stands for others*
- *Providing tailoring services*
- *Manufacturing furniture for businesses and residences*
- *Offering cooking services for families*
- *Selling wireless phones for phone corporations*
- *Providing people to build buildings, houses, roads and or bridges*
- *Offering outsourced call center services from other countries*
- *Providing computer consulting services*

These are the many businesses I looked into and trying to put something together to help me get up outta these streets I'm tired of being stuck out chea without having my own. What's my survival motto "My will to live must be greater than anyone desire for me to die."

I even have the notes you gave me.
What's the brand advantage?
What sets your brand apart from that of the competition?
What is distinctive?
What differentiates this brand from the competitors?
How do customers perceive the brand?
What emotion does the brand evoke?
Who appreciates the brand?
Why?
What do customers get from the brand?
Where does customers find the brand?
What do customers see the founder didn't?
www.businessexampleolchemisft.com

A company owner: Head of company
Sound budget: Testing a business model will require funds.

Qualified human resources: The leader gets to choose his team (key individuals not buddies)
Laughing a loud Sin realized that Badoo no longer desired being at the bottom. So, after we went
to the library, I see you've been staying active cause it's a lot in ya book?

I did all you told me to, Sin! Realizing that his people in the field no longer desired being comfortable
Sin would go to the library getting information to help others escape the same hell he was attempting
to escape in every manner. The focus was not who get out first just get out. Each one reach one teach
one. We were a team fighting as a tribe to figure out avenues to help all our people not just us. It
never was the design the design was for us to makes ways out so others wouldn't be trapped in the
land of the exile. So we all felt, we were abandoned and left for dead. No one would help us but us!

Who could muster such will upon his mental, what is complex to some are the norms of his daily
turns? After each fight to step, each walk was learned. Life reality is no coastguards comes out at this
sea its either sink or swim.

My greatest Sin ....

...is when my pen stop being my oxygen!
How can I pretend, that wind doesn't create electricity!

As nature speaks, I continue listening, never missing a note.
That was wrote as I devote my actions to each instruction.
Every random hint keeps me blushing, ya consistency reminds me that love is nothing without
substance.
I'm forever searching for beauty as if you were 16.
Whether it's note, number or dream!
The reality is you're my everything.

Sin returning from the window of his thoughts. The car door slams as Sin notices Gangsta and
Gizzle arguing. All I really catch was Gizzle holler I didn't tell you to become a junky if you go
check somebody check ya self. Snatching the black bandana from his neck covering his knuckles with
it Gangsta tells Sin to hand him the fye. Yo seat down yo you doing too much. You see how this cat
just tried me yo. How he tried you by giving you a reality check you gotta remember just cause you
accept who you are doesn't mean everyone else has embraced it as of yet. If I wasn't on no drugs, he
would've tried me. Sin said well get off the drugs and beat him up and began laughing. Gangsta
said oh you think it's funny. Sin realizing Gangsta was yet sensitive as well as embarrassed about
admitting to his family the drugs had took a hold of him and he was out here. Get in the car and

chill, look this is not no counseling session we all abuse something in some way or manner of life they don't fuck with you guess what they were never really fucking with you. People pretend well and the moment you no longer are of benefit to them guess what its curtains. Sin began rolling up and said hit this blunt and stop wearing ya feelings on ya sleeves cause people go eat you alive now. Get out the funk for real for real. Yo, I don't got the time to counsel you but I'm bout to slide to the crib and eat you good brody? You know I love you! Sin embracing Gangsta cause its real but life will not slow down for none of us so we must stay focus and continue embracing our wave to the best of our ability. Many people wave differs it doesn't mean that we cannot ride the wave. It just means we must just adjust to the wave. Ducking off in between the projects in Lil Miami Sin decides to park where in seclusion so the radar isn't as attentive on his location like many people in the streets would call him. Mister Stay Out my Business! As he pulls up Sin blows his horn pulling up to one of his favorite spots Mary Head house her name really was Mary Head, but she became a supreme representative of her last name, good lawd! As Mary ran to the door "What's up Sin!" Is the kid good enough for a meal with ya good cooking ass? Yes, you know you always good for something to eat and I am going to always cook I got 4 heads to feed. Give me a minute ill fix you up a plate. Sin got out the car and grab his lap top which he took everywhere with him. It was like his oxygen it's no telling when he would want to write plus he always tried stay sharp for open mics and spoken word venues when he would step out in the land of strangers he was never afraid but in his own confines you could not get Sin to spill a bean no one knew he was a poet. Connecting to Mary Wi-Fi he immediately started chopping it up with the multiple inboxes he had Aura was numero uno.

11/26/10, 5:09 PM

Aura
i SAID THEY WERE GONNA BE MAD... BECAUSE OBVIOUSLY WE HAVE CONNECTED ON SOMETHING OTHER THAN PHYSICAL THING...THATS MORE INTIMIDATING THAN SEX ANY ONE CAN HAVE SEX...BUT IF U CAN CAPTURE MY MIND, THE PHYSICAL ASPECT WILL BE PHENOMINAL!!!!!!

GhosstfacePoet
Eye responded 2 urs tell me what u think

Aura
hmm for some reason Jill Scotts longwalk just popped in my head......

GhosstfacePoet

Neva heard it...eye am on Jazz and Gospel more than anything these days

Aura

oh wow u need to hear it....

GhosstfacePoet

Eye will take a listen 2...whats the name?

Aura

Jill Scott "Longwalk"

GhosstfacePoet

Eye am bout 2 write a piece walk with Ghosst...

Aura

cant wait....

Sin, I fixed ya plate. As Mary stood in the door, she'd put you in the mind of Kerry Washington with more tazz the devil you dig me, ok. Ok baby girl gives me one second. Let me find out you just came over to steal my Wi-Fi its go be an issue you heard me. Did you hear me Sin? Yea I hear you chill out I'm getting off the computer now. Logging off locking his door while taking his laptop and bag in the house. Oh, you staying the night. It's a problem you know how I move I'm staying down here in lil Miami you gotta know that. That's cool if you stay just know I don't need ya other hens in lil Miami to act out I'm so for real. Chill out yo you be doing too much I'm so serious, ugh you doing too much don't kill my vibe! You always vibing lawd knows you smoke more than a chimney. Mary toting her nose up and hit Sin in the chest with the back of her hands. As he was blowing on his blunt Mary pressed closer into Sin. Oh, you are gassing up with me so I can eat you up like I'm bout to eat this plate. Looking clear into Sin eyes, you are so freaky, but I love that shit! No ceilings and no brakes. Hmmm, you so mean you not going to run from me. You're just going to feed me until I eat up all portions of ya mango? That's ya favorite fruit, wetter than any well. Mary pressed her lips on the other end of the blunt and Sin released it as she blew a shotgun leaving clouds that left tears running down his eyes. Grabbing the Dutch, he grabbed Mary by her throat while kissing her as his tongue began brushing crevices upon her body painting every dry spot above her oceanfront. Pinning her against the wall as she surrendered to his ever-inviting aggression with no rebuttal. As Mary clothes became puddles that were from thoughts that rained more passionately. Pushing Mary upon the table ideas jumping into the lap of her heartbeat backwards on my knees in need of more than prayer. Searching for love feeling not prepared to grasp life greatest gift after every fall exhausted from it all. Mary turns around and lift me with a kiss to remind me effort yet exist in the midst of life windows of doubt Mary softly wipes my mouth to always remind me I am not riding the smoothest road but there is a gps that will guide one to its correct route. After multiple culvusions of passion Mary was sleeping on the kitchen floor as Sin was propped against the refrigerator blowing away the reality of his pain. Mary, Mary get up so you can get in the bed yo? Sin getting Mary up walking her to the sofa laying her upon it. As he gets lost in thoughts blowing clouds and desiring to write. Penning his thoughts after escaping the life of madness that didn't exist in his pen, Sin was able to make lemons and lime taste like a mixer of vodka, fruitiness mixed with a splash of water. An untamed beauty he held and loved to apply to escape the world. In his polo brief Sin now was able to eat so food that wasn't mobile and rock out on his laptop.

11/30/10, 1:34 AM

Aura
u sure dont have much to say anymore...about the things I write.....

GhosstFacePoet
Eye just commentd bay...

11/30/10, 1:41 AM

Aura
NO TALK FOR AURA HUH?

11/30/10, 2:07 AM

Aura
The seduction plus words is the fantasy we all desire to inhabit

Moments when fully clothed words can touch your core set your soul on fire

Expose you feeling vulnerable and naked

I need to be touched by something inspirational

That transcends the monotony of everyday existence

Goes to the soul of who we as people

When words penetrate and titillate our senses

11-24-98…12:36pm

11/30/10, 2:39 AM

GhosstfacePoet
Wow dat is concrete a great write…ur sharp my writing hasnt evolved dat indepth as of yet

11/30/10, 2:49 AM

Aura
I didn't write it babe someone else did but it was something I wanted u to read!!!!

GhosstFacePoet
Thats a hard piece of work

11/30/10, 2:57 AM

Aura
Why did u erase ur comment…wow eye dont adore u huh?
… im getting caught up in my feelings eye may need 2 fall back?!

Aura

Maybe I just need to stay off your page.........

11/30/10, 3:41 AM

Aura

your voice softer than a whisper in my ear making love to my mind with words of explicit and erotic acts of love....your hands barely skimming my skin touching me ever so slightly exploring every inch every curve of me....your mouth and tongue placing soft kisses and tiny nibbles all over me....fingers in my hair massaging my scalp...lips on my belly making wet trails to my center....breath blowing my skin leaving me shivering from the sensation...hands and finger parting my nether lips...your mouth and tongue french kissing those lips and clit...fingers probing finding that spot with that come hither motion on that "G"....ur joystick rubbing gently against my wetness causing it to throb...when u enter in ur words become more explicit and when u expand my walls we dissolve one into the other...... ok thats enough SHIT!!!!!!

GhosstFacePoet

U turning me on...

Aura

As u can see I like to be made love to.....I like F#Kin too, but I'd rather be made love to completely......*

GhosstFacePoet

Eye use 2 f&ck when eye was upset but eye make love like every moment da first & last time..

Aura

eyes closed.....hands in hair massaging and twirling hair.....caressing a cheek....fingers in mouth.... hands kneading my flesh...fingers dialing my nipples....parting my lips thumbing my clit until its firm and stands at attention...fingers probing my pussy in search of tht spot finding it asking it to cum!!!! Fingers diving in exploring until I erupt with a volcanic force.....gushing that cum all over those hands.......

GhosstFacePoet

This is it...dis is it

Aura

is that better?!?!?!? lol

GhosstFacePoet

Fuck yes...
Again eye ask what is manscape or scape

Aura

Manscaping is when u shave and groom ur area around your privates...babe u know how women shave there mound....

Mary waking up witnessing Sin on the laptop. Do you ever go to sleep Sin? Not really, I sleep when I am dead! Sleeping is the cousin of death, so I tend not to lean towards death. Do you ever put your thoughts to rest? Should I? I would believe you should for the most part, you're constantly in your thoughts. I am a thinker that's how I run all of us not created the same. I feel some people think strange as I do believe they think I have weird thoughts. I feel some people are simply enslaved with a mindset; you are being a teacher answer this. Do they desire freedom? Is hate just the most common drug? It's easy to tear something down with the seconds minutes hours, yet building is such a longer process. I have gunned So many people down to where is in, I was left numb to any understanding. People say they desire love the reality is people are content with a fix. That's not love that's lust what is temporary effects surface of replication. Solace decided to switch lanes. Sin! Look! What solace? This bump irritating my leg?! What bump?!

Instantly she pointed at a print lips full as a garden. Ugh, you always know how to seduce me. Is that pussy shaved or got hair?

You go eat whatever pussy I have in stock?! Sin begins dying laughing and smiled graciously you're always on time. I came to the knowledge when real was looked up on as one's daily bread. Not only was everyone promoting many was representing it at an all-time high. Tupac was the leading ambassador. So, you feel like the streets not real no more, how could you say something of that nature just because generation after you present themselves different? No that's not it at all Solace, what it is that people are to look as society puseudes them to and we're being pushed from Real to unreal wearing the make up to remind us we look like the role. Yo Sincere you be going too far! Explaining that you say that when our men are walking around looking like women and I women are walking around looking like men but they're not going too far. It's a difference between freedom of choice and force, this has been forced on us from fear. Fear of what Sin? One has become comfortable with familiarity in saying that one has become dependent upon a structure so you believe something can change that. Truth is only one can change order is the one who intake order and what does his standards consist of.

Its neither here nor there let me not alter your view of how I see things you gotta go to work correct? Yes, Sin?! May I take a shower with you so I can be spoiled with ya energy I may not see you for a week or what not?! You know I'm fucking with you no matter what.

You yet leave me in Awe.

A woman beauty can be alluring as a tattoo to one's eye lids, once one appreciates its value of true Art. The ink becomes the perfect blend of your blood and reaches the depths of one Heart.
Thank you, God...
.. for the essence of your undying beauty, that was created from the music of your lips.
Her existence alone is a pure gift!
As you continuously kiss upon my temple and walk in & out my mental, I adore how a rib could hold such uniqueness yet be simple.
You are the greatest Artist by far!
You yet leave me in awe...☺☺☺☺☺!

Cee-Cee jumps out the car to where she sees Sin car backed in, staring thru the tint she notices that Sin seat is lounged all the way back and he is asleep. Cee-Cee begins saying to herself I'm go scare this nicca but I'm going to video him on my phone as she laughs about the entire idea. Cee-Cee turns the phone on in her as the light blinds her. Adjusting the phone trying to video as light gleams thru the window as Sin mouth is wide open "yeah this is what it looks like when you in the trap with no sleep, I'm about to scare this nicca watch. Views climbing up in her phone as she begins crawling on the other side for a better view as the light sits more closer to his face with phone in hand. Sin noticing a glow that instantly awakens him followed by the lights blinding him off instinct he grabs his 40 out the console of the driver's door. Unsure of what's what not to be caught off guard he lifts his 40 up and wave it while squeezing shots he bust the window. After the barrel breaks the glass Cee-Cee screams while dropping her phone ducks as the window breaks. It is followed by more shots from where Cee-Cee was I looked as if a dragon was breathing from the window. Sin it's me Sin it's me, immediately Sin jumps out of his car pissed as smoke still was breathing from the barrel. Yoooo, you play to fucking much. Ugh! I was just trying to catch you on live with ya mouth open. Really, so you ready to die for likes. What a few many of fame ...Sin realizing the phone was still recording he shot it. Now buy another one since you keep begging for attention that's so lame yo. What you been on? All that was not called for!? Sin, still looking down at Cee-Cee as she laid on her butt unsure of what to do? Find something safe to do cause now you gotta go sell some pussy to fix my window cause Jackie Chan can't pay for this window nicca frfr. Damn you play to much yo! Lights all thru the hood began lighting up in a domino effect from all the things that was at hand. Push yo for real …. got my trap hotter than fish grease. So, I know I can't get no quarter off you now huh? Quarter of what Cee-Cee? Loud! My family from Detroit down here they wanted a quarterback for Bledsoe number oh they don't wanna a quarter they want a quarter, quarter?! Smiling Sin said fuck the window I'll get it done for the low, stop acting out for likes you see it almost cost you your life. Yall and this social media …get this money you aint got time to socialize ya heard me? Slapping her on the back of her blonde braids she said I am sorry Sin I get it. Matter fact imma tell you how you can straighten ya face "How Sin?" Ya sister from New Jersey omg Dee-Dee, what was ya momma doing anyway spelling her alphabets when she had yall who call they kids letter of the alphabets? Laughing she was cool with all that, she aint fine as me but hey you know I'm taken. Plus, you my sister on somebody side! Both began laughing in unison. Cee-Cee and Sin had been childhood friends that grew to be so tight he was like family to me family everyone accepted him as fam, and he protected everyone in the exact same manner. Thoughts been disturbed and by the way pussy and selling like it used to so you must take 3-4 trips with ya sugar daddies to get up my 300 hundred dollars. Sin, imma cook you some breakfast grab a quarter from you we go blow and you go be straight with just that nicca I'm not stunt that. Sin shaking his head what could he say ok we even I want pancakes nicca and grits not no oatmeal we not in New York no more we in Georgia. Sin, you so stupid I'm for real for real. Cee-Cee was really someone who Sin viewed truly as an elegant shorty with hood tendencies. Welcome to the slums of the lowlife where savages love good girls and where hoes tricked good guys but were straight fools for the niccas who were knee deep in the trenches. How can one not love such beauty where enemies knew they were enemies but still rocked with them clicked up telling one another bitch I love you, but we all knew the true loyalty was more concrete than love in the jungle. Love isn't blind the person who fails to see it is. Many still don't understand a coin is a coin yet it holds two different views as is life but for the most part the jungle has a set of eyes many could never grasp. It's nothing you can act out or listen too stories and fall in suit this avenue of living holds many chapters that could never be decoded only by walking it one would understand elements many still can't grasp or understand. The closest equivocal essence of hell with heaven keeping you in the blazes of the quenching fire. If one can survive the tides of jungle waves any if not everything else is a cake walk. The confusion lies in loyalty over love cause one to believe that even if you don't love me your having my back is loyalty in reality love endures and create loyalty as an umbrella to the windows of the many other body parts that stem from love. They don't tell us that because love is deemed as a weakness in a field where numbness is the norm. Love has always and will always be Sincere Hollis cheat code it kept me from the madness of selfishness. The jungle is the home of selfishness many people end up losing themselves because people prey on a giver. Guess what tho! I said Sincere lived off love.

Sin has no understanding know that. Keep things that away...to the left to the left! Cee-Cee laughing I wasn't always ya sister now you want my sister you so lame yuck! Lips poked out looking at Sin all twisted recollecting on their past encounters. Jackie Chan was a well-rounded junkie who sold drugs and used every drug I just could never understand the reasoning behind that, but she loved him along with an entire flock of others. Indeed, he was the Martin Lawrence of the trap gone off the white girl while keeping the trap on their feet. During one of his feining moments when he was broke, and Cee-Cee really couldn't keep up with the ticket to his addiction but not many knew that her so called brother was actually someone she called daddy when others were nowhere in sight a secret only, they knew about. Geeking and joning he knew it wasn't nothing that Sin wouldn't do for his Ummm so called sister, but he let it be what it was because he never disrespected and always saluted his place in his ummm sister life. These streets don't love nobody Jackie Chan would always say when I slid up, I knew it was his sarcasm from popping all the beans, he spoke how he felt and didn't care who didn't like it. Cee-Cee never used to the mood swings knew the only way to shut his mouth was to feed him something so he could leave her the hell alone. So, she thought! The verbal abuse if he couldn't get what was needed after all the irritation each situation was beginning to cut deeper and deeper his demons was eating at Cee-Cee spirit and she was tired. Jackie Chan screamed you slut bucket you got your daughter following ya lead sucking dick for a sport. Cee-Cee Staring hurt not believing he could stoop so low with her daughter in the other room. Cee-Cee left riding in circles she called Sin. What's up with ya Sis? Where you at Sin? I'm over here behind Lil-Miami dear what's good? I'm on the way now, stay right there! Bet! Pulling up she tells Sin to hop in & Sin jumps in. Cee-Cee was beautiful in everyone eyes a nicca dream and every girls desire. A redbone 5'2 maybe all white shorts that came up to the middle of her thighs, with paws tip toe-ing out her lap as if a kitty literally walked from between her legs. Not to mention how her body was built you couldn't miss the idea of how her crouch looked as if it was always stubborn lips poking all thru her shorts. Wearing white and blue 95 maxes with a white and blue halter top holding cups that spilled not 3D but double D. Lawd she was true art work. Two fishtail braids one white the other blue she was before her time. Eyes covered by some all-white shades that kept everybody out her busy. "This what I be talking about you go make Jackie Chan shoot at me I swear; dam you taste anything like you look you know you got my mouth watering.!? Sin, I am not stunt in you with ya big head self. Can I kidnap you from the trenches momentarily or you stuck in the trap? We can slide where ever it is were going I am cool with that! Cee-Cee pulls up at the store "Sin you want anything to drink?" Nawh, I'm good babe!" "You sure I got my stamps now!" Looking out the side of her eyes, Sin lifts up his head and said oh yea let me get out. Hold up Sincere I didn't say were grocery shopping...Sin looked while jumping in the mobile cart for the handicap. "You don't know how to act nowhere you go." "Chill yo I'm getting older than you think" Speeding her strut up looking back, "You don't have to take the hood everywhere you go Sin." 'Don't judge me yo!' Grabbing some Nutrageous cookies and Nutty Bars plus 2 orange juices Sin was good. Cee-Cee will you grab some gars cause I already know how adventurous you tend to be. Ok I am ready lets go Sin. Get off that buggy you are embarrassing me. Lip turned up looking at Cee-Cee but these niccas you with aint don't do me homie! Leaving Sin snatches the bags outta Cee-Cee hands, "I don't care how or what you're use to when around me you will allow me to be a gentleman it's me allow me to be me." "How and why you won't allow no woman to encounter who you are completely?" Sin began laughing I mean I am still a work in progress so I am and will be real with who I am and what I represent I know I am not ready for no relationship, so I openly let people know I aint shit. Laughing Cee-Cee said you not lying cause you got so many women til its stupid. I call em family look at us we still here and nothing has ever changed I'll never switch up and will forever support you in whatever it is you choose to do that's love in my eyes. I can only be expressing of love in the best format I know how to be never subtracting only growing deeper in it. Tossing a Game Natural leaf Cee-Cee states get out ya feelings and get emotions off ya sleeves ole soft as always nicca. Yea I knew you thought I was going to curse you out but its ok to feel. Seat pushed back sunroof all the way back on her Altima as she puts on her playlist which may have been the best part of being involved with Cee-Cee her music seemed to spill into ya Soul as if a more in-depth intimacy was being performed as SZA Love Galore featuring Travis Scott tap dance upon ones soul. Placing about a grammy in the gar he rolls up two so that could blow without no breaks back 2 back like the Lakers. Blowing on the gas Sin begins staring at Cee-Cee as paws crawled from under her shorts intoxicated from the movement he begins drawing imaginary notes on Cee-Cee thighs as Amanda Perez follows Sza with Angel it was crazy how life always seemed to speak on a more in-depth chapter than ones soul was prepared to receive. Cee-Cee vibing from the melodies as she grabs the blunt feeling. Sin playing with her fishtails if as if Sin always gave her the attention. That were craved for and he did it patiently as if he wanted me to lie in the confines of such an act that was surreal. Poking me in my side while following Amanda I pray only if he knew these acts are my prayers. Reaching for the ashtray dumping the ashes Cee-Cee grabs her phone and suddenly Mary J. Blige begins singing Everything. Sin fingers begins rambling under the back of her halter top fingers leaving a trail as if the warmth of her skin and release from his fingers was lost in his own realm that didn't involve earth. Cee-Cee leaning more towards the receiving end of adoration and admiration. She longed from no one compared to Sin essence was soothing as if he held a healing aura. As Sin began massaging Cee-Cee collarbone his only desire was to escape on a mental vacation that he seemed to get lost in. While in the window of his imagination he was a dreamer he saw nothing less. Vibing for over an hour high off more than gas Cee-Cee looks over at Sin who was asleep. It was crazy how someone so innocent was such a gentle Beast he held a loving spirit, but the streets never indulged in this portion of his energy. High cheekbones chocolate that glowed different than ya typical dark skin guy. Waves running down his head like waterfalls as his Polo hat was hanging slightly off of him. Arriving to Olive garden the back of her hand's brushes against Sin face and it awakes him. As Sin wakes up, he then grabs Cee-Cee hand kissing the back of it while their hands are cuffed and locked together. "You good, babe?" "Yes, I am good you ready to grab a bite?" Sin begins to let his seat up realizing they've arrived at Olive Garden his favorite restaurant. Oh, so who spoiling me or you? Today we rocking out so if I have to pay for your day away from work I will in your voice!? You must be getting ya taxes or a lump sum, I'm saying tho! You know it's a nice ticket but no flex you make me feel extra special all the time that alone is more than any ticket ya dig!? Cee-Cee said by the way can I be ya girlfriend a few hours? You sure you ready for that Sin said followed by him blushing cause Cee-Cee was the shit in his eyes. Pulling Cee-Cee closer to him stating if this rehearsal Jackie Chan may lose ya I'm for real for real kissing her softly on her neck. Chills running down her spine from Sin kiss while butterflies were running rampant all thru her body, she was ready to enjoy the festivities of the day clearly. Sin opened the door allowing her to walk in staying close to her as the host told them they would seat them in a minute. Sin really riding the wave lies his head on Cee-Cee shoulder and said while face was close to the right side of her face what would you do to ya boyfriend at this point. Cee-Cee looked down at Sin indulging in the closeness he was conveying listening to him she responded by kissing him upon his lips. While wiping her lipstick from his full lips idk what am I supposed to do? Sin smirking broad as ever cause she had already performed in such a great manner. While her sealing such an act was clarity that the both was in harmony with life tune in unison everything was one. How is it that one's imagination can create any element one yearns for in totality? Grabbing his hand leading him where the host led us after sitting in a corner Sin felt comfortable at because he was a person of seclusion. You sure you want the ticket cause I am open to take the bill you know I love this spot. Sin, with her eyes locked in on him. You not the only one eating I work stop playing with me. Rubbing his hands as if he was Birdman Sin said let's get it! Grabbing her phone Sin took her phone and turned it off, replacing her phone with his with it being turned off as well. If you will be my girlfriend, I don't need nothing to steal any of our moments can we just bath in them? Ok, Sin I am with that Cee-Cee said as the waitress asked could she asked did we know what we wanted to drink? Cee-Cee ordered a Strawberry/Lemonade while Sin grabbed a harsher one a watermelon Margarita. Ok can I get you guys an appetizer as you wait to place your order? Is it something specific you desire Cee-Cee? No if its aite with you I'll ride your wave? Ok can you give us the Spicy Alfredo Chicken? Ok coming right up. Relaxed at ease away from the cares of the world Sin was indeed in a great place. Extra thing was at ease nothing moving fast nor slow and this indeed was something he needed. Escaping the jungle of life. Must be nice to pick up and just escape life responsibilities Sin stated to Cee-Cee. It is, especially when your kids are grown! Plus, when you control your own freedom win/win situation. Tell me this honestly, it's just us? How is it that in your being involved why you not where you should be in ya happiness? Yall niccas not shit! Sin, refusing not to response because it wasn't about him it was only pertaining to her. In saying that he was willing to be an ear. Most of you are cheaters and once you betray trust in a relationship it's like what do we have? It's hard for me to trust again. So, may I ask why is it that you're available to someone you clearly do not trust. I am not with him yea we fuck from time to time that's it. That's why I am living my best life being Single. Ok I hear ya Cee-Cee! I wanna know that when I'm not in your eye sight I can be able to trust that you are being trustworthy. It's all about trust with me ijs! Consistency establishes such an attribute; do you not agree? You right! What is Love to you? Love is when we choose to be at our best the word love is a very strong word. Love don't suppose to hurt if you say you love me prove it. It's the little things that matter. Is it hurt or is it that in being uncomfortable or unfamiliar mindset cause uncertainty so I believe that can be depicted as hurt? Love is a beautiful word why hurt it? Hurt is the wrong word is all I am saying. Maybe abuse, deprive or neglect. Sin why hurt someone you love? As Sin rambles thru his phone he googles hurt definition: to inflict with physical pain. Love isn't tangible so nothing tangible can injure it. How you ever been in love, do you know how it feels? Yes, pain has been my greatest guide in my journey of encountering love. Your momma should've named you Riddler cause your dialect is the body of riddles. Yadda, Yadda, Yadda. Making it back to the trap after making a few plays. Sin gets caught up in his phone as notifications kept buzzing.

12/10/10, 1:14 AM

Aura
Marriage huh? Be careful u might wake up one morning in love with me!!!!

GhosstfacePoet
Is dat a bad thing...

Aura
Being in love is a wonderful thing!!!!

GhosstfacePoet
Yea if its pure

Winter midnight breeze covering the entirety of my physique. The air conditioning unit interrupted my thoughts as it cuts through my silence. I inhale another drag for my Dutch as the aroma answers multiple questions. "Babe, I'm ready!" she says, as I stare in her eyes Innocence mixed with confusion followed by tears stares back at me. I can tell, from her puzzled stares that the outcome seems uncertain. As she reaches out touching my face I draw back, determined not to be derailed from my journey at hand. Tears racing against her cheeks she whispers you have a son that loves you, Sincere! I'm only called by my government when she is trying to convey a message. I brushed you off with the music. Lil Boosie and Lil Webbie betrayal becomes the louder voice. Feeling ignored she quickly gets out of the car. I re lit my blunt high off more than life. I'll look up for the last time to witness her struggling with carrying my son into her mother house. I called White Boy he picked up second ring. What's goodie sin? My response was I got this Irene, want to blow some music with me? He laughed and said you can find me in Lil Miami. I smile I'm sliding through. I reached up under my seat pull out my fifth and I'm not talking liquor. The 45 cover my right thigh, I popped another bean pulled out. In route my phone vibrates Music in background screaming. As I place my Dutch in ashtray, I answer my phone. Oddly they hang up I'm in the front of the elementary school and a church which has a digital billboard that stores different messages. The message that pops up after the phone has hung up, makes me hit my brakes pull to the side and I begin to read" God is trying to get your attention!" I pull over confused, hurt, lost and begin crying talking to God. Lord I don't want to kill anyone I just want them to know I'm not to be fucked with. Blunt, yet truly speaking to God from my heart.

12/12/10, 5:14 PM

Aura
I ♥ this.....
The Floacist - Let Me
Check it out on youtube.

12/12/10, 8:11 PM

Aura
Hmmm...bless me with the unmasked Ghosst!

GhosstfacePoet
You not ready for that, no one is thats why i walk lite ….i mean that literally! U wanna a pic..?

Aura

Yes...I want wht u seem to be willin to gve to everybody else!!!!

GhosstfacePoet

There you go, no one gets more attention than you babe! Okay but u have it & u have 2 tell my status what eye look like 2 u...deal! Allow your words to be the photograph of ya art work.

Aura

Ok

GhosstfacePoet

Ok sending it now..

12/13/10, 2:25 PM

Aura

You came to me in my dreams lastnight...quietly making your presence known..felt your lips kiss my eyes and cheek, then brush gently across my lips...hands on me but not... depositing ur energy on my skin...kisses on my breast, tongue and teeth on my nipples...making a trail down onto my belly, tongue dippin in and out my belly button....on to my shaven mound....soft kisses on her to say hello down to her awaiting lips... u kissed them softly and they kissed back...thumbs opening up displayin the the pink glistening flesh and the eager bud.....tongue flickering and lips sucking me in making me grind and moan from the pleasure fingers in and out finding that fleshy spot...asking it to quench the thirst you have for me sugar water...ravenous lips and tongue make me so wet I fear I may drown u in the flow.... I cum so hard from the pleasure ur giving...and while yet quivering from the force of the orgasm you blessed me with...you take that chocolate dipped joystick and rub the head down the slick wetness of me and u enter...upon entry ur breath catches in ur throat and you start ur slow grind..pushing in inch by inch until im completely filled with you...thrusting deeply...faster and harder the stroke becomes....my name whispered in my ear....calmly tellin me how good it feels...me pulling u in deeper opening myself up to the stroke...calling ur name "QUAN"...I feel another one fast and furiously approaching...... then it washed over me like a Tsunami...the contractions of her were so powerful and overwhelming that with out notice you let out the loud guttural "AURA".... and I woke up... heart beating fast and throbbing in my love below...welcome to my dreams!!!!

89

GhosstfacePoet

(Mouth agape in Awww)

Descriptive details cover my vision eye that could see your deepest thoughts it seemed Albina sunflower was standing out um on the field of an array of things without one word her lips spoke volumes with the honey complexion that would have track any bee as if it was sketch from plate and if are smart school out her metal leg longer than drawings from any artist pencil it was simple a beauty was captive am fully bloom this issue was groomed in Portland Oregon rose garden physique for annoying Ali you believe she was in the Dolly Parton Melodies of beauty playing tunes underneath my eyelids. Miguel hums thru out my mental as if I've been awarded life most precious gift.

A voice with squeaky yet distinctive. Her hair is waving with them my vision to get my attention. Heaven got to be tired of you gawking at an angel. Precious tugged at sin shirt. I want her is all sin could say!

Angel Wow pictures of her yet running through my mind as silence intrudes myspace the breeze yet brushing my face. A coffee complexion, almond shaped eyes, eyebrows pool with an arch, eyelashes so full some women become envious of this man. Lips boasting of his define roots groomed as if he was preparing for a photoshoot. Pencil sketch tape that leaves his waves attempting to cover each border falling sideways. Many women have just decided to touch his hair and awe of uniqueness. Mother raised me in a manner to appreciate who I was the guy is Sincere Hollis born in Miami Florida raised in the state of New York reside in talking Ville Georgia home of Charles Johnson from the Carolina Panthers. The beauty of my confined essence of the country a city kid who enjoys the sound of crickets, being attacked by gnats in the city most of these bugs do not exist. More so then anything I was in awe of swimming in creeks to where as you could see the beautiful fish and encounter Wildlife.

I was every bit of 9 or 10 most! I remember riding on the bike with my cousin in the country, dirt roads of red clay. Wine on the main road where we encountered coyotes, deer's and even wild hogs; this day we encountered a bear that stood up was more so 20ft or better once I see him, I jumped from the bike and ran. Precious screamed Sin what's so funny. Nothing, Precious. I responded. While rambling throughout my thoughts. Precious was Angel's cousin as well as my baby mother's best friend. I can give you stories of precious that would exceed the pages of this book. Precious with what you call eye candy hands down. Beautiful like she kept braided in a ponytail that hung round ear length. To bottom gold slugs with cheetah tattoos covering her shoulder, paws climbing up with eyes peeking out her cleavage the tattoo by her ankle that had ice cream running off a comb with the words you want to lick. Under it, a honey complexion small version of Serena Williams Garfield eyes face powder with freckles.

Precious was my smoke partner, I desired her originally, but I ended up with her best -friend. Me and precious has done everything but have sex grateful cause then our relationship wouldn't be what it is. I recall one moment it was a birthday now precious had her flock of fans, who would jump at her command yep we appreciate each other. I took her to my favorite restaurant olive Garden; I'm such a fan of pasta. We went Shopping, we even tripped out and laughed the beauty of it all was we were in South Carolina. Palm trees, big body bands, navigators it was upscale this was Hilton head. While there we got a room, laying on the beach at the walking and blowing out thoughts in the clouds we decide to go to the room. Truly, if it was just for the pleasure of our desires, we would have been cross that line. Promising, rare, one of a kind my greatest fear was tarnishing her purity. So, with that being said I decided within me we'd never cross that line. This night was like no another the few drinks not thoughts together we went to the room. Somehow, somewhere I doze off and was awaken by precious who wore a tank top and thongs. Hands raced under my shirt I was locked in a trance, hypnotized! Soft butterfly kisses covered my chest to my neck. Nails raking my torso as if it was a cat trying to climb to safety. Fully erect as if a hundred and five men were exiting my briefs. Head swollen from confident one on one attention like a magician she made me disappear completely. I grabbed her then she kissed me, the depths of our passion Excel any encounter ever embraced. I've yearned for such a moment as this. Lost in anticipation bathing in desires freely. Regaining consciousness her nails fumbling at my jawbone. My lips meet at her lips this more deeper than any French kiss. Tongue patting her second heart she begins releasing like a super soaker her fluids become the darts that leave me messy. Eyes rolling it seems her soul lies in midair and Sin said I love you babe we can't do this? Wow for real Sin! How is it so easy for you to make other special yet overlook me? I went to the bathroom and jump in the shower with no words spoken. Instantly the curtains were snatched open, Sin you know I love you. How is it, you place your energy in everyone else yet deprive me?! Am I not loyal, am I not consistent! I'm more Loyal than Shunna. For real precious!

Is all I say before I exit the shower dripping wet.

What don't I do? I work, I go to school like you told me to I never took anything from you not even your money? You said you love me Sin, tears covering her face. So, what you saying I don't love you if I don't sex you? What is this about sex or money? If it's about the money you can have the bag. You can have every coin in your account graduation gift! Go hard to make sure. None of my people struggle I do it for who I love and yes, I do love you enough not to hurt you. What's good about me? Huh, Tell me one thing? I have all these women I'm with, you don't see what's going on. I appreciate them but that's where it stopped. You want me to lie to you, to make it seem fly to you? I am a realist so I can't give you make believe, we are pulling down imagination and illusions. Its either the truth or nothing. My life is a promising, I've hurt more than I help and niccas don't make it no better. What's real is they want my head and I know this. So, it's eat or be ate, before they leave me slumped at the light. This my life! I never asked for it, what I give you is the purest form of me. You think I enjoy hurting women, No!?

I mean who is faithful frfr, so I rather bless you with the truth if you accept it, I never misled you. Precious sat on the edge of bed in tears. Listening to Sin who had his back to her looking out the window, thinking as if why I can't encounter someone real that don't tear me down with lies. Someone who rather build me than destroy me. As she arose and walked to the window she whispered to her heart. I'll stay here and experience any portion of Real no matter what. Sincere was indeed a sincere guy your mother spoke you into fruition. Sin felt Precious cover his back as she gripped him closer to her. Sin could feel the warmth of her nostrils and her heartbeat. Sin spoke softly to his heart I am tired of hurting people and instantly he said grab your clothes. This your birthday get away we about to enjoy this. As we jumped in the charger 2010 mode my feet pressed forward as if 110n felt like 45 easy. Precious vibing dreads swinging following Plies chorus "Shawty…!"

Sin, looks over and see that she is enjoying herself he says lowly "that's all that matters, babe for real for real." As we reach the bridge which leads into Savannah we go to Deja Groove. After a weekend getaway Precious was totally in awe of the string of events. Chatting on the phone with her bestie, Shunna. Who she considered her Ace, its nothing that they haven't spoke on? Shunna felt as if she could give her many of her darkest secrets just to name a few. Precious laying in boy shorts and wifebeater, always desired being comfortable. Reminiscing thru string of events Precious told her. He is a dream come true. Girl, he is all you can desire We went shopping in Cacky -Lacky (Carolina nickname) all on the beach." Shunna on the other end intaking things excited that no one was taking advantage of her friend. Shunna and Precious were classmates who grew up together. Nineteen out of school they yet stayed side by side, her oldest brother and Precious had messed around in the event of that their relationship was rocky until she put it down like you all grown what you all do has nothing to do with me. Shunna was five two hair fell down like Pocahontas, pecan tan full face teeth tight and white as if she came straight out of a Colgate commercial. A smile that would light up the darkest region. In Sin head Shunna was his Key. When Monique was on Anthony Hamilton Sista Big Bone, Shunna deserved the strip a beautiful woman she was her inner beauty was more radiant than anyone I've crossed Sincere thought. As Shunna was riding thru the rain, Sincere was sleep laid back in seat embracing his Bill Blast coat which laid snug underneath him. Shunna staring at him wondering will he change, or can he change, only time will tell. Precious, screaming in the phone "Bih I know you hear me?!" Coming back to realization of her talking to Precious, I am sorry babe I'm in traffic we need to chill get our feet's and nails done maybe enjoy a facial?! Okay Precious say when, I'm up for it! What you doing tomorrow? Nothing, girl! Tomorrow it is call you later I love you boo and I am looking forward to meeting your new, new. They both laughed in unison. Sin, Sin! Wake up, boy! Shunna started to snatch his coat but reconsidered not knowing would Sin wake up or Sincere. Siiiincere Hollis she said after tapping him across the head. Wake up corn head ass. Sin, eyes yet closed said you love this head when you're racking these waves tho. Stepping out her black and pink Acura RL rims shining from glistening rain drops. Sin began stretching in the parking lot as Shunna slides underneath his arms. Psss, have I ever told you by any chance today I love you my guy? Teehee, I aint ya guy I'm ya girl. You and your smart mouth just accept a compliment. Oh really, who else you loving? Are you prepared for the truth? Sin, realizing the hesitation in her factual reaction. As Long as you prepared to get boxed in ya shit you say the wrong thing and I aint you thotties in the street. Ok I might as well keep it raw. Cupping his hands around her ears as if she didn't desire others to be informed by his ignorance. The person name is Divine I love him a tinier bit more than you. Shunna smiling realizing their destination and reasoning for being at the outlet was for Divine. Sin youngest son who in his eyes was different a very rare breed. Born pre-mature many gave up on him making it. Sin left everything cold turkey to be at his side. Truth was clear, chances were that the child could his or another cat whom Shunna cheated on Sin with. Sin made a promise if Shunna bless me with truth my loyalty would place me here a rose growing outta concrete. In tears felt as if she betrayed Sin outta his betrayal Hope had exposed Sin skeletons. Ones tic for tac nature held her hostage instead of leaving she cried it could be yours or Mann baby. Sin pulling her in closer to him told her hurtful as it is lil buddy Imma support you. It's not the child fault and we all fuck up but you fuck up one more time you're going to get fucked up, ya heard?! Laughing as she begins wiping her tears away. Sin kissed her and then he kissed her belly and begin talking to the baby. You will be one of the wisest and strongest young men to walk earth I promise you. Not once did he reconsider Divine placement in his life. Truth be told he was the turning point no one foreseen these strings of events that worked things in a greater direction. Before the harvest first the seeds must be planted. One foot in front of the other. Puzzled by his lack of understanding unsure if he was getting older or caught up in his feelings. It seemed no matter what when meditating on the idea that if his son was not birthed, he'd still be attracted to a lifestyle that became less appealing. WW3 was World War 3 the 3 represented m which was me. Sin and Sincere I was at war with myself. Ridding myself of an old mindset transitioning into who it was I desired not who society desired me to be of representation of. A Beautiful disaster in the world eyes I was depict as the ideal guy who held bad tendencies, but I held all good attributes to the natural eye. Money, Power & Respect! Sin was my alter ego. Precious snapping her fingers trying to get Sin attention realizing he was day dreaming. Well damn if it's not Divine (Clapping), the trap (Clapping), gambling (Clapping) or women Can I yes me Shunna please let me get my time everybody else do. Opening her palm while pushing Sin forehead, let that register I shouldn't have to beg for no attention ugh you irk me! You with that, matter fact you got no choice bring ya ass. Shunna and her theatrics were something else, but it was her. "Oh, yea it's time

---

to turn it in cause I'm not doing no fighting no more. Suddenly stopping full stride Shunna hands open I calmly turned my phone off & gave it to her. Thank you ugh you make my job so hard this why I make sure you pay me for my duties fucking with you is beyond a job Sincere. You be acting like you go die if you can't have this phone, Sincere Hollis. Shunna only called me by my first name when conveying a point. I can't say that's why you with me cause you spoil me more than I spoil you. I don't know if you wanna be my shorty or the nigga in the relationship. So, Sin whispered in her ear I got half on a baby Shunna said I got my half. Sincere and Shunna loved shopping a baby in their lingo was a rack (1 thousand). Exhausted and irritated Sincere starts walking to the car hand full of bags. While Shunna complains you always won't let me help you, I'm a lady but I aint handicap neither. I know you can't stand for a woman to do any form of labor in front of you. So why ask if you know these things you be talking just cause you got lips.

Arts & Craft
Martyrdom Picasso as leaves from my branches fall in the streets of Gotham.
Drinking shot after shot from life bottle, taking light swallows.
Shadows of tomorrow will i be consumed by the gossip that follows?
Hour after hour, second after second; how is it that i am fully clothed yet my Soul feels naked.
Love has been the topic, so what is the subject?
Art among the masses, displayed among the public.
Am I a puppet toying with my own strings?
Words create poem after poem, scene after scene.
Far from a dream not even animated, a small voice falls from heaven reminding me you're one of my favorites.
Tasting David sincerity as my sanctuary is engulfed in its personal symphony.
By means of empathy no sympathy needed, bristles of my paint brush continue bleeding.
As painting of my work comes to life as if its breathing.
As my canvas continue seeking to speak with no lips a gift of a blessing dancing among curses. That embrace you verse after verse.

3/14/11, 2:36 AM

Aura

Hey babe can u talk? Give you 10 minutes? Yeah ok you better hope I don't cum before then..call me when ASAP I need you... You call: whispering...hello...no babe he isnt here! I'm feenin for you..I want you to hear my pussy talk to you....its ur name I wanna call when I cum not his....I'm running my hand down into my lace panties. legs spread wide rubbing over her...taking my finger and suckin it into my mouth babe gettin it nice and moist then back down to my slit...I'm already wet just layin here thinkin about you running your tongue over my clit...I'm rubbing my clit nice and slow for you dipping into that hole ....mmmmm you hear that sound? Rubbing in circles and up and down, in and out, grinding on my fingers all for you babe, pussy making that wet suction sound....mmmm I wanna feel you...my clit is gettin harder shes peeking out tryin to see what all the noise is about.... its the sound of my pussy your pussy gushy wet and me singing Ghosst's Anthem...damn baby this shit feel good wanna taste? Come on baby make Vette gush...Baby its coming I.. feel ...it can...u...O' my fuckin GHOOOOOOSSSSTTT!!!! mmmm...baby I made such a mess wanna help clean it up? Hello? babe are you there? I hear you breathing heavily babe...hello?

GhosstfacePoet

Eye dont wanna add nothing just use dat cause u went in....

Aura

that was not the deal.....

2/14/11, 10:56 AM

Aura

URGENT TEXT Lover: Hey babe can u talk? Ghosst: Give me 10 minutes….. Lover: Ok, but you better hope I don't cum by then…call me ASAP!!!!!!!….I need you now!!!!!! Ghosst: Wait hold on, I'm calling you now let me slip in the bathroom…… Lover: (whispering) Hello….. Ghosst: What's up Boo? Is Ghosst clear? Lover: Yes babe, he isn't here….I'm feenin for you…… Ghosst: So what u wanna do? Lover: Our pussy wants to talk to you…. Ghosst: Its Ghosst I wanna hear when u cum boo, not his name! Lover: I'm running my hand down into my lace panties. legs spread wide rubbing over her... taking my finger and suckin it into my mouth babe gettin it nice and moist then back down to my slit...I'm already wet just layin here thinkin about you running your tongue over my clit...I'm rubbing my clit nice and slow for you dipping into that hole ....mmmmm you hear that sound? Rubbing in circles and up and down, in and out, grinding on my fingers all for you babe, pussy making that wet suction sound....mmmm I wanna feel you...my clit is gettin harder shes peeking out tryin to see what all the noise is about....that's the sound of her gushy wetness and me singing Ghosst's Anthem of praise…. Ghosst: Golden rule boo…u must cum in my mouth…. Lover: Damn baby this shit feels good..wanna taste? Ghosst: Replace my face with nothing but cum, let ur clit marry to my tongue…dats my wish Lover: Come on baby make this pussy gush… not once but 3 times…baby …mmm…its…coming I can feel….it oooo…can you? Ghosst: (whispering) say it…call my name boo… Lover: mmmm…ba.. by..O my fuckin….Ghoooossssssttt!!!! Ghosst: Keep dat water flowing…. Lover: mmm….babe I made such a mess..wanna help clean it up? Babe hello..are you there? I can hear u breathing heavily…hello! Babe… hold on, someones knocking on my door!!! (opening the door) Hey babe…. Ghosst: Nickname me Water God…go hard or not at all…you ready!!! Lover : Cum on in…….

12/14/10, 3:33 PM

Aura
Obviously you have me mixed up with someone else if you think I was pushing to upset some chick I don't know from a hole in the ground…All i was simply sayin is wow on my comments, now if thats what upset her then maybe she knows more about me than I know… I haven't even put my personal feelins on ur page I just go with the flow….I find it funny that you would say pay back because she got upset…and if she can't deal with what people are goin to say she shouldnt comment…better yet don't worry bout me commenting again, cuz its not my page and I can't tell you how to run it so I'm gonna stay on mine….And yes I'm bothered….

GhosstfacePoet
Wow…dont do dis please eye tend 2 run frm negative energy & im feeling u eye think eye may end dis freakshit

Aura
Naaw don't….I'm a firm believer of when people show who they are you should believe them!!!! So keep being Ghosst its who you are….I'm not being negative at all just expressin my feelings and defending myself I'm allowed…now if run away then you were never here to begin with….don't trip!!!!! I've said my peace…now what u wanna write next?

GhosstfacePoet
MIKE & PIPPEN…

Aura
whaaat?

GhosstfacePoet
Im Mike ur pippen…

Aura

do you feel what I was sayin earlier? just like the txt I just sent you Kiwaina was apologizing...i guess she thought she hurt someones feelings..dont you find that odd? I mean if its not serious then why get in ya feelins or is it serious? nobody should be apologizing...you have to watch how you handle these women....but if theres something i need to know plz enlighten me....and what is Mike and pippen!!!

GhosstfacePoet

Ur my pippen defense Michael Jordan Scottie Pippen eye need u 2 win championships

Aura

is there something u wanna tell me? I'm being for real....

GhosstfacePoet

Like what dat im considerate of ppl feelings

Aura

Ok babe I got it...., i see you not feeling me like i am feeling you?.

GhosstfacePoet

Sexually & poetically

Aura

i mustve missed something....explain this...

GhosstfacePoet

mike & pippen is an analogy now use dem as reference 2 sex and poetry....exp...tongue out do you got your spongelet me assist u and ride wing right we balling doing devilish things ur my queen im ur king let 3peat win more rings sex in ova drive hot like a 45 outta retirement u knw eye can fly

12/16/10, 10:33 AM

Aura

Since you asked that I not step on any toes I will not comment on your post...I won't censor myself... because I'm sure no one else does and haven't been asked too...I guess I was takin the things you were sayin to me to heart and now I'm trippin cause...I was in your constant dreams and now you're askin me not to step on toes...I don't get that....its like you go from one extreme to the other...so I guess I'm not holding your attention anymore...Well Mike the ball is in your court...Pippen needs to know whats up....just like you asked me the other night I feel like ur keeping something from me and if so please enlighten me....the hot and cold is not cool.....u came to me again in a dream and that shit weirds me out don't know if u can understand that...just let me know what REALLY goin on!!!!!

GhosstfacePoet

Im not a rude or person of dismay what is hard bout dat babe...

Aura

So what about me? So its ok for everybody else to say what they want and because I put mine in a different way I gotta be steppin on toes? I mean u got women basically sayin they want you to lick their puss, but if I say bow down in my santuary and worship at my alter...thats steppin on toes? lol I don't get that...them being vulgar about it is ok but me being suggestive isn't hmmm go figure....

GhosstfacePoet

Lets do it then

Aura

DO WHAT?

GhosstfacePoet

Display ur ability show out with me...

12/17/10, 1:20 PM

Aura

Make ya tongue hard and spit on dat clit...diggin in dat hole like you lookin for some shit...ya dick growin hard and you can't concentrate but its from me, not dat pussy you just ate... ur losing focus listening to me masturbate....its the sound of me all wet and gushy and the sweet smell cummin from dis pussy that got u thick...tryin beat her pussy up ur whispering damn Vette quit... my cum is like a drug and you need ur fix......its callin u and start to feen damn u know you wanna taste of my cream.....And just when u thought you couldnt take that shit no more I let you lick that shit all up not letting a drop hit the floor...leaving her all open and shit .....taking that shit in like ur last hit....u don't apologize but tell her baby imma feen and Vette is my drug.....

IaokimGhosstfacePoet

Yes fuck yes

Aura

U don't wanna add anything...finish it!!!!

12/19/10, 4:30 PM

Aura

URGENT TEXT Lover: Hey babe can u talk? Ghosst: Give me 10 minutes….. Lover: Ok, but you better hope I don't cum by then…call me ASAP!!!!!!!….I need you now!!!!!! Ghosst: Wait hold on, I'm calling you now let me slip in the bathroom…… Lover: (whispering) Hello….. Ghosst: What's up Boo? Is Ghosst clear? Lover: Yes babe, he isn't here….I'm feenin for you…… Ghosst: So what u wanna do? Lover: Our pussy wants to talk to you…. Ghosst: Its Ghosst I wanna hear when u cum boo, not his name! Lover: I'm running my hand down into my lace panties. legs spread wide rubbing over her…taking my finger and suckin it into my mouth babe gettin it nice and moist then back down to my slit…I'm already wet just layin here thinkin about you running your tongue over my clit…I'm rubbing my clit nice and slow for you dipping into that hole ….mmmmm you hear that sound? Rubbing in circles and up and down, in and out, grinding on my fingers all for you babe, pussy making that wet suction sound….mmmm I wanna feel you…my clit is gettin harder shes peeking out tryin to see what all the noise is about….that's the sound of her gushy wetness and me singing Ghosst's Anthem of praise…. Ghosst: Golden rule boo…u must cum in my mouth…. Lover: Damn baby this shit feels good..wanna taste? Ghosst: Replace my face with nothing but cum, let ur clit marry to my tongue…dats my wish Lover: Come on baby make this pussy gush… not once but 3 times…baby …mmm…its…coming I can feel….it oooo…can you? Ghosst: (whispering) say it…call my name boo… Lover: mmmm…ba..by..O my fuckin….Ghoooosssssttt!!!! Ghosst: Keep dat water flowing…. Lover: mmm….babe I made such a mess..wanna help clean it up? Babe hello.. are you there? I can hear u breathing heavily…hello! Babe… hold on, someones knocking on my door!!! (opening the door) Hey babe…. Ghosst: Nickname me Water God...go hard or not at all… you ready!!! Lover : Cum on in…….u want it? I got it dripping like water!!!!!

12/20/10, 9:58 PM

Aura

Just as quickly as you appeared to me you have gone…. no longer willing to haunt my thoughts or dreams. The essence of you was felt with me daily as you have imparted in me much more than just a physical yearning, but a mental longing. Your presence was more to me than just some masked apparition spitting your lustful brilliance…you were the face and mind behind, "like the air one breathes eye need you…ur in my constant dreams." I felt your words deposit themselves and I took the most intimate of thoughts from my mental being and let them flow through my physical and spill onto paper.….like no other and for no other. Your ability to believe that I cared for you fading back behind the masked specter and turning from your true face… "eye need you like thoughts yearn to think." Were your words, but I guess the yearning is no more … And I am left with Love Interrupted.…..

IaokimGhosstfacePoet

Got it…

Aura

Wow that's all u hve to say?!?

GhosstfacePoet

Ur more indepth wit me than anyone eye know but yet how do eye justify pain…

Aura

Am I inflicting pain on you?!? If so how?!?

GhosstfacePoet

Eye viewed u differently, i seem to be the afflictor.…

Aura

Sorry to hve caused u any pain wasn't aware tht I was doin so.…definitely wasn't my intent.…hope ur view of me jasnt changed much…I'm still Yvette can't change that!!!!

12/21/10, 2:34 AM

Aura

Make ya tongue hard and spit on dat clit...diggin in dat hole like you lookin for some shit...ya dick growin hard and you can't concentrate but its from me u taste.... not dat pussy you just ate... ur losing focus listening to me masturbate....its tempting you like bait.... the sound of me all wet and gushy and the sweet smell cummin from dis pussy got u thick...tryin to beat her pussy up ur whispering damn Vette quit... my cum is like a drug and you need ur fix......its callin u and u start to feen.... damn u know you wanna taste of my cream.....And just when u thought you couldnt take that shit no more I let you lick dat cream all up not letting a drop hit the floor...take dat shit in like ur last hit.... let it course through your veins...leaving you slobberin, shakin and grabbin ya dick....got you spewing ur seed ... leavin her wide open and in need....u don't apologize but tell her Vette is my drug and I'm her feen...she got dat good shit I need..... I gotta get to rehab I just can't get clean..... Ghosst, Ghosst i feel like i am on repeat?!

12/31/10, 2:09 PM

Aura

I just wanted to tell you I wish nothing but the best for you in the New Year...I also want to thank you for the support you've shown me with my writing...you helped to give me confidence that I didn't have before....and whether you believe it or not I care about you...but it seems your view of me has changed, just by me taunting some dude on fb....whatever is goin on with you I hope it gets better and I certainly don't want to add to that.....If I don't speak to you before then....HAPPY NEW YEAR!!!!! plz be safe if you're goin out....

Do I even matter to you Sincere Hollis? I guess it was many things I faced but I constantly ran from becoming a man and I was haunted by this great responsibility when facing Angel. Sincere am I talking to myself? No ma'am! Okay so let me ask you this question again?! Do I even matter to you Sincere Hollis? I don't know if I was prepared for this. THIS? What's this? Not wanting to unravel Angel he was slow to respond because Angel could be aggressive, he didn't want that. My familiarity is constantly warring against my unfamiliarity. Dam yo I am scared, scared I'll fail. All my life I have won at what I desired winning in. Now I am in a place I have no knowledge of, so I only do what is expected of me which is to fail. Angel was the only person who exposed Sincere in his rawest state of being. So, he always avoided her, marrying her but staying away from the responsibility of manhood. In his eyes if he supported her financially, he did what he was to do as a man. Miseducation can be rotting to one's soul. Sincere can we ride and talk I wanna take you somewhere?! Yes ma'am! Sincere if you don't mind will you turn your phone off, I need your undivided attention? Yes ma'am! Unsure of what to say Sincere felt naked and vulnerable. You remember how things started with us? You were focused on your family Sincere now it's as if you're unsure of anything. Not desiring to blame her for his lack of application Sincere just listened. Do you want your family Sincere? Immediately looking away his voice was lower than normal a yes cut thru the silence with a crackling. Doubt begin to climb in the pits of his stomach. I love you flaws and all I will forever carry your name. I know who you are Sincere not who Sin is he doesn't exist to me. Not once did she ever judge my error she always felt as if i could be better than I saw myself as being. Wiping my tears away with her hands she kissed me as we stopped at Tucsawhatchee Creek. I love water and Angel knew the spots I'd go to get away from the world's madness, this was one of them. Stepping thru the brush Angel grabbed Sincere holding him close and said do you not remember our signature. Using hand language she held her pinky up representing I then she threw up the peace sign representing 2 then she dropped the thumb representing death two balled fist right arm crossing the left as the right fist held a one against the other balled fisted representing do opening hands embracing union representing us and separating representing apart. Corny to probably the world so sacred to me because she was the makeup of my world. Peeling off my clothes she revealed my wounds with no bandage. Were about to swim in this water. Angel peeling off all her clothes we were naked while the currents washed away the doubts that tried bathing upon my essence. On my way back to the town unsure if I missed some bread, I powered my phone on by habit it wrong and I answered it. What you got going on Sin wya? Shunna asked ya phone been off ugh. I'm off the radar? Angel looking at Sincere said this what I am talking about tell em you with ya wife. Sin, that's Angel? You be doing the most one minute you go do right then the next you wanna be with ya family you confused. Angel hearing the conversation from the silence as Sin tries looking out the window Smashing him and his phone as his face hits the window it begins leaking. Sin screams let him out Angel locks the car doors and speeds up in an attempt not to bring hurt to him his busts the window with his fist. Dam, yo I am not perfect stop putting ya hands on me. I am tired of you disrespected me I am ya wife not those hoes. Feeling like a failure wanting all the madness to cease Sin unlocks the door and jump out the car on the interstate. Looking in her rearview as cars weave to avoid Sincere Angel could not believe what just happened. Pulling to the side while running towards Sincere. You alright Sincere? Realizing his clothes were ripped while his arm, hip and leg was bruised along with his ego. Sin had panicked and trying to escape his arena of not being what people craved from him he was losing himself and wanted out it seemed. Kissing the crown of his head while holding him crying as others pulled over. You're leaving those streets you need me as much as I need you were one. I will not fail you Sincere let those streets go.

1/23/11, 6:24 PM

Aura
I MISS YOU!!! I HOPE ALL IS WELL!!!!

1/25/11, 12:06 PM

Aura
I guess since I didn't get the memo...I want u to know I've been really concerned about you! I hope everything is ok!

1/27/11, 11:59 AM

Aura

1/28/11, 6:50 PM

Aura
Damn it!!! I jus wanna know if ur ok!!

GhosstfacePoet
Yes ma'am

Aura
Wow ok!! I tried callin sendin txt but I guess u weren't takin calls! I'm glad to know u are ok!!!!

GhosstfacePoet
Ur Beautiful

1/30/11, 8:10 PM

Aura

obviously u dont want any communication with me so....I hope that everything is well with you.. take care babe!!!! tried txtn u several times with no response so i got it!!!!

1/31/11, 1:34 AM

Iaokim

Bay eye have been in the hospital!? ill txt u asap eye promise....u all eye got Stop tripping!

1/31/11, 10:40 AM

Aura

Whats wrong? U might wanna be careful with the pics u post as profile pics.....dont want u to get flagged....

GhosstfacePoet

Ok whats up babe you dont fuck wit me no mo smh

Aura

what do u mean?

GhosstfacePoet

U actn distant eye feel ur essence but ur a ways off

Aura

how am i actin distant babe?!??! I logged and saw ur profile pic and sent u a message......U know I have been concerned about you!!! I missed you!!!

GhosstfacePoet

Eye need 2 c you u 4real

Aura

why didnt you tell me u were gonna be MIA!?!??!
and im not just talkin facebook....u were just gone!!!!!!

GhosstfacePoet

Had alot goin on ppl stalking & shit

Aura

ok babe...

2/1/11, 1:38 PM

Aura

seems u have no need....u got plenty of pussy fuck and suck all out in the open!!!! lol

GhosstfacePoet

U crazy just doing sumthin 4 da fans ppl request cause sumone may suggest dem Entertainment boo

Aura

im not trippin...im just observing trust!!!!

GhosstfacePoet

Lol eye miss u 4real

Aura

miss u too....

2/1/11, 8:06 PM

Aura

my chocolate pink she staring at ya and I must admit shes a bad bitch so she daring ya.... to let your mouth juice make her wetta and wetta, slick and thick while your erect tongue sticks... in and out of her pink pussy hole lips and tongue out of control like you sucking out my soul.... ya hands on my hips your taking hold riding and grinding, fucking ya face in just one minute your about taste Angel

---

105

Supremes heavenly cream..... dripping, dropping and raining down covering your face you're sure to drown bubbling, gurgling and oozing out the sides of ya mouth as you take this cum down...... face completely erased from just this sticky paste which is why I reign supreme, remember I wear my halo tilted cuz I'm a cum freaks wish and a sinners dream…. *PUSSY ANGEL SUPREME

2/1/11, 9:09 PM

GhosstfacePoet
Eye love it

Aura
U want me to put it on ur page?!?

GhosstfacePoet
Yes ma'am

Aura
Posted it!!!! Now go call MiMI!!! Lol she feenin!!!! Smdh

Aura
Wow

Aura
wow what?!?!?!?!

GhosstfacePoet
Eye dont have her number

Aura
she seems to think so....lol

GhosstfacePoet
Word, you stay in ya feelings?

2/2/11, 1:58 PM

Aura

I got one question? if u miss me so why haven't u at least sent me a txt or something....we're adults say what it is....

GhosstfacePoet

Eye lost ur number txt my other fone 478.6363920 no call me now Plz

Aura

Funny I got a call from that same number right there and thought hmmmm...I wonder if Quan changed his number!!!! its still in my phone....U lost my number wow ok....501-563-8988 smdh!!!!

GhosstfacePoet

My touch screen is damaged dats what had da most stuff n it

Aura

ok babe.....it is what it is!!!

GhosstfacePoet

Eye need u to stop acting as if my mental dont desire u

Aura

well heres something for your mental im tagging you now!!!!

GhosstfacePoet

Change ur screen name

Aura

why whats wrong?
do you even know what it means?

Aura

Nope but eye want ur Middle name 2 be PussyAngel Supreme

Aura

u crazy!!!! lol

GhosstfacePoet

Cool

Aura

whats that mean...

GhosstfacePoet

U good!

Aura

Here we go.....

Aura

u know what i just saw where ur girl changed her name for you....I guess since I'm not a groupie it doesnt rate on ya list...

GhosstfacePoet

U dont have 2 do it babe plz did eye said u were a groupie, you be doing the most.

Aura

The only reason I changed my name in the first place is because everyone knows me on different shows and in chat as beautifuldizasster and they're always askin how to find me and one of the chicks I met on blogtalk started callin me bdizz and it stuck...

2/4/11, 7:54 AM

GhosstfacePoet

Whats wrng boo?

2/4/11, 11:52 AM

Aura

I'M OK.....

Aura

I need to take a ride on ur face!!!!!!!

2/4/11, 2:42 PM

Aura

*Ready to slip and slide take me on your fantasy ride leave the mask off no need to hide take this pussy you can have it do what you will be savage while my clit spits on ya lips making me durty whine my hips stick ya tongue out make it erect get it from the inside a good taste of AuraWette my girl Nitafreak says lick her stupid trust I have no doubt you can do it but for me go above and beyond that claim I want you to lick me insane I'm talkin straightjacket fame when you're done I don't even wanna know my muthafuckin name now you're singing and dancing in my rain my essence and fragrance taking over your brain I'm embedded in your mental staking my claim Soon I won't be the only one going insane…. *Pussy Angel Supreme it took me 2 seconds to write this and I laughed when I was done if u want me to post it I will..didnt know how you were gonna feel about it!!!*

2/4/11, 4:42 PM

GhosstfacePoet

Post it….eye love it!

2/15/11, 5:31 PM

Aura

*Gripped tightly around my waist Hips slow seductive nasty grind Overpowering urge to rain Showers of pure ecstasy Soaking you, being consume by you Tongue fucked by you, pulsating and dripping wet my thoughts…look closely at it u may see something unexpected *AuraWette*

GhosstfacePoet

Pussy throbbing like ur heartbeat on da tip of my tongue..grind me like ur trying 2 scratch dat spot… intoxicating juices imma call those pussy shots!!!

Aura

DID U SEE UR NAME IN IT?

GhosstfacePoet

Yes ma'am sexy & creative...

2/22/11, 10:00 AM

Aura

I wrote to your status..if your interested in reading it let me know!!!!

GhosstfacePoet

Write it on there eye wanna witness it

2/24/11, 2:58 AM

GhosstfacePoet

SO CHRISTINE CALLS U Sin HUH!?! SMDH

2/24/11, 9:49 AM

GhosstfacePoet

She wants Ppl 2 know she knows my first name...So, is that a problem?

Aura

No...I don't know her personally, but I know of her ...be careful!

GhosstfacePoet

What does that pose 2 me...bay!

2/24/11, 2:10 PM

Aura

I'm not hatin or nothin I just about her and because I care about you and I know you've had experiences with stalkers...be careful she has those tendencies...

GhosstfacePoet

she doesnt have my number bay

Aura

She was friends with a friend of mine and he said she's nuts so be careful!!!

GhosstfacePoet

ppl cant get close 2 me any more

Aura

Yeah I know.....its unfortunate for those who wanna be for the right reasons!!

2/24/11, 3:55 PM

Aura

Wanna make a movie...then lets proceed...got ya face buried so deep in it to the point of suffocation...a beautifuldizasster there's no imitation...told you before this pussy iconic..having you floating on air like a toke of the best chronic...tongue fuck me good and then lift that pussy hood...suck dat clit and she sure to spit...intoxicating and fruit juice flavored...the best you never savored...glazed and amazed you're now punch drunk...no its my turn to give you something else you want ...assume the position 69...I'm bout to make it disappear...yes all 9 and that half too..don't forget I'm pussy Angel Supreme and thats what I do!!!!! sorry meant to respond earlier lemme know what u think...... *AuraWette

2/25/11, 1:41 AM

GhosstfacePoet

Hello bay eye need 2 be closed 2 u

Aura

HEY BABE.....U DON'T WANNA BE....

GhosstfacePoet

Im 4real can u plz stp b.s-ing a moment bay

Aura

IM LISTENING

GhosstfacePoet

U who eye want...real shit eye love ur mind its beautiful!

Aura

BEAUTIFUL MIND?!?! U WANT ME?!?!

GhosstfacePoet

Nawh...eye need u!

Aura

TELL ME ABOUT IT!!!! I WANNA KNOW!!!!

GhosstfacePoet

With u at my side...Jigga and Bee cudnt grasp our swagger

Aura

SO NOW WHAT?

2/28/11, 5:38 PM

Aura

You went from tellin me you wanted me and how beautiful my mind is to not returning txt...I mean which is it?

3/1/11, 12:11 AM

GhosstfacePoet
Maybe eye dont wanna b let down

Aura
WOW!!!!
this emotional game is too much....

Aura
hope ur enjoying this....

3/1/11, 8:51 AM

GhosstfacePoet
Enjoying what...

3/2/11, 2:36 PM

Aura
I just have one question...why are you encouraging that woman (Christine)?!?! I guess you just thought I was hating on her when I told you she has stalker like tendencies..But for your sake i hope she doesn't show you that side of her!!! Now I'm goin to take my tired ass back to work...lovin your stats and of course I wrote to them..have a great day Sincere!!!

3/2/11, 3:45 PM

GhosstfacePoet
Put dat response up

3/5/11, 11:51 PM

GhosstfacePoet
Hello Beautiful...

3/6/11, 11:36 AM

Aura
Hello Handsom....

3/6/11, 1:17 PM

GhosstfacePoet
Just going thru it

Aura
what are you going thru?

GhosstfacePoet
Eye wanna do a piece with u cause their one in the same...plz!

Aura
whats the problem Sincere? I have no problems writing with you u know that...I write to ur stats all the time....

GhosstfacePoet
No its really ur piece then eye wrote off it plz

Aura
so u want me to write and then u write to it?

GhosstfacePoet
Its already ben done eye just want 2 do it on Poetically Spoken show

Aura
lemme guess "Urgent Text"

GhosstfacePoet
Nope...What the F...!

Aura
wow really?

GhosstfacePoet
Yes ma am uve read my part rite

Aura
yes...and I just revisited it again....wow its really relevant to our situation right now!!! Kinda strange... so I think I'm gonna write more.... I'm surprised you went back and read that....

GhosstfacePoet
What u mean write more

Aura
Jus cause I want to!

3/7/11, 2:05 AM

GhosstfacePoet
If u write 2 da poem eye wanted 2 do its taking frm it

3/7/11, 9:33 AM

GhosstfacePoet
Eye need u asap

3/7/11, 11:45 AM

Aura
u said u needed me so there it is she doesn't know I wrote that yet....

Aura
Since you and Blaquerose got each other I digress!!!! LMAO!!!!!

GhosstfacePoet
Eye Love ur Work and ur tripping

Aura
not trippin at all!!! believe that!!!!

GhosstfacePoet
So where did dat cum from

Aura
ur stat boo....

3/7/11, 3:40 PM

GhosstfacePoet
Huh

Aura
huh what? I'm just sayin you got her she got you yall good....no worries!!!!!

GhosstfacePoet
Wow, you stay in ya feelings im just writing.

Aura
wow what?! im not understanding....maybe Nevaeh will throw her words on what I wrote on ur stat!!!!

GhosstfacePoet

Her dude wont allow it...dats why she stays quiet and just like stats dats how dey met.

Aura

ok well I guess i wrote enuff for the both of us.....

3/8/11, 1:01 PM

Aura

Did u change ur #? I've txt u a couple times with no response...either way I guess u didn't wanna respond....

GhosstfacePoet

No bay eye be changing numbers

3/9/11, 8:28 PM

Aura

thumbs expose...parting perfect chocolate pussy folds...tongue erect...strokes glistening pink inner set... clit hard and challenging you...bury your face in it you know what to do...plunging in and out of that hole...in so deep...out stretched tongue French kisses my heart...this pretty pussy is beauty marked... pussy pulsates her beat on that tongue...making that wet suction sound as mouth juice spits and clit drips...hips grinding and whinding...pussy smearing and glazing....skeeting and squirting cum flow is raging.... head game fiyah...fucking blazing...you and me together could be...ABSOLUTELY AMAZING!!!!!!

3/10/11, 4:22 AM

GhosstfacePoet

Yo...where do these thoughts cum from...Omg eye love it

Aura

Its what I thought of after reading some of the things on ur page....btw the line about the beauty mark is true...she's beauty marked on the inside!!! Lol

GhosstfacePoet

Lol...talked 2 Passion smh she loved what ur doing plus da fact dat u asked 2 shout her out...eye miss my Potna her dude has her isolated

3/10/11, 9:22 AM

Aura

SMDH have fun!!!!

Aura

On a serious note...DO I SCARE YOU?!? I'm just trying to figure out our dynamic...

GhosstfacePoet

No ma'am just into u so 2 keep frm falling eye use guardrailing up

Aura

So in other words yes....Quan if u want me to fall back I will....I barely come out to play, but if u need to put up guards me maybe I need to stay in my lane...I don't understand it, but if thats what u need.....
by the way have you ever considered how you putting up ur guard makes me feel!?!?!?!

GhosstfacePoet

Yes ma am dats why eye walk lite

Aura

If you think what ur doing is walking lite I'd hate to see you stomping....

GhosstfacePoet

Eye am into u damn...u feed me with attention eerrr now and then ur miles away u were n my every thought so eye had 2 fall back

Aura

Im gonna say this..and its not meant to make you feel any certain kinda away, but you say that I give u attention every now and then but thats because of how you relate to me...u want me to show you attention but you show me none...and the distance thing is something that could be worked on...but u play this indian giver game where you give me a lil then you take it back!!! Some of the ladies on ur page u don't seem to have an issue with giving them anything...And yes I understand ur an Artist, but at the same you want me to believe that you don't have personal relationships with them and its obvious, but me who you claim you're into, you act like I'm the damn stalker....and if I was in your every thought I would've never known by the way you act! Theres so much I could say, but I won't...

GhosstfacePoet

Wow only if u knew da truth

Aura

You always say that...

3/10/11, 4:49 PM

Aura

can u receive voice notes on ur phone I wanna send you something....

GhosstfacePoet

my fone tripping

Aura

sooo u can get on fb get it while its tripping on ur phone?!? Smh lol ok

GhosstfacePoet

Yes actually eye can!

3/11/11, 11:23 AM

Aura

I CAN NOT BELIEVE WHAT I'M READING RIGHT NOW!!!!!! YOU........

3/11/11, 1:05 PM

GhosstfacePoet
Huh

Aura
You and Blaquerose just gave me perspective on the things you say to me...obviously you have focused your attention elsewhere, but you claim you put up guards with me, you have no interest in me SINCERE, and its amazes me that these thirsty dudes that I barely interact with will show me and you won't, I don't even entertain them but you have definitely been showing love to yours...I can say.. that I was being more true to you than u even know...SMDH @ me!!! It is what it is...

GhosstfacePoet
Wow...u neva amaze me yo...eye mean 4real

3/14/11, 9:46 AM

Aura
Hope you had a great weekend Sincere....

GhosstfacePoet
Yes ma`am what about urself

Aura
BLAHH....

Aura
I still feel the need......

GhosstfacePoet
Huh...

Aura
for you....

GhosstfacePoet

For me..

Aura

yes for you, but I'm tryin to give you what u need...

GhosstfacePoet

What is it eye need

Aura

you say you're guarded with me, so I try not to impose myself on you..

GhosstfacePoet

Eye know eye wud fall n Love with u but eye Love hard so its 4 da best

Aura

I just wish you had told me this before I got caught up in my feelings....
Now what am I supposed to do with what I feel for you?

GhosstfacePoet

How do eye knw u wont eventually hurt me

Aura

I could ask you the same question...seeing as how its so EASY for u to turn away from me....

GhosstfacePoet

Ttyl

3/14/11, 3:09 PM

Aura

He says he needs to be close to me doesn't want, but needs me...yet he puts his emotions on pause and his heart on lock...disconnecting from me...for fear of falling in love...hard wired into them...those who can't see...the other face he's shown me...cyber space groping them stroking them...giving them intimate parts of him flaunting it...taunting me with it... obtaining pleasure from it...leaving me haunted like the ghost of lovers past...our essence intertwined...mentally enraptured...guarded yet *still drawn to me, but unsure of what he feels...turning his face from me...fading behind ego and temporary affection the two sided coin continously flips... leaving me with hearts double jeopardy.... posted this in my notes this morning after our conversation...I tagged you as well but I know you will read it here.... *AuraWette*

GhosstfacePoet
Wow

Aura
Wow good or Wow bad?!?

3/16/11, 1:12 AM

Aura
I am going to put "What the Fuck?" on my blog and was wondering if I could add your part as well... giving you credit of course....lemme know AuraWette

3/16/11, 5:47 AM

GhosstfacePoet
Yea its cool eye wud help u get bread but our feelings involved dat and money aint a good fit

3/16/11, 10:07 AM

Aura
What do you mean?!?!

GhosstfacePoet
Nuthin

Aura

I really wish you would stop acting like you can't talk to me...we are adults not children....you can talk through your poetry but you can't talk to me....not that I think any of what ur sayin in ur poetry is directed towards me...quit acting like i did something wrong!!!!

GhosstfacePoet

Im cooking breakfast let me pipe down...

Angel waking up to Melodies awakening her with the aroma of breakfast. Sincere was indeed a great man, when he stayed focused. Suddenly Sincere steps in the room with a tray with scrambled eggs, grits, turkey bacon, strawberries and kiwi with orange juice. Lay back babe? As I laid upon the headboard, he placed the tray upon my lap. Can I watch you eat? I just wanna be a better me, I do know it's a lot I don't know but if you're willing to be of help to me I'll try my best as we trust in God completely. Biting her strawberry while feeding Sincere the rest. Eat this and enjoy us. As Angel began feeding me her breakfast, she leant my crown into her lap and asked can I adore you? Taken by such a gesture, I was speechless. You always checking for me, allow me to cater to you even if its 3 minutes. Take me there I'm willing to be submerged in ya essence.

3/19/11, 3:15 PM

GhosstfacePoet

Hello Beautiful..also eye didnt like da fact u said ur Dna is n my ink

3/19/11, 6:21 PM

Aura

Still tryin to understand why u don't like that line...all it means is I feel that connected to you that I could write it without having known you long....

3/19/11, 11:30 PM

GhosstfacePoet
Eye was jokn bay

3/20/11, 2:33 AM

Aura
Eva Been licked by a Ghosst? dirte ideaz of Oral Sex...tongue licking Ur Hot Spot Fucking My Ideas with mental visions of your tongue in matrimony with my clit those feelings of intense Pleasure got my Pretty in Pink thumping to the beat of your tongue...Pussy Angels no longer a dream a reality for a cum freak fein...Urgent Text made me Supreme on your team...caught up in the rapture you Slave Me with Black Hannibal Lector like tongue tricks and that chocolate 9 1/2 inch joystick...Blowin Ya Mind with mental sex...Selfish not wanting to share with the next...except for the Angels your heavenly harem... Love Interrupted was a Secret Pain...with Haunting thoughts of What Dreams May Come...tiptoed through my mental...leaving footprints of your essence and gently seducing my soul...two faces...one man...Double Jeopardy...which are you willing to give to me...your true face or the masked apparition...fading to black seems to be your mission...but before this poetic love affair ends let me ask...have you been touched by this Angel? she has definitely been touched by you...some may not get it or can't understand...you know what this feeling is.....I think you feel it too... goodnight bae...if u want me to post it I will!!!

3/20/11, 9:30 AM

GhosstfacePoet
No dont post dis...2 personal stop dat

Aura
Wow why is it too personal cuz I used titles from our writes? And why do u want me to stop you asked how I felt! Or is it cuz I said Black Hannibal and I'm not the only one u sent that pic too! Here we go I'm goin back to sleep bae!!!!

GhosstfacePoet
Write it...

3/20/11, 11:29 AM

Aura
Write what?

GhosstfacePoet
Ur poem boo

Aura
Already wrote it...u don't seem to happy about it....

GhosstfacePoet
I love it u just be so deep 2 where as u leave me vulnerable

3/20/11, 3:19 PM

Aura
Don't worry I won't post it on fb...I'll post it on my blog...u don't have to worry bout anyone seeing it from ur page...none of them knows I have a blog!

Aura
Oh yeah I'm too personal but yet o girl talkin bout people wondering if she's ur wife...get tha fuck outta here!!!!

3/20/11, 6:48 PM

GhosstfacePoet
Wow

Aura
Luv u tho bae!!! Its cool......

GhosstfacePoet
Im not going 2 say a word its Real

Aura

What do u mean Sincere?!?

GhosstfacePoet

Nothing u draw up sumthin but da smallest thing yet eye say write it then dis

Aura

I said it was fine bae no worries really!!!

GhosstfacePoet

Eye enjoyed us talkn yesterday thanx

Aura

U don't wanna talk to me anymore?!?

GhosstfacePoet

What Fuck yes eye was thanking u 4 brighting my day is all

Aura

Call me...

Iaokim

Eye dont know why my phone be acting up ugh bay my fone cant get nocalls but i can get on fb weird but true

Aura

ok : (

GhosstfacePoet

Dats how eye feel eye feel like we just starting getting at eachother dam

Aura

So now what?!?! I gotta tell u I keep reading that poem and I'm pretty impressed by it myself to have written it in like 5 minutes...

GhosstfacePoet

Thats ur feelings ive walked in sumone spirit in da same manner

Aura
Wow ok umm.....I guess we're back at square one.....

GhosstfacePoet
We can talk 2 one another here til eye get it to act right

Aura
ok bae...

Aura
this sux cause I wanna talk to you......

GhosstfacePoet
Me 2 4real eye didnt wanna get off da fone with u

Aura
You and Candy went in on that post got me pushing my pen over here!

3/21/11, 3:19 AM

Aura
I want you to write to the poem....respond to it, but I want Sincere sprinkled with a lil bit of Ghosst!!! Can u do that?!?!?!

3/21/11, 3:44 PM

GhosstfacePoet
Babe...

Aura
Hey babe...

GhosstfacePoet
Sumone eye trusted crossed me again

Aura

Who babe?
This sux I need to be able to talk to you!!!

3/21/11, 6:25 PM

Aura

Why aren't you talkin to me today!?!

3/21/11, 9:00 PM

GhosstfacePoet

Eye havent been on here remember BlaqueRose she disrespected me 4 what eye didnt understand why she was getting so jealous eye blocked her

Aura

Wow!!! I told you to be careful with these women babe...she got caught up in her feelings!! What did she do babe?!?

GhosstfacePoet

She post a poem called Ode Ghosst lol held truth mix with alot of lies trying 2 talk down on me she went so far as 2 say dont let me expose u...u asked me 2 put money on ur lights eye neva asked her dat i just said eye didnt have money for my lights and its off payments.

Aura

Wow did u respond?!? I knew she was a gonna be trouble...I'm just sayin couldn't tell u that cuz I didn't want you to think I was hating!!! I read between the lines babe I know when someones catching feelins....I kinda tried to say that when I sent u that message that morning, but u think I be trippin!! I hope she doesn't cause anymore problems for you...

GhosstfacePoet

Eye felt dat as well but what am eye going 2 lie 2 pacify her fuck dat if eye dont want you i just dont, she married

Aura
Damn babe!!!

GhosstfacePoet
Im just tired of having 2 plz ppl, who will plz me...nobody

Aura
I'm tryin......
I'm tryin......

GhosstfacePoet
Are u 4real everyone wants 2 b happy but will u truly make me happy

Aura
I'm tryin.... that's something u have to ask yourself...do u want ME to make u happy....if so we'll have to work on it!
Can we make each other happy is the question....

GhosstfacePoet
Yea eye just want u 2 make me happy

Aura
I'm willing if you are.....

3/22/11, 8:29 AM

GhosstfacePoet
Im willing boo

3/22/11, 10:03 AM

Aura
Are gonna post ur new piece?

GhosstfacePoet

No...it bothered me and eye was unsure shud eye respond 2 BlaqueRose but eye did a piece eye had 2 write it she went 2 far eye really wanna post it its Called Thorns of a Rose

Aura

She mustve taken it down cuz I didn't see it!!! We're not friends but her notes are public!!! I wanna read it...

GhosstfacePoet

She smart not knowing she was falling 4 me sum of her female friends was falling 4 me so if she post it 2 her notes it makes her look bad dis my response if eye were on a laptop eye cud at u 2 da Poetry group im not on a laptop...

Ghosstfacepoet

Thorns of a Rose- Roses are red violets are blue
truth is who will shit on who?
You havent been what i been thru!
Aggravated stalking im not a stranger 2.
Ive seen dis often ...
...Im not a fan of drama but my pen started walking.
First it started here!
I birthed alot of your thoughts I should own your ideas.
Tears who?
Youre comical boo truth is at 11 I didnt cry at my moms funeral.
As a young one she said keep ur eyes open.
Distingush da real frm da fake, Not realizing u were phoney was my biggest mistake.
Wait, while ur caught up in ur feelings ....
...Long dreads hang like wool from a sheep.
Youu followed me as if these were Jesus feet.
I Speak truth dont b controlled by emotion.
I would pitch my slogan Eva been licked by a Ghosst but Rose its showing!
Believed I was da Ghosst...
...Thorns of a Rose exposed ya face your mask fell off So now u mix lies with truth.
Thats what u sell us?
Honestly in da land of the Ghosst u got Jealous.
How u mad and got a Man at home only thing I ask is....WILL YOU PLEASE LEAVE ME ALONE!

Aura

That's hott babe...plz be careful with these women though...u can't be personal with some even if its just friendship...they take what u say too far! I understand it though...not to say u did it to me but u showed me u were interested in me so I returned the same interest had u not I wouldn't have...I'm all in now!!! Lol

GhosstfacePoet

Lol eye can dig dat...its just how can u slander sumone 4 not wanting u

Aura

Because in her mind you said you wanted her so now she feels like a woman scorned!! I tell people be careful with words they are powerful!!! How many women are hooked on you and have never seen your face!! U gotta watch how u handle them....u need rules or something on ur page like Nita!!!! Lol

GhosstfacePoet

How did eye knw being nice cause disarray

Aura

the thing is babe the subject of what ur talkin bout most times is intimate for a woman...no matter how hard she try and play...you talkin to them personally...and I have to say sometimes you do pay more attention to some more than others and thats where the problem begins...POETIC LOVE AFFAIR!!!! You need to make it known what your intentions are upfront and if you feel another way about someone you would let them know....I'm here to tell you its more than just her feeling you like that and you know it.....

GhosstfacePoet

Why do u like me da way u do

Aura

I guess because I kinda saw you differently..the words at first caught me not just ur writes but what u wrote on my notes or on my page....I never felt disrespected by you.....Its not just about the sexual stuff although if I'm being honest I'm curious for sure...but its a mental connection I feel with you.... you understand the art of making love to someones mental and I appreciate that about you...so when ever you and I become physical its gonna be explosive!!!! I could keep going...lol

Aura

I see the potential in you the brilliance of your mind and how it works, I love how passionate you are about poetry and your art. You work and go to school as well... And honestly maybe I'm being foolish but I feel like you do care about me....

3/22/11, 12:51 PM

GhosstfacePoet

Lol ur right all around da Board...yes dis is my passion

Aura

So am I being foolish?!?!

GhosstfacePoet

Whats foolish have feelings 4 others wow

Aura

smh!!!!

GhosstfacePoet

DIS IS WHAT U WANT RITE

Aura

Stop questioning it.......

GhosstfacePoet

.....done!

Aura

WHAT DOES THAT MEAN QUAN?

GhosstfacePoet

Im done questioning it

Aura

i KNOW YOUR GUARDED....SO AM I!!!!

GhosstfacePoet
Lets flow

Aura
OK

3/22/11, 11:08 PM

Aura
Babe.............

3/23/11, 12:54 AM

GhosstfacePoet
Yes dear

3/23/11, 2:38 AM

Aura
ummmmm.......

3/23/11, 11:13 AM

Aura
Hey babe..... whats up no talk for me today?

GhosstfacePoet
Dont u start its 2 early 4 dat how u

Aura

Start what babe? LOL Im good how r u? I wanna ask you something and plz don't get upset about it.....I've wanted to know this so I'm gonna ask...I never assume anything!!! Have you and Passion ever been romantically involved? Just asking don't trip!!!!

GhosstfacePoet

No she has a man Passion is how Urgent Txt was birthed

Aura

ok maybe I asked it wrong....but nevermind got it!!! what do you mean thats how Urgent Txt was birthed?

GhosstfacePoet

We shared ideas ☺ she is a Great friend dats my babe 4real she made me who eye am so im 4eva n debt 2 her

Aura

WOW!!!

GhosstfacePoet

Wow what

Aura

Nothing...so anything else from Blaquerose?

GhosstfacePoet

Neva posted just had 2 get it off my chest

Aura

So tell me how this is gonna be.......

GhosstfacePoet

Idk just let it Flow

Aura

I guess when u want me u'll come for me!!!! lol

GhosstfacePoet

Huh...one minute u were going 2 cum now dis guess what ur rite

Aura

No thats not what I meant babe...I meant on here if u wanna talk to me you will come talk to me....!!!!thats what I meant

GhosstfacePoet

Eye always talk 2 u if im not scared....yea eye yet get butterflies thinkn of u

Aura

R U being serious right now?!?!?! Scared of what?

GhosstfacePoet

Nervous

Aura

I won't bite...unless you ask me too!!!! LMAO

GhosstfacePoet

Eye want u 2

Aura

Lol!!!! I bet u do!!! Just remember I'm kinda spoiled and like some attention so....

3/24/11, 2:55 AM

Aura

goodnight.........

3/25/11, 10:08 AM

Aura

just came back to tell you I didnt delete you.......

GhosstfacePoet

Huh

Aura

I took my pic down...my acct was deactivated but if u wanna talk u can....

3/25/11, 4:46 PM

Aura

Hmmm I guess u have time to like folx stats, but no time for me...hmmm funny I turned my acct back on just so u could have a way of contacting me wow!!!

3/26/11, 12:04 PM

GhosstfacePoet

Thanx

Aura

That's all I get really Quan?!? Wow!!!

GhosstfacePoet

U toy wit my intetellect 4 what

Aura

I'm not toyin with you...I don't what u mean if u would talk me u would know what was goin on! I deactivated my acct I was bein harassed, but I realized u would think I was dissing u or something so I turned it back on and this is what I get!! Seems like to me u the one doin the toying...

GhosstfacePoet

Eye hate how u have me feel u then u just ugh

Aura

I got some dude fuckin stalkin me and I open my acct back up so that I can have some type of communication with you and you all over fb liking stats, but ignoring me...I know how to control my personal feelings I made a comment yesterday on blaise post on ur page and realized it sounded personal so I deleted it, and cause me and Nita are friends here I read where some chick talking she bout she bout to hit u up, but ur probably in class, but I didn't say a word to you about it, now whos toyin with who? This is what I'm talkin about you wanna give me something and then take it back...I don't know why u feel like you need to do this but if this is how you want it then so be it I can't convince you otherwise...you should find out whats goin on before you assume anything.....

Aura
my feelings are hurt just so you know!!!!

3/26/11, 2:29 PM

GhosstfacePoet
Don't get deleted trying to hurt me

Aura
what do you mean Im not tryin to hurt you im trying to be with you!!!!

GhosstfacePoet
Erase ur status thanX

3/28/11, 4:05 PM

Aura
As usual here we go again all over fb and not even a hello!!!!!

GhosstfacePoet
Hello dear

Aura
ok got it.....point is taken!!!!

GhosstfacePoet
Why dnt u txt my fone

Aura

u said this was the only way of communicating so why would I text ur phone if u cant get the message.....

GhosstfacePoet

Txt my fone bay

3/29/11, 10:32 PM

Aura

I just had to drop in your box to let you know how disappointed I was today....I have been in severe pain for 2 days and you laugh at me when I tell you I'm at the doctor...all because you think I'm ignoring you cuz I hadn't responded to you on fb!! Now i'm not gonna point the finger and tell you how you've been with me cuz you already know. Everything is all about you, on your time, when you want and its not fair...No Boo you ok...nothing just LMFAO!!! not once but twice...and when I got home I did write something to post but my feelings where hurt simple and plan.......

GhosstfacePoet

Eye thought u didnt recieve my first 1 im sorry 4 any form of dismay u told me dnt assume so eye felt ud tell me also eye laughed cause u said dnt assume 4give me and it seems all is wrong when eye approach u so in likeness of dat eye will fall back

Aura

thats all you wanted in the first place is to walk away so just say that!!!!

GhosstfacePoet

Yo ur not feeling me really im confused but its peace

Aura

IM NOT FEELING YOU PLZ...YOU GIVE ALL YOUR TIME AND ATTENTION TO YOUR FB LADIES AND IGNORE ME, BUT IM NOT FEELING YOU OK!!!!

GhosstfacePoet

U dnt txt me and have my number what is dis about F.b Ladies fuck dem u want me 2 prove it

Aura

here we go again with this prove it shit!!!!! umm u just told me to txt you yesterday and I did....and yes ya fb ladies fuck them exactly....what is it u want me to do when I try to put it out there your like naw too personal or stop that so what is it!?!?!?!?!?

GhosstfacePoet

Eye want u stop dis up and down shit dat dnt turn me on it turns me off

Aura

done......

GhosstfacePoet

So how is everything going bay

Aura

not good ....pain
my hands are killing me..if these meds dont work i may have to have surgery....

GhosstfacePoet

Talk 2 me whats wrong if u dnt mind my asking

Aura

I have carpel tunnel syndrome in both my hands and its just gettin increasingly worse....and because I work with my hands all the time its getting harder....but everyday isnt like the last 2 actually i havent had problems with them in a while but damn when they hurt they hurt like hell!!!!

GhosstfacePoet

What is da cause of it

Aura

doin the same repetitive motions with my hands for a long period of time (doin hair) causes the tendons in my hands to swell sometimes..its common in hairstylists, secretaries and factory workers....

GhosstfacePoet

Oh

Aura
lol im not disabled or nothing...

3/30/11, 10:06 AM

Iaokim
Eye realize dat bay dis da only place eye can catch u

4/5/11, 5:22 AM

GhosstfacePoet
Bay...dont do dis plz!

Aura
do what?

what ru talkin about....

Aura
I'm not sure what you're speaking of, but I am not doing anything Quan....

GhosstfacePoet
Babe do u think eye knw a lil about u...

Aura
Just tell me what you think I'm doing....plz

GhosstfacePoet
Ion ur so complex mind boggling

Aura
I'm not complex at all....

GhosstfacePoet

So what is it u truly want frm me

4/5/11, 9:40 AM

Aura

I'm confused... I thought we had established what this is, but obviously I was mistaken...so the question then is what is it you want from me? What type of relationship do you want with me Quan... you say u want me but in what capacity, because I seem to overstep all the time so tell me whats up!!!

4/5/11, 11:42 AM

GhosstfacePoet

Eye want u 2 myself so we can enjoy da many endeavors we may witness

Aura

Still a vague answer....

4/5/11, 3:15 PM

GhosstfacePoet

Eye wanna grow with u explore fantasies and highs or lows side by side...plz!

Aura

there seem to be rules and limitations where this is concerned its not that simple for you.....

4/5/11, 6:53 PM

GhosstfacePoet

Talk 2 me im listening

Aura

No you're not....
Ok

Aura

See that's what I'm talkin about....why is it so easy for u to talk to everybody else but me?!?

4/5/11, 8:38 PM

GhosstfacePoet

Im here u talk and just cut things off sarcism

4/6/11, 2:33 AM

Aura

No I really don't understand this....

4/6/11, 7:49 AM

GhosstfacePoet

OPEN UR MOUTH AND TALK IM HERE BABE

4/6/11, 10:22 AM

Aura

DO YOU WANT ME SINCERE?!?

GhosstfacePoet

Yes

Aura

THEN ACT LIKE IT!!!!!

GhosstfacePoet

How is it do eye pose 2 act

Aura

WOW REALLY.....so ur good with how we are?

GhosstfacePoet

No but u entertain other why not use da same energy into me if not more

Aura

thats funny...I always come to you....I txt...I come to your page and say good morning I send you messages all the time..and txt jus because im thinkin about you....can u say the same? Listen to what u jus said. "u entertain other why not use da same energy into me if not more." I'm feeling that statement for sure!!!

GhosstfacePoet

Eye knew u wud cause eye know u

Aura

I'm really confused now!!! U added blaquerose back?!?

GhosstfacePoet

EYE 4GIVE DONT 4GET

Aura

SPEECHLESS!!!!!

4/6/11, 2:03 PM

Aura

So I send you a text ask you to call me and I get what.... crickets....so this is how I see this...you want me but only on your terms!! so I guess when u wanna talk you will...

4/6/11, 3:14 PM

GhosstfacePoet

Babe im in a rut is dat what u wanna know...dam!

Aura

"Eye wanna grow with u explore fantasies and highs or lows side by side...plz!" thats what you said... so how are we supposed to do that if I don't know whats going on with you? and then u acting like I'm on your nerve!!! OK!!!!!!!!!!!!!

GhosstfacePoet

Nawh sumthings just 2 personal eye try avoiding answering but u neva let up

Aura

Stayin in my lane then....hope what ever it is it gets better for you! ttyl

GhosstfacePoet

Wow....

Aura

wow what...first you tell me im in ya business and won't let up and when I say I'm gonna leave it alone, and I hope whatever it works out i get wow!!!

Unknowingly to many i no longer desired living reckless. I was a King to my people this who i did it for but in truth it wasn't my truth. In learning that i was leaving to compliment everything around me it was time that i started my own way. Which i held no idea of what it would be i desired to be of help no longer of hurt. Lowlife is all i knew, i could not leave them out to dry so i had to find myself so i could be of help to them. The bible was beginning to make sense to me i recall reading 1 Corinthians 15:33
Be not deceived :evil communications corrupt good manners.
It was time to separate myself from ole habits if i desired creating new ones.

GhosstfacePoet

Thanx dear 4 everything

Aura

what does that mean Quan?

GhosstfacePoet

We good know dat!

Aura

All I want is if you want me act like it....its not that hard...I ask questions because I care not because Im tryin to get in your business....I'm supreme for a reason I don't play second position...

GhosstfacePoet

Eye understand

4/8/11, 3:37 PM

Aura

I think I care about u too much that's why everything bothers me... U don't hve 2 prove anything... uve been showin me all along I just didn't wanna see it!!! I guess will never understand how much I've grown to care for you...just bcuz I'm not posting it all over ur page doesn't mean that my feelings are any less genuine..

4/8/11, 5:55 PM

GhosstfacePoet

Eye agree

Aura

What do want to do the SINCERE?!?

4/9/11, 9:05 AM

Aura

U have never hurt me like u have this morning...I'm too out done!!! Tears...SMDH!!

GhosstfacePoetYo dats my Homegirl who is a Great friend ok im done pacifying others 4 what...2 yet complain she is an Angel

Aura

it has nothing to do with that..i sent up a prayer for her.. whatever her situation and Im not complainin I hope that whatever she is going through gets better believe that....

GhosstfacePoet

Oh Doll....wow!

Aura

Wow what and who is doll?!?
you called me Doll...who is that?

GhosstfacePoet

Pay me no mine

Aura

u never answered the question....what do u want Sincere?

GhosstfacePoet

Idk any longer

Aura

So u ask for me and then I give you me and then now u don't know? because I want you to be here for me when I need you?

GhosstfacePoet

Ur 2 confusing, idk i never gave no one all of me.

Aura

how am I confusing you? u said you wanted me so I'm trying to give that to you....because it bothers me that you show me no love or attention thats what my problem is and if we're being honest you were having the same issues with me..u said u didnt like some of the interaction on my page, but I show you love everyday in some way if you were paying attention you would know that...I care so much for you and you don't even know it!!! its a shame....

GhosstfacePoet

Show me physically

Aura

Why do you always test ME? The fact that I was sitting in a hospital room txtn you, or the fact that I'm yet still in your inbox, even though I know you don't want anything from me...so what do u want me to do? plz no vague answers this time.

GhosstfacePoet

Eye need 2 talk 2 u...when im able 2 get more minutes eye will but if u want 2 talk 2 me before then get me a verizon minute card...eye want u but ur sarcism is sumtimes irritating

4/11/11, 11:16 AM

Aura

I was in no way trying to start SHIT or digging at her...and if thats what you think it was then I won't attempt to change your mind..And since you say I always have something to say and that I irritate you (smdh), I wanted to make sure that I wasnt being overly sensitive so I copied and pasted her post and sent it to a friend for their opinion, not having told them any other details of the situation, and what jumped out at them was the line "got bitches crying they love you" they then went to your page to see the whole exchange....I have nothing but LOVE and respect for you, you know this, but I also have respect for these ladies who speak to me daily and show me love when I post on your page..I would never assume that I am the only one with feelings for you...I know better..but yesterday you expressed your "feelings" for the first time publicly and so in return I did the same...Im not trying to make anything more than what it is and if you look at it again, you would understand why it was questioned...I hope you can respect this!!! *VETTE

4/19/11, 1:37 PM

Aura

Well since ur not responding to my text I guess I'll assume that you're not talkin to me anymore....I don't know why its so hard for you to see.... *AuraWette

GhosstfacePoet

Eye write my pen brings da Art 2 life

Aura

Why can't you jus answer? were you talkin to me in your stat!?!

4/20/11, 10:14 AM

Aura

so I guess ur still not talkin to me?!?!?!?!?!

GhosstfacePoet

Was up babe

Aura

Why are you doing this?

GhosstfacePoet

Doing what?

4/20/11, 12:24 PM

Aura

I've been sitting back stayin in my lane but still paying attention...I figured if u wanted to talk you would, your post yesterday dug in me and I didn't know why but i know now..u wanted to keep me to yourself and I was like ok and I literally ignored people who wanted my friendship that were friends with you, I didn't put whatever our business was out on front street for all to see....even in my posts if they were too personal I wouldnt post them or i would change the words as not offend anyone, making plans to come visit you in the next couple weeks, but none of that do you respect, yesterday was the first time I put my true feelings on blast on your page for real....then you iggin me but talking to others all the time you been playing a game with me. Its just so sad and I know that you and Nita have a closer relationship than you let on, that has been obvious to me for weeks now....especially after yesterday!!!!!

4/20/11, 1:51 PM

GhosstfacePoet
Word...how many people tell me daily they can wash my pain away so tell me do u not believe alotta ppl interested in me guess what im interested in truth anything less than dat is non existence

Aura
And that was all I was givin you, but you were playin games I would be a fool not to think that other women werent after you I see it everyday...but why would you play with my emotions if u had no intentions on following thru with anything you said....

4/20/11, 4:41 PM

GhosstfacePoet
U didnt...!

Aura
explain that.....so what did I do now!!!

GhosstfacePoet
U funny how is it u ask da same question different...will u violate da fact eye care not 2 talk about dis manner then u insult my intelligence

Aura
point taken...written down and filed!!!!

4/21/11, 1:26 PM

Aura
Im gonna keep this in your box...your physical, your financial, none of that was ever any issue for me...do you know how many pics of you I have and I hardly ever look at them? Funny thing is you think I'm just like every body else and I'm not!

GhosstfacePoet

Wow...tell me are u, like wats ur strengths eye love and dislikes u hold eye dnt care 4...are u really paying attention

4/21/11, 4:40 PM

Aura

couldnt txt all this, but you know what drives me crazy about you? We're having a great conversation and then you just stop responding....HATE IT!!!!!

4/22/11, 7:45 AM

GhosstfacePoet

4give me

4/22/11, 9:38 AM

Aura

?

4/28/11, 6:52 PM

Aura

said I was gonna leave u alone...cuz thats how you like it, but i just had to say...I think Poetically Spoken said somethings that I wouldve said but differently I'm glad you have a friend that you allow to be there for you......

GhosstfacePoet

Dats my friend more than eva

Aura

I know thats why I appreciate what shes says more than anyone....I respect her!!!!! I have told you in countless pieces how I feel about you and what you mean to me...your not just some dude talkin bout sex to me....I think about you daily I know you're going thru and it pains me that you won't allow me to be there for you, but i can't make you, so with that said let me fade back into the shadows and be there from afar.....

5/4/11, 10:08 AM

Aura

YOU JUST DIDNT UNDERSTAND IT DID YOU....THIS RIGHT HERE WAS WHAT I WAS DOIN BOUT TO SPEND MY MONEY AND FOR YOU TO COME TO ME TODAY AND ASK ME DELETE OR BLOCK ME FROM YOUR PAGE.....i'M SPEECHLESS!!!!!

Wow!

Riding thru the city with Lil Wayne Mirror blasting. After looking myself over and over i am not well pleased. Living a triple life married, these streets and a virtual reality relationship we someone i loved deeply but afraid to commit not wanting to hurt no one in all this. I slowly begin to strip the layers of me away i no longer wanted to be involved with desiring God to help me recognize who i was. As i park in the projects the t.v on my dask comes on. Its Paid in full my favorite part. Money Mitch ask will the streets still love me?

5/22/11, 10:59 PM

Aura

I was sittin here earlier thinking about what u said about me being funny acting and I thought to my self but this is what he wanted...for me to just go with his flow, not to react to everything I see or question it because I still react but I don't say anything...I come to your page at times and read your post and or posts from others and I'm like why is it so hard for him to communicate with me? I see Nina and the lil word games she plays and just the same type of thing thats always been there and I just feel like I'm not someone you wanna share yourself with....You just turned and walked away with out any hesitation...My silence and lack of participation on your page isnt because I'm *acting funny...I'm just dealing....But I'm still around just giving you want you showed me you wanted....*sighs*

5/23/11, 9:14 AM

GhosstfacePoet

Eye just dont want u catching a attitude just live

Aura

I am Living, but at the same time it does bother me...that you are so nonchalant with me but seem to give yourself freely to others...but it is what it is...

GhosstfacePoet

What do eye give dem

Aura

you share things that you have not with me and at one time I was someone you say you wanted to be with, but now I'm some stranger....I'm dealing....

GhosstfacePoet

Sorry is only 3 ppl eye wantd here but hey eye can make sumone want me...ur yet a friend when ur ready 2 apply da friendship get at me

Aura

What do you mean there was only 3 people you wanted here?

GhosstfacePoet

its not da same ppl change 4 strange reasons dats why im alone

Aura

since your not really sayin I guess I wasn't 1 of the 3, but as far as changing...I didn't change...you did, but I continued anyway...and then u picked up with someone else as if I wasn't a factor.....I have remained your friend, but my friendship is reciprocal ....can't be one sided...the feelings are enough to deal with let alone having to deal with a friendship that one sided...I take any relationship I enter into seriously whether its friendship or not....thats why this bothers me...

Aura

Of Course Silence....yeah you keep doing you catering to them thirsty broads....who are only concerned with what you look like and ya tongue and dick tricks....instead of finishing this conversation with me you are yet again entertaining some chick who is so damn concerned with what you look like.... uggghhh and you wonder why?!?!?!?!

GhosstfacePoet

Bay why do u do dis?

Aura

SIGHS......

5/23/11, 6:28 PM

Aura

DRAMA....

GhosstfacePoet

Whats da Drama

Aura

I PRIDE MYSELF ON BEING INTELLIGENT AND I KNOW THAT I AM, BUT I DON'T GET IT.....

GhosstfacePoet

Wow where did dis cum frm

5/24/11, 1:09 PM

Aura

In the beginning it was just your words pursuing me...seducing me...and then our poetic love affair began...before your face shown I saw you...looked right past the mask and the groupie love into you... felt an electric connection with you...and so I gave you the purity of my poetry...scribing beautiful and passionate words for you...and in those words I found a love for you, my muse of dark chocolate *skin...full inviting lips...bedroom eyes and beautiful mind...and soon our poetry spilled past paper and became a desire for one another....but no sooner than it began...with no warning it abruptly ended...we don't make love anymore...dare I say the desire...respect and appreciation you had for me has faded...tried to give you what you wanted ...what you needed...a place of love and refuge...a place to be something other than the Ghosst in the mask...just Quan the man...and just like a Virgin who's poetic cherry you popped you will always have apart of me...but if the Ghosst in the mask is what you would rather be...then I guess its not you I see.... **just random thoughts at 3am....*

5/24/11, 4:11 PM

GhosstfacePoet

Wow...ur pen has always stayed close before da Mask was removed u knew beyond da Ghosst...hid fears behind sex, money and music! Hoping Cupid yet shoots me...da attention from da Groupies may have been 2 much, truly im desiring ur touch? Do u feel my hurt? Day in Day out im kissed with wet promises...honestly who wants me? Many fix lips 2 spit temporary Pleasure, measure happiness? 4give my soul 4 its dark road of torture...who control da future, do we provide our truest light hoping da energy we recieve is mutual 2 what we gave...so am eye da worlds slave doing things 2 makeup 4 my past acts!

Aura

Ok this the part where I let u read something I wrote about a month ago...was really feeling hurt and this was my expression..no one knows who and what this is about but when u read it u will understand I know u better than u think...I'll tag u shortly...

5/31/11, 3:26 AM

Aura

you got what u asked for....

5/31/11, 7:48 PM

Aura
U asked for me to let u be..so I hope u know what that means to me...so you will forget any traces of me...but this is what u asked of me...just remember I didn't leave you...you asked for me to go...so like Ringling Brothers on with your show!!!

GhosstfacePoet
Stay...4 a lifetime!

6/12/11, 10:50 AM

Aura
You had that didn't want it...referring to ur stat!!

GhosstfacePoet
U neva stayed down u always tried 2 bring about why why why just be u

Aura
Smmfh u are a mess!!! You don't care who feelings u hurt!!

GhosstfacePoet
Hurt...how did eye hurt ur feelings babe what did eye do nothing...just said u wasnt into me u were trying 2 change me wow dis is crazy

Aura
I wasn't tryna change you at all...ur so blinded by those women u can't see a good one when she's in ya face...never said I wasn't into u me being into was the problem it wasn't reciprocated and obviously u had ur back up plan!!! Yes this is crazy!!!!
I wasn't tryna change you at all...ur so blinded by those women u can't see a good one when she's in ya face...never said I wasn't into u me being into was the problem it wasn't reciprocated and obviously u had ur back up plan!!! Yes this is crazy!!!!
I never stayed down are u kidding me...man plz if I weren't down for you...no worries now I really know what's up u told me to let u be...

GhosstfacePoet

Yo u neva wud call fall da sleep on da fone...indeed eye was starving 4 u but u are involved boo... it dnt take a rocket scientist 2 knw dis im not mad just hot dat im not able 2 get da attention im so deserving of...we dont have a rift do we babe? Im not with anyone just thanking sumone how ive ben hurt but listen is dis a issue my stat...bay even u wrote shit n stats we not ignorant why dis heat becuz my feelings

Aura

And I just the confimation tht u been dealing with her for a minute too.. Are you kidding me Sincere?!? U ought to be ashamed of urself playin with peoples emotions like that...and I'm not making the shit up she said that shit!! Tisheena

GhosstfacePoet

Am eye da only person u been dealing with Honestly plz playn with ppl emotions nawh just not believing bullshit flowers

Aura

I'm gonna stop now because I'm bout to get in my feelings and I don't wanna say something I may regret...but again I don't know what type of woman you thought I was but obviously u thought I was some youngster u could gas my head up and play with my emotions...I don't divide my heart up into pieces and serve it up on a platter to different people...so what ever bullshit followers ur speaking, but YVETTE was not one of them!!!

GhosstfacePoet

Nawh eye watched u just because u tell me sumthin dont mean eye go 4 it ur involved u cant give me what eye want u give me portions of attention wud

Aura

How do u figure...u never gave me any attention time or anything u never called I was always the one contacting u!! So don't go and make excuses she said yall hve been talkin for 6mo!! Wow Quan u never had any intentions with me and that's fucked up...I tryna be down for u and u didn't want it so don't try and put this on me I made myself more than available to you!!! 6months Sincere wow!!!

GhosstfacePoet

Ok if in anyway im at fault forgive me but its hard 2 trust and Believe eye delete ur girl she get on my page frm her other page and do what eye told u BlaqRose did 2 crush me...Love wow aint no love anymore Real shit

---

Aura

U never had any for me thts for sure!!! How silly of me..and even when I knew about you and Nita the money and everythin I was still down and this what I get...

GhosstfacePoet

Yo wow are u 4real money eye neva askd her 4 nothing she said all these things 4 what reason she always askd did eye need sumthin umm yea its cool

Aura

I never said u asked but u did accept it and but what ever ur relationship with her it was ur decsion to make who ever u wanted...and I wasn't it....gave u space to make ur decision and u made it!!

Aura

Further more I'm such a damn grown ass woman I never once discussed anything about me and u to Nita ever only friendship...its sad u didn't recognize the woman in me!!

GhosstfacePoet

It was screaming but u gave me bits and pieces

Aura

I never gave u bits and pieces I made myself accesible to you and chose other things so again this is on you...I watched u with other women I watched show affection to other people and all that...I feel so disrespected right now u have no idea!!!! If not for anything tht u would treat me someone who is a friend...wrote countless poetry with u and for u...that u would disrespect it like that!!! Wow

GhosstfacePoet

Tell me how eye disrespected not once did eye say bye just xpressed myself why u handling me like dis

Aura

Me handle you...u didn't have to say bye u walked away....and for 6 months u been giving some other chick the exact thing u claimed u wanted from me... So yeah I feel disrepected becuz u played this game and not jus with me others as well....there is definitely no misunderstanding from me right I know exactly what it is....

GhosstfacePoet

Wow...is dis 4real! OK COOL...SAY NO MORE!

Aura

Quan plz don't she said yall hve been involved for 6 months! And ur trippin...talkin bout she didn't wanna step on toes!!!

6/12/11, 4:38 PM

GhosstfacePoet

Ok so now what...u know eye am very interested in sumone ok...is dis what u keep asking me

6/12/11, 5:54 PM

Aura

And then u say u love ur Angels but Tisheena gives u Butterflies!!!! U just said that same stuff to me a month ago!! U are a mess!

6/12/11, 9:23 PM

Aura

I gave you way too much respect...and instead of asking me about certain things you assumed...so no I wasn't with anyone else, but there are a few guys thanking you right now, believe that!!!!! smdh

6/13/11, 7:17 AM

GhosstfacePoet
Ok

6/13/11, 10:04 AM

Aura
I can't believe I put myself on pause for this!!!!

GhosstfacePoet
Why are u doing dis...ugh eye hate negative energy

Aura
I am not being negative bae just being real with you and myself....be happy in your decision....

6/13/11, 12:06 PM

GhosstfacePoet
So u leaving me?

Aura
What do u want from me Sincere!?!?!?!?!

GhosstfacePoet
Who is 2 say ill eva see u...broken promises!

Aura
The funny thing is....I was making plans to see you then I found out you were whispering in Nitas ear as well...so no broken promises I even inboxed you the flight info...had planned to come last month!

GhosstfacePoet
Ok cool well it is what it is...im not going 2 go crazy bout make believe ppl...

Aura
Make believe? ur a mess...Im more real than most!!!!!

GhosstfacePoet
Ur rite cause idk anyone on here but 2 ppl personally they knw me eye knw them

Aura

Sincere honestly you never wanted to know me...you never acted like a man that wanted to get to know me this woman who I am....hardly ever called me and then when you didnt have minutes I was always the one contacting you...even when u felt like I was gettin in ya business I fell back... you just liked the idea of me, thats why it was so easy for you to just walk away and you did that....

GhosstfacePoetic

Ok ur rite...im tired of staying depressed bout NOTHING so ttyl

Aura

Why R u depressed when u just admitted that you didnt really wanna know me...I don't understand...I made myself available to you and you thought you could get something better and so you walked away....so I'm NOTHING wow!!!!

7/5/11, 6:20 PM

Aura

deleting my comments...smh

GhosstfacePoet

Huh

Aura

comments aren't there but I understand...

7/6/11, 6:42 AM

GhosstfacePoet

Yo what u say makes no sense

7/6/11, 10:02 AM

Aura
why does it not make sense, commented on ur post and I guess it was deleted...

7/6/11, 4:43 PM

GhosstfacePoet
Eye neva saw it

Aura
No worries...

7/6/11, 9:32 PM

GhosstfacePoet
Da games ppl play

Aura
Ur funny...games... I have no need or use for them...that's ur arena not mine....

7/7/11, 7:17 AM

GhosstfacePoet
Cool...why are we even friends

7/8/11, 6:25 AM

GhosstfacePoet
Eye keep askn myself da same question

7/8/11, 9:17 AM

Aura
What question is that?

7/13/11, 10:44 AM

GhosstfacePoet
Delete my page plz eye dont want no parts of any Angels

Aura
Say what it really is u don't want no parts of certain Angels...cuz I know damn well a few u didn't send this message to...don't get mad at me for you and Nitas mess!!!

GhosstfacePoet
She said Angels so since everyone lying eye give 2 fucks what 4 but eye dont want no more Angels but 4 ppl eye know neva crossed me and havent been with Drama im good just like dat

Aura
Smh ok....

GhosstfacePoet
Thank u

Aura
Funny how I didn't spill all the shit between us and I get lumped in with the rest but u know what its cool...I told u along time ago about playin with people...but u know what I appreciate the connect with PS you and ur girl be happy good luck!!!

GhosstfacePoet
Sorry ur girls rite u and Cheri just was upset dats why eye seldom write on here anymore

Aura
Explain that...

Aura

And by the way I hope u didn't mean everyone lying including me...lol I have no need to lie for what...it was what it was...you claimed to be into me... when I wasn't I guess doing or saying what you wanted you were like Jayz on to the next one...Yes I was upset cuz I knew EVERYTHING that was going down when it was going down...and I still didn't air your business with me out...always remember I am a grown woman and conduct myself in that manner...write whatever you want on YOUR page...do you boo..be happy!!!!

GhosstfacePoet

Im saying sorry dear...yes, u and cheri were rite u guys told me along time ago...when eye was digging Cheri she had a man then she wud get irritated and say why mess with them but eye wantd 2 knw yu

Aura

And wanting to know me was fine but you didn't have to pretend with me...you could've still gotten to know me without all that extra, when someone tells me they are into me I take it for what it is, but when you show me differently yeah I get upset...its all in the past now....I just hope you have learned from this mess with Nita!!!!

GhosstfacePoet

All Women da same.... learn what, plz ill just not deal with them anymore

Aura

Wow!!! well unfortunately you'll keep having the same issues and sweetie all women aren't the same... lol I'm definitely not the norm no matter what u think...I'm far from the usual!!!!!

GhosstfacePoet

No one has shown me different so until then my mind set

Aura

I tried....EPIC fail though...you know why, you like the usual... too focused on the same kinda chick. Even after all the stuff that went down I'm still talking to you... I call that more than usual, truth be told Poet even now I don't really know what ur name is...and no matter how much of a victim you try to play...this mess was orchestrated by you...you got that woman all wrapped up in her feelings and played off her emotions and I told you to stop, but you knew exactly what your were doing, you didn't think that she would blast you like she did and I'm sure it makes you no difference that she did it but there were so many women saying the same thing and its definitely not a good look...so no matter what your intentions were you need to learn to tread lightly when dealing with certain women..

7/26/11, 11:24 AM

GhosstfacePoet
Eye love ur profile pic pen and lips dam

Aura
Thank you bae they are mine...one of my favs...its my logo for now!

8/13/11, 6:31 AM

GhosstfacePoet
Send a picture of ur lips 2 my fone im so into u u just dont knw

8/16/11, 4:23 AM

Aura
hehehehehhe got these women mimicking your flow....hilarious

8/16/11, 9:46 AM

GhosstfacePoet
Who mimicking my flow

9/5/11, 5:27 PM

GhosstfacePoet
Who are u...eye just witnessed sumthin u told me its falln in place!

Aura
what r u talkin about?!?

GhosstfacePoet

Its u, it was 2 personal it was u yo

Aura

I don't understand what u mean...just talk to me...tell me...

GhosstfacePoet

Write on my wall eye need 2 witness ur pen eye wanna see sumthing plz then ill say why

Aura

Since u don't wanna tell me what ur talking about....enjoy ur birthday babe hope its a great one!!

9/5/11, 9:23 PM

Aura

Now if u wanna discuss whatever it is ur talkin about without the riddles and rhymes we can...u know how my pen spills better than most so I dunno what u need me to prove...

9/6/11, 12:39 AM

GhosstfacePoet

It dont matter thanx eye fell 4 u thru what, is dis even real ppl on here

Aura

Again Ive said this 1000 times Im real as they come if you have something to ask just ask Im the one to question you I dont even know your name

GhosstfacePoet

How do eye knw u Real

Aura

what is this about? you're the one

GhosstfacePoet

What wow knw name wow u must lost site of who eye was...Sincere duh u knew dat yo

Aura

I never lost site of who you were that was the problem I saw you more clearly than most and you didnt and dont like it...so what is his all about?!?!?!

9/6/11, 9:56 AM

GhosstfacePoet

It dont matter eye c da deception

Aura

What deception are you talkin about?! U are really wiggin out I haven't deceived you and if someone is writing like me or using my words u should really let me know so I can handle that...I have no need of games trix are for kids and I'm about to be 38 yrs old in 2 wks....so yall play on the playground I have kids to raise...

Aura

There are posers on your page for sure, but unfortunately sir I am not one of them...I was straight up with you and you misled me, so that's that...

9/15/11, 12:54 PM

GhosstfacePoet

Eye haven't placed a finger on everybody but eye truly kno da essence of u

Aura

is that right?

GhosstfacePoet

For some reason ur words hold da same mass as others if u place my pieces 2gether u hold my Heart n ur palm

Aura
what r u sayin Sincere?

9/15/11, 2:38 PM

GhosstfacePoet
Nothing I'm just riding da waves

Aura
ok

10/14/11, 3:07 AM

Aura
Just checking to see if you were good...haven't seen anything in my news feed from you lately..hope you are well Sincere...

10/26/11, 12:12 AM

Aura
hey there...
or not...lol

10/26/11, 6:36 AM

GhosstfacePoet
Huh...what's good?

10/30/11, 8:45 PM

Aura
Hey Sincere!!!

10/31/11, 2:31 PM

GhosstfacePoet
Whats up...Beautiful you...!

10/31/11, 6:46 PM

Aura
Just checking on ya... been reading your posts...ur pen seems a lil different now....

10/31/11, 9:09 PM

GhosstfacePoet
Guess u snatched dat Savage outta me, call it growth!

Aura
How so?!?

11/1/11, 8:26 AM

GhosstfacePoet
Eye guess i am coming into a man more so than anything eye love what YOU do!

11/1/11, 9:34 AM

Aura
Well whatever has caused the shift...its nice to see the versatility in your pen....always a fan....

11/9/11, 10:02 AM

Aura
Wow you sure are introspective this morning....Regrets?!!?!?!!

11/29/11, 9:26 PM

GhosstfacePoet
Eye am sorry

Aura
Forgiven.....

12/7/11, 11:54 AM

Aura
hope you are well....

GhosstfacePoet
yes maam im good why u say dat

Aura
just because...

GhosstfacePoet
......?????

Aura
cuz I hope you are doing ok thats all...

GhosstfacePoet
indeed
how u

Aura
im good thanks....

GhosstfacePoet
youre anti y

Aura
?????

GhosstfacePoet
anti social

Aura
no im not...lol

GhosstfacePoet
what u thought eye was talking bout

Aura
ijs im not anti...

GhosstfacePoet
bet...so y dont eye witness ur pen at times

Aura
on your page?

GhosstfacePoet
what eva

Aura

oh I think you just miss it, then I post all the time...lol
haven't been posting in my notes as much, but there are a few collabs and things if you wanna be
tagged I got you...

12/9/11, 10:24 AM

GhosstfacePoet

psssstt...

Aura

pssst.....

GhosstfacePoet

how is my friend doing today, may eye ask who are u? Real shit...im deserving of that to dat least, rite!

Aura

What do you mean who am I?

GhosstfacePoet

u hold some form of significance but eye cant finger it...eye feel im being finger fucked tho!!!!!

Aura

I dont know what you mean, Im the same Supreme Ive been...

GhosstfacePoet

eye do realize dat but eye didnt discern what eye have discerned as of late...

Aura

and what is that?

GhosstfacePoet

its something abnormal, eye feel a different vibe many ppl eye tend to open to its something bout u my
spirit warns me to be delicate....thats why eye have always been super cautious but are u indeed whom
u say u are plus at times its like im kissing u but being seduced by a supposing other person...be real?

Aura

WOW really...I don't know what to tell you other than I'm just me...everyday all day ME!!!!

GhosstfacePoet

and who else?????????HINT HINT (Sincere thinking like her and these many faces.)

Aura

theres no hint just me....
if theres something you would like to ask just ask it... no riddles and rhymes

GhosstfacePoet

remember eye said someone reminded me of u....dis person was more indepth with me than any honestly what has ur attempt with us as friends was there a destination?

Aura

So because someone reminded you of me, that makes you what think I was a poser...lol I have no need for the games I told you that before, but I guess you didn't believe me until all the drama hit...I can't say what wouldve happened, you only let people in so far....

GhosstfacePoet

eye trust none

Aura

I see so I guess that answers your question then...if you couldn't trust me then I guess we would've just been stuck where we were...

GhosstfacePoet

most time ppl arent who they draw themselves up to be so there for the mindstate is make believe and im a reality fein
u seem authenic originally but idk shit didnt add up

Aura

I'm still lost...what didn't add up?

GhosstfacePoet

substance of ur truth....

Aura

sighs...ok lol

GhosstfacePoet

thats funny but eye gave u what u asked of me and what eye get

Aura

no you really didn't you gave me half truths...

GhosstfacePoet

no lie just didnt tell the entire story dats no lie just portions of truth
this shud be a fifty fifty thing...u give me eye give u

Aura

I gave you truth and you gave me bullshit end of story...sorry if you dont see it that way..unlike most what you looked like or how good you licked a clit never really mattered to me, but I guess that superficial is what you like and label it truth...

GhosstfacePoet

fuck sexual fantasies im talking bout u

Aura

exactly but you seem to thrive off that more than when someone was being real with you....

GhosstfacePoet

nope its just my freedom to escape bullshit...Poetry and sex eye digg str8 n cause its something eye enjoy very much so...this me unmasked no erotica

Aura

I understand that...the erotica didnt bother me at all...it was the lack of belief and trust in someone who was tryna be genuine with you even warning you about certain individuals...never disclosing anything that may or may not have been happening between us...

GhosstfacePoet

smh...its cool even among da drama and turmoil eye wasnt bother...negative energy finds me cause hating is a disease dat will always follow me

Aura

but you put me in the category with everyone else and I'm not that chick....

GhosstfacePoet

wso what chick are u?
so

Aura

If you don't by now I certainly can't tell you...

GhosstfacePoet

wow...bet

Aura

Im just sayin...you should know and the fact that you're questioning it well I guess you just didn't pay attention...

GhosstfacePoet

irregardless to what u assume give me u uncut and raw
its something about u dats why eye need to know where do u stand in my life, ugh

Aura

what do you want?

GhosstfacePoet

YOU

Aura

I don't believe that....

GhosstfacePoet

its so many things dat point in ur direction...is dat my hearts gps cause eye yet keep being directed towards u with my heart puesuasive chain

Aura

really? u barely speak to me and you want me to believe that?

GhosstfacePoet

we speak....just in codes, its no secret! Dont try me like im crazy yo

Aura

lol

GhosstfacePoet

dats funny tho, UUUUGGGHHHH!!!
you like da games u play

Aura

i dont play games....#grownwoman

GhosstfacePoet

LLH...neva said it wasnt u hell yo!
how is it u yet stay behind ur mask and uve seen me unmasked...BD

Aura

im not behind anymask at all...

GhosstfacePoet

ok so its more than one BD...ugh! Why are we fighting truth when the simplicity in truth isnt erasable

Aura

theres only one BD...lol
and one Aura
...2parts of the same whole...

GhosstfacePoet

my point exactly....eye have a memory like an elephant eye wud go back a few yrs but we in the future and im dumb in the present time
U have a blessed day imma stop harrassing u, its love babe...if no one knows how eye feel u do, so ive told u numerous times numerous ways they all mean I LOVE YOU...Peace!

Aura

excuse me what?!?!?!?!
ur not harrassing me

GhosstfacePoet

o....let me see Yvette pen eye am use to BD pen

Aura

Whispering his scriptures into my thoughts...scribing his Psalms across my soul...infusing my spirit with his doctrine...binding me in knots of Love.... He is my Religion
thats Aura pen right there....

GhosstfacePoet

YOU who im looking for...marry me?
eye love ur pen but ICU really eye do?

Aura

months would diminish into days and days into minutes until the communion of our souls...I'd allow you to spill me...to fill me... only to spill me yet again, until our desires are sated,
thats Aura as well.....
backward glances and naked frame dances...he coaxed me...stroked me...suspended and opened me, parting my barriers until the levees broke....ok I'm done but you get the picture....

GhosstfacePoet

DAMN....dat last line backward glances and naked frame dances...he coaxed me...stroked me... suspended and opened me, parting my barriers until the levees broke....ok I'm done but you get the picture....

Aura

lol
candle waxing...legs trembling... breathing staggered...pornographic moans low and guttural...up against walls...bending...bullying...until one of us is broken...
done for real this time....

12/26/11, 7:43 PM

Aura

You're such a pretender....smdh!!!

GhosstfacePoet

huh....

Aura

All this time you've been so concerned about whether or not I'm real and there's something about me...lol and all this time you making babies and talkin about a wife on Nitas page...YOU ARE A MESS...I hope all these revelations you're having are real!! #tickled

GhosstfacePoet

bout real as the entire mind state of you....Yes you know eye was trying to get a divorce but life press me to and fro but hey Im glad u did what u did...u help me ALL of YOU, the eye opener was Chyna Blue....eye realize my mind state was slipping deeper ninto darkness

Aura

Chyna Blue? damn you were involved with her too!!! I didnt do anything but try and be something I thought you needed....fuuuuuny..if this wasnt so funny I think I would be pissed!!!!

GhosstfacePoet

eye know who you are im saying she made me put a finger on the ochestry of music ive heard but didnt put together

Aura
SPEECHLESS!!!!!!

GhosstfacePoet

when she stated he trying to sell his soul....eye was lost but You help me realize my weakness eye was at my lowest point

12/29/11, 10:43 AM

Aura

While I really appreciate the change you seem to have made, I wonder do you realize the damage you did or could've done? I sit and watch your stats some days it makes me happy to see them other days it infuriates me...Again I am happy to see you happy thats all I ever wanted for you, but have you made amends for all the people you hurt? I mean up until 3 days ago I knew nothing of a wife and children absolutely nothing you misled me even in friendship...I don't know just speechless....

GhosstfacePoet

Forgive me at the time me and my wife was separated eye wantd a divorce eye didnt back and forth but she neva gave up on me...no disrespect 2 you but you told me you were involved eye needed a ear a friend and eye found that in you yes im not as open as most but im apologetic 4 any hurt or turmoil eye may have caused cause in my search 4 happiness eye was worried bout self again plz 4give me that was my past plz dnt hold my giving you me totally against me...this is the true me friend im sorry eye truly am

Aura

I won't debate this with you, but I never told you I was involved had I been I wouldve never gotten so wrapped up in OUR situation...but again I'm glad your happy and I'm glad you acknowledge the selfish reasons behind your actions...Im glad I didnt take it further with you as well I see I would've been hurt in the end...happy I was a friend to you at least Take Care Sincere...

GhosstfacePoet

Thanks its a brand new start

12/31/11, 12:02 PM

Aura

Now that I know who your wife is..this makes so much more sense to me now...she requested my friendship months ago, but because we had no mutual friends I never responded, as a matter of fact shes still sitting in my request box...everyday I find that I never knew you at all...its sad that I was real with you as much as you would allow me to be...Sincere Hollis...you really need to step back re evaluate your actions because I think your taking the easy way out I feel betrayed by you and you were supposed to be my friend, although I know this is face book I take my friendships seriously... you were never honest about anything inn your life, but expected TRUTH from everyone else and it pisses me off when I think back at how you would speak on truth and reality when it was you who was living this lie...regardless if you were trying to divorce or trying to resolve your relationship you should've made that known...but I do thank you for revealing who you really were back then, it took my eyes off you and put them where they should've been all along... so for that I thank you!!!!

GhosstfacePoet

Eye started this page eye said eye neva wantd 2 b involve just friends sumhow u became a close part of me and u who eye knew nothing about dats y eye felt you were just toying with me but 4give me cause eye was so selfish

12/31/11, 3:57 PM

Aura

SORRY FOR MY LANGUAGE BUT THAT IS COMPLETE AND UTTER BULLSHYT.....IF YOU THOUGHT I WERE TOYING WITH YOU YOU WOULDNT HAVE DEVELOPED ANY FEELING FOR ME AT ALL...BUT ITS COOL AGAIN THANK YOU BECAUSE NOW I HAVE THE PEACE I NEED....

GhosstfacePoet

Not toying in dat sense its just you were limited 2 what you wud give me Vette why do you always cum off mean 2 me dats hurtful as well ugh eye messed up dnt punish me 4 ignorance im sorry babe plz give me what we had Love and sincerity at one time eye read it in ur words now eye guess im da enemy of state thru it ALL EYE NEVA TOLD YOU BUT SOMEHOW ITS LIKE EYE FELL IN LOVE WITH YOU AS WELL EYE CLOSED MY EYES 2 WHO YOU WERE AND FELT YOU ALL WERE AND BELIEVED YOU ALL REALLY LOVED ME AT THAT POINT N LIFE EYE HAD NO ONE EYE WAS LOST AND HURT AGAIN 4GIVE ME

Aura

I'm not trying to be mean or punish you at all...its funny you sit here and say that you somehow fell in love with me...how could you?!?! you are forgiven I told you that before, but like I said I find that I didn't know you at all...I went and looked at some of the things we wrote together and asked myself who are these people!!!!

GhosstfacePoet

It was me all eye eva wantd was love sincerely eye went 2 church work fulltime student my wife askd about her ex in my face the was the most crushing blow eva happen 2 me so eye wrote frm freedom neva foresaw any of these things happening then eye abandon her being selfish 4 a long time eye yet was blaming others but in looking 4 Love eye was in search of who eye was eye expressed who eye was we were no longer 2gether she felt threating by you cause eye wud txt and talk 2 you always no one was an issue but vette she put effiences into you til eye didnt knw eye was n2 you as indepth even

Passionate askd did eye love you eye was scared of the reaction truth is truth you all help me in my toughest moments im greatful sorry again 4 da hurt or strife eye may have caused

1/1/12, 6:13 PM

Aura

Tell her there was no need in blocking me....there was no malice meant in my message, but just so she can feel comfortable...delete me!!! I am glad you're happy take care!!!!

GhosstfacePoet

She wants a divorce ugh what was ur reasoning 4 inboxing her

Aura

U and ur wife have issues that don't have anything to do with me...if she wants a divorce because of a sentence she doeant wanna be married to you...I meant no malice in my message I was simply tryna explain if I had known you were married I wouldn't have been conversing with you @ all whether you were seperated or not!!! Tell her to call me!!! 501 5639838

Aura

After your last message about her having an issue with me I felt bad...I would have never ever engaged in any of the conversations we had...the writes nothing!!!! now if she wants to Divorce because I simply asked why she requested me yall got problems.....

GhosstfacePoet

She thinks it was more than eye spoke of, she thought u were trying 2 be funny she deleted her page not block you she said facebook isnt 4 her...smh call u nawh the Lord will work it out sum how

Aura

Please.....being funny I'm a grown ass woman, I dont play games like that...she was the one trying to see what I was about and again if I had known you were married we wouldnt even be here...the fact that you playing victim is hilarious to me...tell her there is no need for her to be concerned, I have a MAN...I didnt know you at all....so no harm no foul!!!!

GhosstfacePoet

Yep

1/4/12, 12:18 AM

Aura

YOU NEED TO QUIT...YOU ARE NOT A VICTIM!!!!

GhosstfacePoet

Eye thought u were a friend yo really eye knw eye didnt open up 2 u but still, how wud u act if u were married a woman inboxed u ive apologize Aura ugh

Aura

You should've deleted your page after you apologized to everyone anyway and started over...how do you think you can have all the same people on your page with those freaky tendencies and you try to be right with your wife and God....come on! I think you need to fall on your face in prayer and hope that whatever the problem is within your marriage will be healed, cuz frankly dear its not me!!!

Aura

If the woman was beefin then yeah I would have an issue but I wasn't nor did I disrespect her I was tryna apologize to her, but before I could she was gone...you don't seem to get the fact that you led me into something that i wouldn't have ever done...you forgot I am a grown ass woman I have better things to be doing like raising a child with special needs to be beefing with a woman over her HUSBAND!!!!!

GhosstfacePoet

Eye didnt say it was u Aura ugh c why do u always do dis...treat me like eye dnt exist u talk 2 me harsh u outta all ppl

Aura

I read ur post even though I deleted you as a friend I can still see your wall....

GhosstfacePoet

How, eye knw who u is why u do dis make it hard 4 me
U had a man Aura u told me u had a man did u 4get

Aura

I just told you have a man...funny how you choose what you remember...I'm not making anything hard for you, just don't blame me for your infidelity...you took the choice away from me of whether or not I wanted to deal with you on any level by not telling me that....

GhosstfacePoet

Eye just wanted ur ear Aura im sorry really eye am eye was hurt doing dat time eye wud cum crying 2 you and b like u wudnt understand...u help me more than u knw maybe dats why dis is more bitter than anyone else will u 4give me plz im sorry 4 any form of hurt eye may have caused

Aura

I'm not hurt because of any romantic feelings I'm bothered because you betrayed my friendship....its really crazy to me how you forgot that you just told me you thought you were in love with me...lol but thats neither here nor there...I hope God fixes what ever is broken...

1/4/12, 9:12 AM

GhosstfacePoet

He has thnx Aura

1/20/12, 10:10 AM

GhosstfacePoet

forgive me for anything ive done dat eye may not know offended You as well as what may have... we have been friends to long for me to part ways with You forgive me please, Youre a great person eye cant deny dat but within my selfishness eye didnt realize what eye truly created was turmoil as well as confusion

1/20/12, 4:19 PM

GhosstfacePoet

You so stubborn

Aura

I dont know what you mean....

GhosstfacePoet

Ive finally understood eye was 2 blame yet eye reach out 2 an old friend and its like whateva

Aura

I dont what ur talking about....

GhosstfacePoet

You dnt wanna b my friend no more eye knw YOU yet c me but eye want Yvette B. As my friend

Aura

To ensure that I wouldn't to blame for anymore of your marital drama I thought it best to delete myself from your world....

GhosstfacePoet

Forgive me 4 past actions but eye just askd 4 my friend back with no drama included....FRIEND NOTHING MORE NOTHING LESS

Aura

I told you before you were forgiven....

GhosstfacePoet

So why we not friends

Aura

Because u were blaming me for your issues with ur wife...but its fine...

GhosstfacePoet

Ugh stop it let the past stay just there in the past

Aura

It is in the past dear...

GhosstfacePoet

Eye wanna c you on my page stop playing Vette ugh

Aura

Can I ask you something...why is it so important to you all the sudden?!?

GhosstfacePoet

Ok dats fair eye miss my friend there you have it...you are a great friend 2 me eye want that back, eye c ur essence other places but its not Aura dnt act up friend bout time eye count 2 ten open my eyes my wall shld have my friend Aura up there the count down begins

1/20/12, 8:00 PM

Aura

so now im on a countdown? you should know better than that!!! smh

1/20/12, 11:47 PM

GhosstfacePoet

Neva mind 4give me 4 reaching out 2 u neva again will u have 2 worry bout me my word is my bond enjoy life

Aura

hope this makes you happy now....dont make me regret it!!!

1/22/12, 11:02 PM

Aura

Cant really tell you about women only about me....read my stats you'll learn all about me.....much different than you know....

GhosstfacePoet

Wow let me fanatasize so tell me more just wantd 2 know if its not 2 much

Aura

If you pay attention to my posts dear you will get a feel for ME...what you say you didnt really know!!!

2/15/12, 11:43 AM

Aura

I just realized that I was I guess deleted...lol funny you basically beg for my friendship...I give you that and you turn around and delete me....smh!!!! Be Blessed in all that you do dear....
http://youtu.be/O7ofQmeao9I
William McDowell - I Give Myself Away
William McDowell - I Give Myself Away
youtube.com

2/15/12, 2:09 PM

GhosstfacePoet

You got my feelings all in a visegrip thanks buy no thanks dear just seperating myself so eye grow properly sorry if eye offended you no harm intended ....Thanks this is my vision to completely give myself away 2 God so he can use me in the manner he sees fit

Aura

I definitely don't want to hinder your growth...funny how you chose me to separate from but you kept others....I find it odd but please follow your heart and let HIM use you...

GhosstfacePoet

eye removed others it was if u were touching me more indepth. I was completely in another place with you its deeper than keyboards and screens and that was scary cause our relationship became spiritual some how and eye cant put a finger on it

Aura

Again I never thought I was of any threat to you nor am I trying to be...so again be blessed...

GhosstfacePoet

Idk who you are but you have a gift to open eyes you opened mine and eye thank you God loves you dear ur attributes holds beauty but use it as a vessel to open minds, hearts of many to grow be of help Beautiful ur inner Beauty is more radiant than any darkness light cuts thru it all

Aura

You know who I am thats why we are in the position we are in now...I've never had to have this conversation with you, but I am a Christian....God puts certain people in our lives for different reasons....if I was put in your path to open your eyes to a better revelation, then that was my purpose..
GhosstfacePoet
indeed....thanks

Aura

One last thing...instead of running from me you need to reconcile your feelings for me, because just cause you can't see me doesn't mean I'm no there still somewhere tiptoeing around your mental and that is obvious and NO I'm not arrogant I just know what this is....

GhosstfacePoet

eye dont quiet understand ur deliverance but know eye want happiness and true love for anyone eye have came in contact with during my lifetime....nothing more nor less, were all deserving of God's beauty and love but God chasten those he loves like any father....if eye have hurt you forgive me anything other than that eye cant finger God will heal all things if its a true desire

Aura

No don't get me wrong I'm over the whole situation that occurred, I took blame for even letting my self go there, but what I'm saying is you're drawn to me for some reason that you can't explain and until you figure it out it will always be that way.....

GhosstfacePoet

You seem like an Angel honestly
In saying that you helped me in a manner eye just cant finger but somethings arent to be explained

Aura

Funny you're not the only one who says that..had a whole piece written about me in that way!!!

GhosstfacePoet

its shows youre blessed with an attribute you dont even kno exist use it to help that help is thru God or more so letting God lead you.....just view things in this manner if eye place myself in the appropiate situation to where as to recieve what he presents before me so much other things follow just try submitting totally 100% letting God be the driver you will be amazed at the outcome

Aura

You're singing to the choir dear....I am well aware of the AWESOMNESS of GOD...I have a testimony!!!

7/27/12, 3:09 AM

Aura

And what do I owe the pleasure of u requesting my friendship?

GhosstfacePoet

i mizz ur poetry...
iz it A prob. with tht hope im oFF puniShment

Aura

U were never on punishment with me, however ur wife maybe...

A homeless guy held a sign asking for change, Sincere drove up dropped a card inside his hat. Driving off, the homeless guy reads the card that has Homeless Transitional Center upon it and decides to check it out. After arriving to the Homeless transitional Center which held a life strategic class to help one developed and manage life in a sound state. Along with a life coach to guide one in managing ones finances he was very well pleased with the placement of the environment he was in. Along with structuring one for a career setting. In the auditorium to meet the owner of the Homeless Transitional Center I met the guy who dropped the card in my hat and I hugged him thanking him for the opportunity. He thanked me that I could be of help to helping him reconstruct his life.

Printed in the United States
By Bookmasters